A Rob Wyllie
First published in Great Britain in 2
United

Copyright @ Rob

The right of Rob Wyllie to be identified a ... has been
asserted by him in accordance with the ... ...sign and Patents Act
1988

All rights reserved. No part of this publication may be reproduced, stored in a retrieval system, or transmitted. in any form or by any means, electronic, mechanical, photocopying, recording or otherwise, without the prior permission of the copyright owner.

All the characters in this book are fictitious and any resemblance to actual persons, living or dead, is purely coincidental.

RobWyllie.com

The Maggie Bainbridge Series

Death After Dinner
The Leonardo Murders
The Aphrodite Suicides
The Ardmore Inheritance
Past Sins
Murder on Salisbury Plain
Presumption of Death
The Loch Lomond Murders
The Royal Mile Murders
Murder on Speyside

Murder On Speyside

Rob Wyllie

Prologue

'The River Spey (Scottish Gaelic: Uisge Spè) is a river in the north-east of Scotland. At 107 mi (172 km) long, it is the ninth-longest river in the United Kingdom, as well as the third-longest and fastest-flowing river in Scotland. It rises at over 1,000 feet (300 m) at Loch Spey in Corrieyairack Forest in the Scottish Highlands, 10 miles (16 km) south of Fort Augustus. Some miles downstream from its source it is impounded by the Spey Dam, before continuing a descent through Newtonmore and Kingussie, crossing Loch Insh before reaching Aviemore. From there it flows the remaining 60 miles (97 km) north-east to the Moray Firth, reaching the sea 5 miles (8 km) west of the town of Buckie. The area from Aviemore to the sea is generally known as Strathspey, its beauty and grandeur each year attracting thousands of tourists from all over the world. The area is important for salmon fishing and is world-famous for the production of the finest malt whisky.

On some sections of its route to the sea, the Spey changes course frequently, either gradually as a result of deposition and erosion from normal flow, or in a matter of hours as a result of spate. The river spates rapidly as a result of both heavy annual rainfall and the snow-melt from its wide mountainous catchment area.'

Source: Wikipedia, December 2023, augmented by the author.

Notice the article mentions that the famous old river *spates*. Check any thesaurus for that evocative word, and you will find *deluges*, *floods*, *torrents* and *gushes* amongst many synonyms. Yes, each year, almost without fail, and long before the effects of climate change came into such sharp focus, the river frequently bursts its banks at the point, just south of Aviemore, where it is joined by the picturesque River Druie tumbling down from the majestic Cairngorm mountains. And most years, foolhardy anglers or kayakers, sometimes visitors but often locals who should know better, ignore the danger warnings posted all along its banks and are overcome by the power of the mighty river.

Which makes it quite a handy location should you be contemplating the execution of a near-undetectable murder.

Chapter 1

It wasn't exactly panning out in the peaceful way she had envisaged, but that didn't mean that Maggie Bainbridge wasn't enjoying the trip. She was up in the beautiful Scottish Highlands, on the banks of the majestic River Spey to be exact, and she was camping, in a proper *tent*, and at this precise moment it wasn't actually raining and the sharp-toothed midges seemed to be on their day off. What was not to like? Until just a few days ago, the staging of the event had been in doubt, the festival site being under two feet of water due to the river bursting its banks a couple of weeks earlier. It often rained in July in Scotland, Yorkshirewoman Maggie had learnt, but this recent bout of incessant rain had evidently been exceptional even for that often-sodden month, and it had carried on through to mid-August without a break. However, the sun had been out for the last three days, meaning the site had started to dry out and, even better, the weather appeared to be set fair for the upcoming fortnight, if you were to believe the forecast.

She lay with her hands behind her head, musing over the fact that she had reached her very early forties without having ever been to a music festival before, and if she was being truthful to herself, she was very glad of that indeed. For many of her friends, attendance at Glastonbury was a top-of-the-bucket-list must-do, a sort of rite-of-passage, despite the whopping expense and the high probability that you would spend three days with your leaky tent floating in a sea of mud, only venturing out into the rain to watch your favourite artist performing, ant-like, on the Pyramid Stage about half a mile away. In fact, her best friend Asvina Rani, London's go-to family-law solicitor for the rich and famous, had been there three times - still managing to look like a super-model in a parka and green wellies - but had never yet been able to convince Maggie to accompany her. And the great thing was, with tickets for that particular event being like gold-dust, if anyone asked, you could just give a despondent shrug and say of course you'd *tried* but *sadly* you'd missed out once again. Much better, she thought, to watch it all on telly in the warmth of your living-room, with a nice glass of wine and a big bag of cheese-and-onion crisps.

But this one was different. First of all, she was here for work, not leisure, courtesy of a big divorce case her little firm was working on. The case, like much of their work, had come to them from Asvina, who was a Senior Partner at Addison Redburn, the prestigious City law firm. The fact that Maggie's client Cassie McKean could afford Asvina's services made plain the wealth that was at stake in this matter. There was no doubt about it, this was going to be an interesting case, and she was very much looking forward to getting started.

Although Maggie was technically under canvas, her accommodation was decidedly at the glamping end of the spectrum, her tent equipped with properly soft beds with thick pillows and fluffy cotton duvets, and the living area set up with a comfy sofa and a fully-stocked fridge. Her wonderful little boy Ollie had his own bedroom too, with a canvas zip-up door and a rugged camp-bed, the space illuminated by a suspended lantern that looked like an old-fashioned oil lamp, but was actually a battery-powered LED device. It was just past ten o'clock in the evening, and after the drive up from Glasgow on the busy A9, they should both have been sound asleep. But Ollie was, understandably, hyper with excitement, and she couldn't sleep because the bloody *Claymore Warriors* were performing what she believed was called a sound-check on the half-built main stage, a mere hundred and fifty metres distant.

Thunder in the Mountains. It was a fantastic name for a music festival, although if one was to be pedantic, the Cairngorm range from which it took its name was some twelve miles to the south-east of the flat-as-a-pancake festival site. But in actual fact, the ambitious event was about much more than just music. The coming weekend was to be dedicated to the climate emergency, with a veritable *who's who* of planet-saving activists flying in on their private jets to debate a wide-ranging agenda of initiatives, all designed to bolster popular support from the masses and increase the political pressure on global governments to take radical action. The highlight of the weekend was to be a Sunday-evening address by the King, who was spending the summer at his Balmoral hideaway, and so just ten minutes away from the festival site by helicopter, should he risk social-media opprobrium by choosing this convenient method of transport. As to the music, the Warriors, the band that starred the soon-to-be-ex-husband of her latest client, were to be the headline act at the festival proper, taking the stage on the closing Saturday of the event one week distant. Dougie McKean was their founder and lead singer, and from everything Maggie had read about him, he was a particularly horrid man. Despite this, her colleague Jimmy Stewart and his brother Frank were huge fans of the band, and she had listened, bored but dutifully, as the pair enthused about their greatest works, and in particular their huge million-selling album *Oran na Mara,* which, she had learnt, was a sprawling concept album whose title translated from the Gaelic as *Song of the Sea*. Metal folk-rock was how the Stewart brothers had categorised their genre, but listening to them in the flesh for the first time tonight, *a bloody great cacophony* sounded a lot more accurate. Still, everyone to their own she thought.

She zipped open Ollie's door and stuck her head through the gap. 'Having a nice time darling?' she asked, shooting him a fond smile. 'Yeah yeah *yeah*, ' he replied, leaping out of bed and dancing around manically. 'These are banging tunes, aren't they mummy?'

She laughed. 'Yes, they certainly are that my love. Now you try and get some sleep, because we have a very exciting day ahead of us tomorrow.'

'I want to be in a band when I grow up,' he said, ignoring her. 'I think I want to be the drummer. Boom boom *boom*!' He flayed his arms around wildly, an action that caused him to lose his balance and collapse on the bed in a fit of giggles. 'Uncle Frank said he used to play the drums when he was a boy, and he said he might get me a set for my birthday.'

She gave him a wry look. 'Oh did he now? He never told me that he used to be a drummer.' There wasn't much she didn't know about Frank Stewart now, given she was going to marry him in little more than six weeks' time, but this was one fact that had so far escaped her. She was of course crazily looking forward to her marriage, but there was one question that had been seriously vexing her, and that was what her little boy should call him, because obviously he couldn't carry on being Uncle Frank. But should it be *daddy*, that was the bitter-sweet question she had to answer, and was struggling with if she was being honest. Ollie, traumatically, had witnessed his own father's brutal murder and although, nearly three years after the awful event, he seemed to have recovered, he was now beginning to ask what his father had been like. *He was a good dad but he was horrible to your mum* was the completely truthful answer, but not one Maggie could easily share with her adored son. One day, she might have to share her feelings with him, but that day was thankfully a long way off.

'Anyway, I thought you wanted to be a footballer and play for Arsenal?' she said, sitting down on the little bed beside him.

'I want to do that as well. I'll be a silky midfielder and a rock drummer too.' He hesitated for a moment and pursed his lips. 'Or maybe a racing driver.'

She laughed again. 'Well, as long as you don't want to become a lawyer, that's fine.'

He frowned. 'You were a lawyer, weren't you mummy? And so was daddy. And Uncle Jimmy's a lawyer too, although he was a soldier first of all, wasn't he? Yes, maybe I'll be a soldier like Uncle Jimmy was.'

She leant over and kissed him. 'I'd rather you were a footballer darling, then I could come and watch you play every week. I'd be very noisy and shout your name at the top of my voice.'

He gave her a sleepy smile. 'I'll have my own song. All the best players have their own song for the fans to sing. You could sing that when you come along.' He was silent for a moment, evidently deep in thought. Then in a sweet and tuneful voice, he warbled, '*Ollie Bainbridge, Ollie Bainbridge, we'll support you ever more. We'll support you ever more.*' Triumphantly, he punched the air, which she recognised as his celebration for executing a particularly brilliant solo goal. 'You see, I've already got one mummy.'

'That's lovely darling,' she said, kissing him again. 'So let me tuck you in now, because you need to try and go to sleep. Uncle Jimmy will be here tomorrow and as I said, we've got a very exciting day ahead of us.'

Although of course, she had no way of knowing *quite* how exciting the days ahead were going to turn out to be.

Chapter 2

Work-wise, it had all been pretty crazy for Frank, and bloody annoying too if he was being honest. After six months or so of living with his lovely fiancée Maggie Bainbridge back in his native Glasgow -well, in the hyper-posh suburb of Milngavie to be precise - his former gaffer DCI Jill Smart had phoned him to tell him he needed to get his arse back down to London and pretty sharpish too. That command was the reason he found himself back in Atlee House, the scruffy nineteen-sixties office block which housed his infamous Department 12B, and which was located on a nondescript street just off the Uxbridge Road in the west of the city. The department's published remit was primarily as a cold-case unit, but in addition, it had become a dumping ground for the force's problem children, namely those officers - and there was no shortage of candidates - who had been the leading player in some catastrophic screw-up or other, but who weren't *quite* useless enough to simply sack. It also housed those members of the force who, like Frank, had punched out the lights of a senior officer but had escaped instant dismissal on the basis that the brass knew the victim had had it coming to him. Detective Chief Superintendent Colin Barker had been the senior officer in question, and when Frank had laid him out with a single punch in the open-plan first-floor office of Paddington Green nick, the action had been accompanied by cheers and wild applause from his watching colleagues. But obviously such an act couldn't go unpunished, so Frank had been sent out to grass in 12B, where it was expected he'd quickly have become so frustrated that he would have resigned, saving the Met a redundancy payment and a whole lot of hassle to boot. But in the two years or so since the department had been established, it had gone from strength to strength, its role expanding organically to encompass any sort of matter that might prove embarrassing to the higher-ups of the force and so needed to be buried before it could cause any long-term damage. And god knows, Frank thought ruefully as he ambled along the corridor towards the building's recently-installed high-tech vending facility, there was never any shortage of *these*, embarrassing cock-ups seemingly having become the Met's stock-in trade in recent years. So, faced with increasing demand, the department had expanded, and Frank, originally seen as a mere short-term caretaker, was put in charge of the whole shebang by his gaffer, the aforementioned DCI Smart.

The thing that made this sudden urgency all the more annoying was he had actually been in a bit of a quiet period, it having been nearly six weeks now since his last proper case had ended. But the hiatus hadn't been because there had been a sudden outbreak of competence across the organisation, drying up the pipeline to his department. That was as unlikely as his beloved Scotland winning the World Cup at either football or rugby, though to be fair, both of the national sides had punched way above their weight in recent seasons. No, the real reason was that it was approaching the end of the organisation's financial year, and budget constraints demanded that no further expensive investigations should be launched until the following fiscal period. Except of course, where a *really* senior-level screw-up had occurred, one which might have the potential of making some revered member of the top brass look a complete mug.

In that type of case, budget constraints suddenly didn't apply, which explained why in five minutes' time he was going to be sitting down with DCI Smart to hear all about his latest assignment. The recent installation of contactless payment gizmos on the vending machines had made it a whole lot easier to get his regular fix of caffeine and chocolate, requiring no more than a wee swipe with the debit card to deliver the goods, rather than the often-fruitless rummage through his pockets for appropriate coinage. As a result, it was less than a minutes' work to get suitably fortified for the upcoming meeting.

He hadn't seen Smart since he'd moved up to Scotland, and was looking forward to touching base with her again. Technically-speaking the two of them were now of the same rank, he having been made up to DCI as a bribe to move northwards and take on his last case, but he still could only think of her as his boss. Actually, she was a bit of a strange bird in his opinion. Forty-ish, about the same age as himself in fact, and obsessed with keeping fit, she had the rake-like figure of a long-distance runner, but with a well-honed upper body which testified to her daily gym work-outs. Quite nice-looking too, and not entirely without a sense of humour, but somehow she'd managed to reach what some people would consider early middle-age without seemingly ever having been in a serious relationship. That fact, naturally, had fuelled the station's rumour-mill, which speculated that either she was gay, or, more juicily, that she was having a torrid affair with a Chief Superintendent or Assistant Commissioner and had for years been forlornly waiting for him to leave his wife or partner. Frank of course had never dared to bring up the subject of her love-life, even when Jill had shown an obvious attraction for his brother Jimmy on the one or two occasions she had met him. Mind you, every woman on earth fancied his ridiculously good-looking brother, so that was probably of no great note.

The vending transaction completed, he set off along the corridor with the chocolate bar stuffed in a pocket and a coffee in each hand. Smart's preference was easy to remember, a black americano of zero calorific content. Finding the door open when he arrived at the little interview room, he walked straight in without knocking, and plonked the drinks on her desk.

'Morning ma'am,' he said cheerily, 'I've brought you a coffee. I've got a big chocolate bar for myself but I took the liberty of assuming you wouldn't want one.' He pulled back the vacant chair in front of her desk and sat down.

She laughed. 'I'm in training for a marathon, so it's all protein and carbs for me at the moment I'm afraid. And you don't have to call me ma'am. You're a DCI yourself now, remember?'

He grinned. 'Aye, sorry ma'am, I'm never going to get used to that. Anyway, isn't Marathon what they used to call those yummy chocolate peanut bars? That's the closest I'll ever get to doing one.'

'Men of your age need to start looking after themselves Frank,' she said, giving him an amused look. 'All that fat around the arteries, it's not good for you.'

'Aye, I know,' he said wryly. 'I'm always planning to start my fitness programme next week. But next week, I might actually do something about it.'

She raised an eyebrow but made no comment. Instead she said, 'Well as I mentioned on the phone, a matter of some delicacy has landed on my desk, something that falls one hundred percent into the remit of your department.'

'A historic screw-up of gigantic proportions then? I thought it must be something like that when you flew me down from Glasgow, and you came here rather than me coming to you. Top-secret is it?'

She smiled. 'If only. In fact, it's going to be anything but a secret in a day or two, hence the urgency.'

'Ah, I see,' he said, giving her a knowing look. 'The press has got a hold of it then?'

'Afraid so,' she nodded.

'And is it one of *them*? You know what I mean.'

'If you mean a historic allegation of sexual assault, then yes, I'm afraid it is,' Jill said. 'And yes, I know they're amongst the most difficult cases to work on, emotionally and evidentially too.'

He nodded. 'Aye, because it's often just the woman's word against the guy's, isn't it? Nine times out of ten.'

'Sadly that's true. And we tried always believing the woman's story, and that just made matters worse. Well-meaning of course, but misguided in my opinion.'

Frank gave a wry smile. He knew what she was referring to, because around ten years ago, the police and prosecutors, frustrated by the pitiful number of alleged rapes making it to court, decided the start point should be to believe that every allegation was true. As Jill had said, it was well-meaning, but it fell under the law of unintended consequences, with a slim rise in prosecutions but a marked decline in convictions, as a slew of shaky cases were thrown out by the courts. 'Aye, short cuts just don't work, do they?' he said. 'You've either got evidence or you haven't. And if you haven't, you're stuffed, unfortunately. Devastating though that is for the poor victim.' He paused for a moment. 'So what's this one about, and why the urgency?'

She smiled. 'The urgency is because this one's massively high-profile. Specifically, it's being championed by the Chronicle newspaper and it's going to be splashed all over the front page of their Sunday edition this weekend. The actors in this big-budget drama, would you believe, include the singer Orla McCarthy, a band called the Claymore Warriors, and Assistant Commissioner Ian Archibald of this manor.'

'What?' Frank said, astonished. 'Bloody hell.'

'Exactly. AC Archibald I assume you know of course, but have you ever heard of McCarthy or the Claymore Warriors?'

'Heard of them? The Warriors are one of my favourite bands, if not my *actual* favourite. And my Maggie's actually up in

Aviemore right now, would you believe? The band's appearing at a big music festival up there. That's a crazy coincidence, isn't it?'

'It is,' Smart said, smiling. 'But that seems to happen a lot in your world.'

'Somehow it does,' he conceded. 'But about Orla McCarthy. She's the Irish pop singer and she's pretty huge, isn't she? In the UK and Ireland at least. A kind of cross-over of traditional folk and country, with a bit of dance added in too. Gives Taylor Swift a serious run for her money.' And then suddenly he remembered. 'And of *course*. She sang on *Oran na Mara*, when she was an unknown teenager. She did this beautiful lilting ballad passage in the middle of the title track. That's the big stonking rocker that opens the Warrior's biggest-selling album. It's a cracking tune and her bit's an absolute show-stopper.'

Smart shrugged. 'I can't say I've heard of the song myself, but it's interesting, because the gist of the Chronicle's story is going to be that Orla was sexually assaulted during the Oran na Mara recording sessions. It was eighteen years ago apparently, and she was actually only fifteen at the time. You know what that means of course, in legal terms.'

'She was a child,' he said, shocked. 'I didn't know that. Her voice is so pure and sweet on that record, but I'd always assumed she was eighteen or nineteen at the time. So Jill, what's the detail?'

She paused for a moment, then said. 'At the time, there was an allegation by Orla that she was sexually assaulted by

Dougie McKean, the band's lead singer. But the complication was, she didn't report the matter at the time the alleged assault occurred, but waited until she'd returned to her home in Dublin, when she eventually told her parents.'

'Wait a minute,' Frank said. 'So she was just fifteen, and yet she was sent to London unaccompanied?'

'Not quite,' Smart said. 'She stayed with an aunt and uncle in Kilburn, who escorted her on the Tube to and from the studio. They didn't actually stay for the sessions, because obviously once they had delivered their niece, they had every right to believe she was in safe hands.'

'But she wasn't.'

'No, or at least, that's what's alleged. But you can imagine how difficult it must have been for Orla to say anything at that age. It's the kind of thing you probably would only talk to your mother about, and even then it must have been hard. It was more than six weeks after she'd got back before she finally plucked up the courage to tell her mum and dad.'

'Aye, I can understand why it took so long,' he said. 'So what happened then?'

'What happened was that her father went absolutely ballistic. He flew immediately to London and walked into Paddington nick to report the assault.'

'I think I see where this is going,' Frank said. 'Because if I recall correctly, our revered Assistant Commissioner Archibald was a Detective Inspector there at the time?'

'That's right. He'd just been promoted and had come down to London from Strathclyde police. It was his first big case as a DI.'

'But it never got to court I'm guessing?'

Smart shook her head. 'No it didn't. But the thing was, there were complications. Or *a* complication to be exact.'

'What do you mean?'.

'Apparently there had been some arguments over the writing credits on that track you talked about, the one Orla sang on.'

'Oran na Mara it's called. Brilliant tune.'

She nodded. 'Yes, that's it. Apparently Orla claimed the middle passage had all been her idea, that she had come over to London with the melody and lyrics for the passage already written, and that she had sung it to the band and they had used it almost completely unchanged.'

'But she's not credited on the album,' Frank said, giving a knowing nod. 'I know that much because their leader Dougie McKean is down as the sole writer of that track on the cover of the old CD I've got. But what the hell has that got to do with a sexual assault allegation?'

'What it did was, it gave the band and their management a gold-plated opportunity to claim that Orla had made up the assault allegations to get back at them when they wouldn't pay her a royalty for her composition. You see, she'd demanded that she get both a writing credit on the album and a share of the royalties too. Even back then it seems she had quite a business head, which of course she's well-known for now.'

Frank gave her a wry look. 'And are we saying that our golden-boy DI Ian Archibald fell for the band's version of events then, hook, line and sinker?'

'That might be a bit harsh,' Jill said. 'But let's just say the investigation seemed less than thorough. For example, Orla was never examined by a doctor, and McKean wasn't asked to give a DNA sample.'

'Flippin' heck,' he said, with a look of disgust.

'Yes exactly. And it gets worse I'm afraid. You see, the nature of the alleged assault was particularly horrible, and I'm sorry Frank but you'll have to read the file yourself to find out the details, because I just can't bring myself to repeat it. But anyway, rightly or wrongly, Archibald concluded there was no case to answer.'

He shrugged. 'So maybe there wasn't.'

Smart paused for a moment. 'Except some new evidence has just come to light. Some pretty damning evidence at that.'

'And what's that exactly?'

She smiled. 'It's something the recording studio have uncovered, and for some reason the Chronicle have got a hold of it now. As a result, it's going to be splashed all over this Sunday's edition. And knowing the way the press work, the focus will be on the quality or otherwise of our original investigation.'

'Oh dear,' Frank said, giving her a knowing look. 'Awkward.' He paused for a moment then smiled. 'So what's my brief on this? Launch the big cover-up?'

She gave him a sharp look. 'Don't be so bloody cynical Frank. No, the Commissioner wants 12B to do what should have been done in the first place. A proper and thorough investigation into Orla's allegations. But the problem is, there's actually a further complication, one that's just come to light internally.'

'Oh aye? So what's that?'

She gave him a grim smile. 'The AC has just confessed to the Commissioner that after the investigation, he accepted a pair of VIP tickets to go to a Claymore Warriors' gig. It turns out he was a big fan you see.'

'Bloody hell.' He was silent for a moment. 'So now I get it. The brass are bricking themselves about what the Chronicle's going to say on Sunday, and they want to pretend they're ahead of the game and have already been taking action. And what about Archibald? How's he looking in all of this? Is he going to be chucked to the lions, or is there going to be a closing of ranks?'

'Let's just say the Commissioner is happy to let your investigation run its course,' Smart said quietly. 'The AC will of course fully cooperate in your investigation.'

'Aye, I bet he will. That's going to be fun. Anyway, when do we start? Right away I assume?'

'I see you're wearing a suit today,' she said, raising an eyebrow. 'That's good. Have you got a tie as well?'

'Yeah, I've always got one in my drawer. Why?' he said, giving her a suspicious look.

'There's a press conference at eleven o'clock. You, me and the Commissioner. Does that answer your question?'

Chapter 3

Jimmy's train pulled into Aviemore bang on time, at the end of a long eight-hour haul up from London, where he had been on some unspecified business connected with his fledgling outdoor adventure company. The firm was actually based in nearby Braemar, just twenty-five miles away if you planned to walk it, although to do that you needed to traverse some of the most inhospitable and dangerous mountain terrain in Scotland. The train journey would not have had that jeopardy, but it would have been tiring enough. Although to be fair, he would have had plenty of beautiful scenery to look at en-route, the picture-postcard views starting at the beginning of the long climb up through the edges of the Lake District and continuing pretty much unbroken for two hundred miles, save for the change of trains at Glasgow. Even that only involved a gentle stroll from the Central Station up to Queen Street, taking in Buchanan Street and George Square, two of the finest architectural gems of his home city. Maggie had decided to wait on the platform for his arrival, and now she scanned the length of the train, hoping to spot him emerging from his carriage, which, it turned out, was right at the front. She watched as he stepped out then peered ahead, evidently looking for the exit. And then he spotted her, giving her an enthusiastic wave as he swiftly made his way along the platform, rucksack slung over one shoulder like an army kitbag.

'Great to see you Maggie,' he said, embracing her in a warm hug. 'How's Ollie taking to camping? Loving it I expect.'

'Yeah, he's like a mini Bear Grylls actually. In fact, this afternoon he's on a woodland adventure, organised by the crèche back at the festival. I think it involves swinging from trees, and there's worms too, from what I read in the brochure. To eat, I mean. *Yuk*.'

He grinned and gave a thumbs-up. 'He'll absolutely love that.'

She sighed. 'I'm just relieved they're not going on the river. I don't know if you've seen the news, but two fourteen-year-olds went missing yesterday. Apparently they went out on a home-made raft. A passer-by saw it capsize and raised the alarm. But they've still not found the bodies. Their poor parents must be beside themselves with worry.'

'Aye, I saw it,' he said. 'That's why I'm dead against offering that sort of stuff on our courses. Stew thinks it would be a great idea, but there's no way we're getting into that. That river's way too dangerous.'

Stew Edwards was Jimmy's business partner, an old pal from his army days. Maggie had met Stew a few times and found him very likeable and charming, but there was a definite hint of the maverick about him which, she suspected, would blind him to the dangers of any situation, or at least persuade him they could be ignored.

'Wise move Jimmy,' she agreed. 'The Spey can be really treacherous I've found out.'

'It can. Mind you, I like that idea of swinging from trees and eating worms. We could do that on our courses, a kind of *I'm a fat businessman, get me out of here*, or something like it.'

'That would be very popular I'm sure,' she said. 'But the one Ollie's doing has got a height and weight limit. You're much too tall and I'm *much* too heavy.'

He laughed. 'No, you look skinnier than a racing snake at the moment. Anyway, where's this meeting then? Nearby I think you said?

She smiled. 'Just across the street. The Cairngorm Hotel. I told Mrs McKean we should be there by four o'clock, so we're a good fifteen minutes early. We can grab a coffee first if you like.'

'I travelled first-class remember, courtesy of your very generous client,' he said, giving a mock grimace. 'So I've had about two dozen coffees already today, and a wee glass of beer too if I'm being honest. But yeah, let's wander across and see if she's there yet.'

'Well Cassie is very generous. Oh and by the way, thank you *so* much for agreeing to put some hours into this case whilst Lori's not available. I really don't know what I would have done without you.'

It had been a terrible shock several months back when Jimmy had told her he was leaving Bainbridge Associates to start a business up in the Cairngorms with his friend Stew Edwards. It was just after his divorce and then the break-up with a woman for whom Maggie knew he'd had strong feelings, and she knew he needed a big change in order to sort his life out. Now he and Stew ran outward bound courses in the Cairngorm mountains for overweight and overworked business executives, and six months or so into the venture, it seemed to be going well. In the meantime, Maggie had filled the vacant position with the recruitment of a talented young woman - or perhaps more accurately, a crazy young woman - by the name of Lorilynn Logan. Lori had been a waitress at the Bikini Barista Cafe, a cosy establishment that was located just two doors down from her own office on Byres Road, in the west end of Glasgow. As part of the recruitment arrangement, Maggie had negotiated that Lori would help out Stevie the proprietor of the cafe for a few weeks each year to cover for staff holidays or illnesses, and this week was one such occasion. Next week, she would be back in Maggie's employ, and would almost certainly be required to make the journey north to Speyside.

The hotel was a grey sandstone affair of pleasing traditional design, built, Maggie guessed, in the late eighteen-hundreds to coincide with the arrival of the railway in what back then would have been a sleepy Highland village. Thick navy tartan carpeting welcomed visitors into its airy reception area, off of which wound a wide staircase which presumably led to the upstairs bedrooms. To the left, according to a sign mounted on the wall behind the desk, was the restaurant and bar, to the right a guest lounge, and it was here that Maggie had arranged to meet their client Cassie McKean. She nodded to Jimmy and they walked through. The room, large and softly lit, was equipped with a fleet of leather armchairs set around teak coffee tables, the chairs displaying a pleasing crinkled patina commensurate with their obvious age. A scent of freshly-brewed coffee permeated the air, adding to the effortless cosy and soothing atmosphere of this relaxing space. Scanning the room, she saw that only one area was occupied, a circle of four chairs laid out in a wide window alcove. But whereas she had been expecting to meet only with Mrs McKean, whom she had met once before and hence recognised, she was surprised to see her client had been joined by another woman, another woman whom her now open-mouthed colleague had instantly recognised too. 'Bloody hell, that's Orla McCarthy,' he whispered, but not quietly enough so he wasn't overheard. The pretty pop star spun round on hearing her name, then did a double-take as she set eyes on Jimmy for the first time. It was always the same, Maggie thought with great amusement, with every woman in the world, no matter how famous or successful they were, and her dear colleague was so sweetly unaware of the effect he had on all of them. 'I thought you were another selfie hunter,' she said in her rich Irish accent, beaming a warm smile. 'They're the bane of my life, but you've got to grin and bear it haven't you?' She paused for a moment then smiled again. 'But *you* can have one if you like.'

'No, I don't want a selfie,' Jimmy said, with obvious embarrassment. 'Not that it wouldn't be nice or anything,' he added awkwardly. 'But no, we're here to see Mrs McKean, to talk about her divorce.'

The other woman stood up. 'Hello Maggie, good to see you again. And this must be Jimmy, I assume?' She held out a hand towards him in greeting. 'I'm Cassie McKean, but I guess you'll have worked that out already, since you're a detective.'

He laughed. 'Aye, I did. Nice to meet you Mrs McKean.'

'Cassie, please.'

'And I'm Orla,' her companion said. 'But you know that too. Just about everyone knows me I'm afraid. In Europe at least, not so much in America, worst luck.' She said it accompanied by a disarming smile, which Maggie thought was rather nice, given how ridiculously famous the singer was. 'But please, take a seat,' Orla added, nodding to two vacant armchairs.

These were two attractive women, Maggie decided, after a rapid and, she hoped, undetected visual appraisal. McCarthy was slim and willowy and looked barely out of her teens although she knew the singer was nearing forty. Her carrot-red hair was gathered into the matching bunches which formed the defining part of her look, and she wore a short green tartan dress, black tights and ankle boots all of which suited her perfectly. Cassie McKean was older, perhaps early fifties, but looked lean and fit, dressed in black jeans and a dazzling white t-shirt that despite its simplicity, still managed to convey its obvious expense. Her hair was worn short in a pixie style, with flawless skin which Maggie both instantly envied but, rather more uncharitably, decided must probably have been achieved by the use of filler, botox injections and other such cosmetic witchcraft. Nonetheless, Cassie looked fantastic, testament not just to medical science but to a regular and dedicated fitness regime that left Maggie feeling rather inadequate. But then again, she had a busy career and was a single mum to an energetic eight-year-old, so maybe she was being unnecessarily hard on herself. And now she wondered if she was about to get even busier, thinking that perhaps the singer might have a case for her little agency too. No doubt she would find out soon enough.

She slipped her laptop out of its case and placed it on the coffee table. Flipping open the lid she said, 'So Cassie, I'm hoping you've got the financial statement for us to look at? I think you said your husband's lawyers promised it by last Friday? Did it come?'

Cassie nodded. 'It did. And as I expected, I don't like it much. That's why Orla is here.'

Maggie gave her a puzzled look, it not being immediately apparent how a pop singer could help in a complex financial matter like this. But then immediately she reproached herself, remembering that McCarthy had a fearsome reputation as a hard-nosed businesswoman.

'My boyfriend is Vice President of A&R for Momentum Records, my label,' Orla interjected. 'He's called David Gallagher, although you've probably not heard of him. But there's nothing he doesn't know about the music business. He's a cool guy.'

'Right,' Maggie said, thinking she might be beginning to understand why the pop singer was present at the meeting. 'So Cassie, we talked about the fact that we might have to go to court to challenge your husband's declaration of income and assets if we didn't agree with it, and I suggested to you that we might need an independent expert witness with deep industry knowledge to help us. Are we suggesting that Mr Gallagher might be willing and able to fulfil that brief?'

'Too damn right,' Orla said. 'I want to see her horrible husband pay for everything he's done, just as much as Cassie does.' The bitterness of her tone surprised Maggie, making her wonder what was behind that last statement. But then out of the blue something clicked, something that she was unsure whether she should bring up.

'I've read a couple of your recent articles in the newspapers Orla,' she said cautiously, 'about your challenges with your mental health because of that horrible thing that happened to you a long time ago. It's brave of you to talk about it, and great that you're encouraging other young women not to remain silent if they've suffered in the same way.'

'Yes, it was awful,' the singer said quietly, 'and the worst thing was, nobody believed me at the time, especially not the police. And now this is the twentieth anniversary of it happening, which is why I've decided to speak out. It somehow seems apt.' She was silent for a moment, then said mysteriously, 'And there's been developments, I'm very pleased to say.'

Maggie hesitated before speaking. 'What sort of developments, if you don't mind me being terribly nosey?'

The singer smiled. 'All will become clear. It's going to be all over the Chronicle on Sunday. More than that, I can't say.'

'That's okay,' Maggie answered, sensing not to push it any further. 'But I'll make sure I grab a copy of the paper on Sunday, that's for sure,' she added, smiling.

Orla return the smile. 'It'll be worth reading, believe me. But I'm sorry Cassie,' she said, shooting her friend an apologetic glance, 'I seem to be hogging the conversation.'

'That's okay,' Cassie said. 'I'm just so pleased to have you on my side. So Maggie and Jimmy, what's the plan?'

'Well, we're up here to get Dougie to sign an agreement,' Jimmy said. 'Obviously we don't want to have to go to court if we can avoid it. That's never in anyone's interests, except for the lawyers of course.'

'I live in hope,' Cassie said ruefully. 'But I don't give it more than a one percent chance of success. Dougie's obsessed with money, and more specifically, he's obsessed with keeping it all for himself.'

Maggie nodded. 'Yes, well that's often the opening position in a matter like this I'm afraid. But under the law, you're entitled to half the marital assets and also a goodly proportion of his ongoing income, given you still have dependent children. How old are your kids by the way?'

Cassie gave a proud smile. 'Ryan's thirteen and Grace is ten. They're amazing kids, but I suppose every mum says that.'

'Yes we do,' Maggie said, laughing, 'but that doesn't make it any less true. And they live with you I assume?'

She nodded. 'They do. Dougie's not much of a father to be honest. The band's always on tour and he doesn't see much of them. But they still miss him.'

'So what about custody?' Jimmy asked. 'Has that been settled?'

'I don't think he wants custody,' Cassie said. 'But, no it's not agreed yet. Not formally.'

Maggie gave her client a searching look. 'I know we've only been engaged to sort out the financial aspects of your divorce, but honestly Cassie, if you take my advice, you'll shoot custody straight to the top of your priority list. In any separation, it's vitally important that the arrangements for it are made crystal clear.'

'Maggie's right,' Orla said, jumping in. 'He's a total shit and he'll weaponise the kids, believe me. It wouldn't surprise me if he goes for sole custody, just to spite you.'

Cassie suddenly look scared, the colour in her face draining away as this dreadful scenario evidently hit home. 'No no, he wouldn't,' she said, shaking her head. 'He wouldn't do that.'

From what Maggie had read about the musician and his evident disdain for every sort of moral convention, it was exactly the kind of thing he *would* do. But this wasn't the time or place to say it. 'Let's just see if we can close that door before it opens,' she said instead, in an emollient tone. 'We'll slip in a custody clause to the agreement that we're going to put in front of him later this week. You just need to decide what would be a reasonable proposal for ongoing access. Perhaps one weekend a month as an opening gambit?'

The woman gave a weak smile. 'Yes, that would be good.'

'Okay, we'll get that drawn up later today and added to the agreement. I guess we need to go through his management company or something to get to see him.'

'He sacked his management company,' Cassie said, giving a sardonic smile. 'He's *always* sacking his management companies. No, you need to go through that little slut Tamara Gray. I have her number on speed-dial.'

'Okay,' Maggie said slowly. 'And she is...?'

'She was a lawyer with his last management company, that's how they met. And now Dougie says she's managing him personally, but she's just another one of his groupies, except this one has delusions that Dougie's going to make her lady of the manor.' She gave a bitter laugh. 'The stupid bitch doesn't even know that *I'll* be keeping Inverbeck after my divorce.'

Maggie gave her an uncertain look. 'I guess that brings us back to the financial statement that they've sent you. Does it say anything about that house? And remind me, is it the principle residence, the family home?'

'We've got several properties,' Cassie said, sounding apologetic. 'But yes, Inverbeck is the family home. That's where we live most of the year and it's where the kids go to school. It's on the outskirts of Braemar and it's beautiful.'

'And is *he* still living there?' Maggie asked cautiously. 'Technically, I mean. I know you said he's planning to leave you for this other woman...' She paused for a moment. '... and believe me, I know this must be incredibly hard for you Cassie, but he's not actually living with this Tamara Gray at the moment?'

'No, not technically, although he spends most of his time with her,' she said bitterly. 'To answer your earlier question, yes the financial statement says something about the house. He wants to keep Inverbeck, naturally. And I guess he thinks if he walks out, then he'll lose that opportunity. After the divorce I mean.'

Maggie nodded. 'Well, I think we can do something about that. Because that would mean you and the kids would have to move out, and generally-speaking a court wouldn't support such disruption to children's lives. So we could contend that since there are other properties available to the divorcing couple, we could offset the asset value of Inverbeck by granting your husband equivalent value, but that he would have to live elsewhere. I think there is enough combined wealth in the partnership to make that a practical possibility.'

Cassie laughed. 'I didn't actually understand a word of that. But then that's why I'm employing you guys I guess.'

'You get to keep the big house, but he has to get half its value, whether in cash or other properties or whatever,' Jimmy explained. 'But don't worry Cassie, I think we're clear on your priorities. First of course, it's your kids, then secondly Inverbeck. That's what we'll be concentrating on. Now, was there anything else in the financial statement you weren't happy with?'

'Let me answer that,' Orla interjected. 'Cassie let me see it, and his future income projections are ridiculous - ridiculously low I mean. They're massively understated, a quarter of what the band can expect from back-catalogue downloads alone, and that's before you consider any new material they might record. And they still sell a ton of old-school vinyl too, although god knows why. I've talked to David, and he reckons the future sales are understated by as much as half-a-million a year.'

'Really?' Jimmy said. 'That much?'

She paused for a moment, then lowered her voice to a whisper. 'Yeah, that much. And there's something else as well. Something even bigger.'

'What's that?'

Orla paused for a moment. 'Actually, I'm not sure if I'm supposed to say anything at this stage.' She gave Cassie an enquiring look, as if seeking permission to continue. After another contemplative pause she continued, 'but I expect it'll hit the entertainment news websites any time now. So yeah, what's happening is that Global International Studios in Hollywood is making a big movie about Irish migration to the US at the turn of the last century. It's going to be a massive production.' She gave a coy smile. 'And I'm going to be its star. It'll be my first big acting role and I'm really excited about it.'

'Congratulations,' Maggie said. 'That sounds wonderful.' And it was certainly interesting, she thought, without being quite sure what it had to do with Cassie McKean's divorce case. But evidently, that was about to be explained.

'And they want to use *Oran na Mara* as the main musical theme, because of the connection with the ocean and all that. And before you say anything,' she said, looking at Jimmy, 'I know it's Scottish Gaelic, not Irish. But it fits the premise of the film perfectly, you know, desperate people setting off on the long journey across the ocean without knowing what lay in store for them. And it's a banging tune, let's face it.'

Maggie laughed. 'Funny, that's what my eight-year-old called it too.'

'You sung the beautiful ballad bit in the middle of the track,' Jimmy said. 'In fact, when I saw you were here in Aviemore, I wondered for a minute if you were going to do a surprise appearance on stage with the Warriors.' He gave her a wry look. 'But I guess that's never going to happen.'

'Never *ever*.' Her mouth curled into a contemptuous smile. 'I hate that man. You have no idea how *much* I hate him.'

'But he wrote Oran na Mara, didn't he?' Jimmy said. 'So presumably he's going to benefit financially if it gets used in a big film like that.'

'He *stole* it'. Orla spat out the words, the bitterness self-evident. 'And not just from *me* either,' she added darkly. Maggie gave her a curious look, wondering if Orla was going to explain what she meant by that last comment. But evidently, she wasn't, as she continued, 'But I don't care, because my lovely David came up with an *amazing* idea and my management team have already signed off the deal with the film company. You see, we're going to incorporate the ballad passage from Oran na Mara into a new song that I've written. We've already recorded a demo, and David says it's the best thing I've ever done and that it's going to be a massive world-wide hit. And obviously there'll be mega promotion tied into the film.'

'But doesn't that mean that Dougie McKean will get even more royalties from the song?' Maggie asked, slightly puzzled. 'Obviously I'm no expert in this kind of thing, but I'm guessing he would get a writing credit, is that what you call it?'

'I don't care about that,' she said. 'And lovely Cassie will get half of it anyway, if you guys get him to sign that agreement that you're working on. And by the way, don't forget what I told you about that. The financial projections his lawyers have given Cassie are total rubbish. As you would expect, since he's a double-dealing shit.'

Maggie nodded. 'Don't worry, we'll definitely make sure we deal with that in the agreement, I promise.' Although right now, she wasn't exactly sure how she would fulfil that promise, given the expected belligerence of Dougie McKean, but that could be worked out in due course. But as she said it, something else struck her, which she immediately gave voice to.

'This deal for Oran na Mara,' she asked pensively. 'Has Cassie's husband given permission for it to be used in the film? Because I know a little about copyright law and I guess it will be him or his publishing company that hold the rights to the song. Or is it a band thing, I obviously don't know any of the details.'

For the first time, Orla McCarthy seemed less sure of herself. 'Not yet, not formally. But he will,' she said, quite sharply. 'The money involved is massive and he's never going to turn that down. In fact, David is actually meeting with him tomorrow morning to put a deal to him, with an executive producer from the film company. They're flying up to Inverness tonight.'

'And the band,' Maggie asked again. 'Don't they have a say in this?'

'They don't,' Orla said. 'The publishing company is joint-owned, but Dougie made sure that he owned fifty-five percent of it when he set it up. The others only own fifteen percent each. They get some royalties of course, but they've no say on how the music is used, being minority share-holders.'

'Which brings me back to my point,' Jimmy persisted. 'What if he just refuses point-blank to cooperate, or he asks for more than the film company are prepared to pay?'

'He won't,' she answered defiantly, then fell silent for a moment, giving Maggie time to observe the look of pure hatred that suddenly contorted the beautiful features of the famous pop star. 'And anyway, he's going to have a lot more to worry about soon. Because after Sunday, the gilded life of that two-faced pig Mr Dougie McKean will be over. *Over*.'

Chapter 4

From Frank's point of view, the press conference had gone pretty well, chiefly on account of the fact that he himself hadn't had to say a word, save for a muffled grunt of acknowledgment when Acting Commissioner Trevor Naylor had introduced him as the appointed Senior Investigating Officer for the resurrected McCarthy case. Naylor had been in the job for less than six months, his appointment a knee-jerk swing of the pendulum by the London Mayor and the Home Secretary, who were jointly and awkwardly responsible for filling the poisoned-chalice post. Everything about Naylor was completely the opposite of his failed predecessor, that predecessor being - in no particular order - a woman, posh, gay and a fast-track graduate. Five years earlier, and four Home Secretaries earlier too, it had seemed a smugly smart move, the argument being that she was just the kind of radical appointment the deeply misogynistic organisation needed to shake it out of its institutional malaise. The only problem was, Commissioner Hermione Sloan, although an unquestionably hard-working and decent woman, had ticked every box except the one marked competence. After one foul-up too many, she'd been eased out by a genuinely regretful mayor and slipped a dame-hood, whilst being publicly but untruthfully thanked for having left the force in a far better state than she'd found it. Naylor, by contrast, was old-school, joining the force straight from school then working his way up through the ranks in a steady if unspectacular fashion. *An old-fashioned copper* and *a safe pair of hands* were the labels most often attached to him. And dull as dishwater too, Frank thought with a jaundiced air, having just sat through the guy's over-long and cliché-ridden speech. That was one reason for his appointment having been given the hedge-your-bets *acting* designation, the appointing authorities still hopeful of attracting a permanent candidate with better right-on credentials. The rumour was in fact that the current Chief Constable of Police Scotland, one Jennifer McCrae, and herself only recently appointed to her position, was top of their box-ticking list.

But to be fair to Naylor and his performance at the press conference, he'd managed to stick to the script laid down by the lawyers, which had mandated that neither the accuser or the accused could be named at this stage. So Orla McCarthy was described only as a *prominent public figure*, and the identity of Dougie McKean wasn't hinted at either. And to be fair, when Naylor had announced w*e're re-opening this case due to the emergence of some highly significant new evidence*, he had sounded totally convincing, even although, embarrassingly, the police wouldn't actually know what this significant new evidence was until the Chronicle ran their Sunday-morning scoop. Whatever it was though, it was one of the first things Frank himself would need to find out.

But before that, he had a little chore he had to attend to, one that he had partially subcontracted whilst he was attending the Commissioner's press conference. He trotted back down to the vending area, where along one wall they had recently installed a half-dozen red plastic chairs that looked as if they'd been rescued from the local council tip or stolen from a hospital waiting room. As he arrived, he saw that three people were taking advantage of this luxurious leisure facility, two whom he knew well and one who was completely new to him. He approached the newcomer, held out a hand and said, 'So I guess you must be DS James? I'm DCI Frank Stewart and I'm to be your new guv'nor.'

She stood up and shook his hand warmly. 'Yeah, I'm Gemma James sir, but everybody calls me Jessie now.'

He gave her a wry look. 'And we all know why that is, don't we? Anyway, have these two chancers been looking after you?'

'Yeah, pretty well,' she said, smiling. 'I knew Ronnie already. Me and him go along way back.'

'Aye, I can imagine,' Frank said. 'Although I don't like to. But I guess you hadn't met Eleanor before? Our queen of the forensic geeks?'

He looked at Eleanor and saw that she was glowering. Mind you, that didn't mean anything, because the disapproving glower was the quirky forensic officer's default expression. But Frank sensed an atmosphere too, which made him fear that this initial encounter hadn't gone too well for some reason. And it didn't take long for him to discover why.

'I told her it was her dodgy mates over in Maida Vale labs that stitched me up,' James said peevishly. 'The ballistic guys said there was no way that gun could have just gone off in my hand. When in fact it did. *Everybody* knows that it did.'

'Actually, everybody knows that it *didn't*, ' Frank said dryly. 'You fired it up in the air to scare the shit out of that drug dealer you cornered, and we know that because they found the bullet in the ceiling of the warehouse. That's why they call you Jessie James, isn't it? Because you're a bloody bandit.' He paused for a moment before continuing. 'And that's why you got kicked off the armed response squad and transferred to this wee back-water. You're lucky in fact you didn't get the boot, and I mean permanently.'

The DS smirked. 'Yeah, but I don't think that hood will be dealing drugs again anytime soon though. He literally crapped his pants. He thought I was going to blow his brains out.'

Frank gave her a withering look. 'What, do you think you're a female Clint Eastwood or something? What next? *Make my day punk*?'

Ronnie French laughed. 'It would save us a lot of paperwork guv.'

'Aye, I'm sure that's what the mafia say too,' Frank said. 'Anyway James, welcome to Department 12B. It'll be a bit dull compared to what you've been used to, but I think that's exactly what you need. You agree?'

Before James could respond, Eleanor asked sourly, 'So why am *I* here? It's not like I work for you or anything.'

Frank laughed. 'Good to see the spirit of teamwork is still flourishing in today's new and shiny Metropolitan Police Force. No, I know you don't work *for* me, but you do work *with* me, and I like us all to be one big happy family. And as it happens, we've got a brand-new case to get stuck into and it wouldn't surprise me if we have to call on your unsurpassed skills and talents, as we usually do.'

'And will *she* be on the case?' Eleanor spat out the words, briefly nodding her head in the direction of DS James, whilst avoiding eye contact.

'Maybe, maybe not,' Frank said, shrugging. 'That's up to me. But if she is, I know she'll be able to rely on your full cooperation. Especially now that you're the best of pals.'

Eleanor scowled but made no further comment. Frank beamed a smile and said, 'Great, that's the formalities all sorted, so it's back to work for us all. Frenchie, James, if you two would like to gather round my desk at 2pm prompt this afternoon, I'll bring you up to speed. And just to whet your appetite, let me say that this case is *seriously* high-profile. In fact in the meantime, why don't you toddle off and do a bit of googling. Search for Orla McCarthy, pop princess.'

***

Back at his desk, Frank picked up his phone and opened up the BBC News site to see if they were already reporting on the Met's historic sexual assault story. *Unnamed Celebrity Alleges Rape*. Yep, there it was, and it was their leading item too, illustrated by a photograph of that morning's press conference, in which he himself could be seen sitting alongside the Commissioner, looking bored but thankfully not picking his nose nor yawning. He wondered what the bosses of the *Chronicle* must be thinking about it right now, they alone amongst the media hoards in knowing the identity of both accuser and accused, and with the story set to break cover in just a couple of days. Smug satisfaction was what he guessed, the Met's panic reaction placing the story bang in the centre of the non-stop twenty-four-hour news cycle. But now he had to get the investigation up and running, and pretty sharpish too, given its high profile. During his absence at the press conference, the archive team had evidently been down in the basement and exhumed the files from the original investigation, which now sat piled up on his desk, comprising half-a-dozen thick ring-binders and a couple of filing boxes, both so packed with documents that they didn't close properly. He sighed as he thought with some no little trepidation of what lay ahead. The trouble was, this alleged crime had taken place about eighteen years ago, just at the time the Met was half-way through a move to a digital crime-fighting world, a move that had involved the imposition of a half-arsed and bug-ridden new computer system on an organisation that had never wanted it in the first place. As a result, he expected half the files to be on that system, which itself had been replaced half-a-dozen years ago but was still accessible, that is if you could find anyone who, *one*, still had a password and, *two*, knew how to work the bloody thing.

Luckily he knew such a person, which, he reflected rather guiltily, was why he'd got DS Jessie James and wee Eleanor Campbell together earlier for what he had hoped, forlornly, might be a bit of an ice-breaker. He expected the case might involve long hours in front of that old computer terminal they kept in a dark corner of the fourth floor just for the purpose. And he knew that he would have been driven mental if *he* had been the person that had to sit alongside the touchy Forensic officer as she explained in her teacher-to-dim-five-year-old voice how the old computer system worked. Instead James, new to the department and bloody lucky to still have a job, would be allocated to the task and she would just have to like it or lump it. No, that would be a nice wee introductory task for the new DS, whereas he would concentrate on the paper files. Looking at the spines of the ring-binders, he noted that they were numbered, 1 to 6, which was actually a bit better than he expected. Reaching over, he grabbed folder 1, spun it round to face him, then opened it up. As he expected, the first page was the form where the team had recorded the allegation which was being investigated. Quickly he scanned the one-page document in order to get the gist of the alleged offence, an action which brought him up short as the disturbing nature of the assault on Orla McCarthy hit him like a sledgehammer. No wonder Jill Smart hadn't wanted to repeat it, and he didn't much want to read it again himself. It stopped short of rape, but that didn't stop it being unsavoury and upsetting. The thought of it made him feel sick to the stomach, and he had to stand up and walk away from his desk, pacing the floor for several minutes to regain his composure. Of course this was only an allegation, and the police investigation under DI Ian Archibald had concluded that it wasn't true. He felt his anger rising as something obvious struck him. Eighteen years ago, young teenagers didn't have smartphones and didn't have ready access to the hard-core porn sites that today's youngsters seemed to be cursed with. So could a young Irish girl like Orla, with a sheltered upbringing in a good Catholic family, really have been able to make up such a porn-movie scenario? Frank didn't think so, which made him angrier still. So was it incompetence that had led Archibald to dismiss

Orla's allegation, or was there something darker in play here? Whatever the case, he was damn well going to find out. But before he waded further into the files, there was one thing he was really curious about. He picked up his phone again and swiped down to DCI Smart's number.

She answered on the first ring. '*Hi Frank*,' she said, sounding amused. *'Too lazy to pop back down to the interview room? Didn't I say you needed more exercise?'*

He laughed. 'Yes ma'am you did, but this is just a quickie I hope. This new evidence that the Commissioner mentioned. Just for the avoidance of doubt, am I right in thinking that we don't have a clue what it is yet?'

'Why do you ask?' she said suspiciously.

'It's just that I figured if the Chronicle has something hot, their legal people wouldn't let them just run with it willy-nilly. Not if they could be accused afterwards of obstructing the police in the performance of their duties. So they would feel honour-bound to disclose it to us.'

'Nope, they've not been in contact. I would have been told if they had been.'

'That's what I thought. Thanks,' he said, then hung up.

So, no contact. That meant they had something *really* hot. And that probably meant that his old mate, ace reporter Yash Patel, had his grubby little paws all over it.

Chapter 5

There had been doubts right up to the last minute as to whether Maggie and Jimmy's meeting with Dougie McKean was actually going to happen. Five times she had tried to get a hold of McKean's PA cum muse Tamara Gray, and five times it had gone straight to voicemail. But eventually, a brittle-sounding American voice had called back to say yes, Dougie would see them at three o'clock, although he might be running late due to an earlier and important meeting, and if so, they would just have to wait.

'I'm glad we managed to get that sorted,' Jimmy was saying as they finally strode into the foyer of McKean's hotel after the forty-minute drive up to Inverness in their rental car. 'We were up half the night drafting this damn agreement. I just hope he likes it.'

'He won't,' Maggie said. 'Firstly, it's got the custody clause in it, which he won't be expecting. Second, it's saying Cassie gets Inverbeck. Thirdly, it's saying his future income projections are a load of bollocks. To be honest, I think we'll be lucky to last five minutes in there. In fact, I wouldn't be surprised if it turns violent.' She turned and grinned at him. 'That's why you're here. You're my muscle.'

A pleasant receptionist dressed like a Scottish country dancer directed them down a corridor to the left. 'They're in our morning room,' she said, her eyes conducting an approving and undisguised appraisal of Jimmy. 'Double doors at the end of the corridor. You can't miss it. Oh, and there's a sign above the doors.'

'Cheers,' he said, returning her smile. Maggie gave him an amused look but didn't say anything. Looking down the corridor, she saw the doors were ajar, and as they drew nearer, the sound of raised voices drifted towards them. It appeared that a verbal altercation was in full flight.

'We're gonna sue the ass off of you McKean', an American voice was shouting. 'Believe me, you won't know what's hit you when our attorneys get to work. And if you think we're going to use your stupid little song in our movie now, well dream on. That's in the past.'

As she walked into the room, Maggie saw McKean standing face-to-face with another man, the pair of them rather like boxers squaring up at a pre-fight press conference. She didn't recognise the man but he was evidently the one who had been speaking. And now Dougie McKean was about to reply.

'Bring it on pal, see if I care,' he said, speaking slowly, his face wearing an arrogant sneer. 'And I've got lawyers too you know. *Twat*.'

'What did you say?' the American said, taking a step forward, his expression dripping with violent intent. At that, another man jumped up from an armchair and grabbed his upper arm. 'Come on Clay, it's not worth it.' But then he too turned on McKean, jabbing an aggressive finger in his direction. 'Just to let you know, my record company is going to sue the arse off you too. Because we've got one of the biggest hits of the decade in the can, and if you don't let us release it, you're going to be held liable for all the future loss of royalties. Because we had a bloody *deal*.' He was silent for a moment, evidently waiting for his words to sink in, then turned to his companion and said. 'Let's go Clay. I told you this low-life's not worth another second of our time.'

The American, calmer now, said, 'Yeah, you're right David, this guy's not worth it. But you know, I really like that little English word he used.' He took another step towards McKean, stopping when his nose was hardly an inch from his adversary's. 'Because if there was ever anyone in this room who was a *twat*, it's you pal. You could have made millions of dollars, but now it's going to *cost* you millions. Because every hour of pre-production we have to scrap on this movie, you'll be paying for it. And oh yeah, there'll be loss of opportunity damages on top too.' He paused for a moment and then smiled. 'I expect our legal guys will be starting off at about thirty million bucks. So as we Americans like to say, see you in court. Come on David, we're out of here.'

Maggie and Jimmy watched as the men swept passed them, McKean marking their departure first with a one-finger salute, and then a shout.

'Oh aye, and thanks for the Balvenie. That'll keep me going for a wee while.'

He wasn't a tall man, no more than five-eight she estimated, but he was powerfully-built, with a mane of auburn-red wavy hair that was tied back in a pigtail. He wore a red tartan shirt over a white tee-shirt on which she could just make out the distinctive logo of his band, the Claymore Warriors. But that wasn't a surprise, because Dougie McKean wasn't by reputation a modest man. Or a nice one either.

'Twats,' he said again, giving Maggie a third opportunity to contemplate how much she detested the vile word. Suppressing her distaste, she smiled at him and said, 'Mr McKean, is this a bad time?'

He gave them a searching look. 'Who the hell are you two?' He turned around as if looking for someone. 'Hey Tamara doll, are we expecting anybody? You're supposed to be looking after my bloody schedule.' For the first time, Maggie realised there was someone else in the room, a woman approaching them from the corner where she had stood silently, evidently watching the drama unfold. She was slim and attractive, with her hair tied back tightly from a high-cheek-boned face that was heavily but expertly made-up. She wore white jeans and a simple black t-shirt bearing the logo of an international fashion brand, a simple garment that nonetheless would have cost a small fortune. Close up, Maggie saw she looked younger than was her first impression, perhaps barely past her thirtieth birthday. The young woman smiled, but it was a corporate smile rather than an affectionate one.

'They're working for your wife Dougie,' she said in the American accent Maggie recognised from the earlier phone call. 'On the divorce. I suppose we need to see what these guys have to say for themselves.'

He smiled. 'Fair enough doll, you're the boss. You two better grab a chair then. Want a drink? I'm just about to crack open the Balvenie. These boys just brought me four cases as a wee bribe. It's my favourite, although I love all the Speyside malts.'

'No thank you,' Maggie said pleasantly, whilst wondering why the two men might want to bribe McKean. 'You know how hot they are on drink-driving up here. I'd better not.'

'I'll have one sir, if you don't mind,' Jimmy said. 'I love a wee Balvenie, it's one of my favourites too.'

'Good man,' McKean said. 'Tamara, get me and my friend here a couple of wee drams, will you?' He paused for a moment, then motioned to a group of armchairs arranged round a small walnut table. 'Plonk your arses down here and you can tell me what shite you've brought me from my darling wife. And don't take too long about it, I've got things to be getting on with.' It was an interesting reaction. Maggie had thought it more than likely that he wouldn't see them at all, despite having agreed to the appointment, she supposing he wasn't the sort of man much given to follow the conventions of business decorum. Yet here he was, seemingly anxious to hear what they had to say for themselves. This was Tamara's doing, she suspected, remembering what Cassie had said about the woman wanting to become the lady of the manor, and that wasn't going to happen until her rock-star lover got on with divorcing his wife. Sadly, the future Mrs McKean was going to be sorely disappointed as far as Inverbeck was concerned.

Jimmy and Maggie sat down as commanded, to be joined a few seconds later, not unexpectedly, by Miss Gray, who was now equipped with a notepad and pencil. 'Thank you Mr McKean,' Maggie said, smiling. She slipped her shoulder-bag to the floor and reached down to retrieve her laptop. 'Bear with me for a few seconds whilst I get this thing up and running.' She placed the computer on the table, lifted the top and pressed the *on* button. 'Just so you know, we've drafted an agreement based on some of what you asked for in your financial statement, balanced with Cassie's wishes, together of course with some legal niceties concerning the future welfare of your children. Pretty standard stuff, all-in-all.' She hoped the emollient tone would soften the blow of the sledgehammer that was about to hit McKean and his girlfriend.

'It's a pretty thick document I'm afraid, these things always are,' she continued, spinning the laptop round to face them. 'But you probably want to leave the horrible details for your lawyers to scrutinise. It would send you to sleep, believe me. But we can go through it all now if you really want to.'

'Cut the crap Miss Bainbridge,' Tamara Gray said sharply. 'Let's hear what you're proposing. And just the headlines.'

Maggie smiled sweetly. 'That's exactly what we were proposing to do Miss Gray.' She paused for a moment before continuing. 'So I guess there are three main points that are central to the agreement. The first and most important is of course the future welfare of your children, Ryan and Grace. Both are still school-age and Grace is only ten so it means that you, Mr McKean, will be legally obliged to support them until they leave full-time education, which in most cases means until they reach the age of eighteen. By my calculation, that means for the next eight years.'

For the first time since they'd arrived, a smile broke across McKean's face. 'Aye well, we wouldn't want to see the wee brats out on the street, would we? But anyway, they'll be living with us after me and my baby-doll here are married. We're all going to live in Inverbeck and play happy families.' He took a swig of his whiskey and nodded at Jimmy. 'Do you like fishing mate? Because I've got my own wee salmon stream that runs just outside my back door. Pure magic it is. You should come down there one day and we can have a session. A couple of beers and we might even catch a fish.'

Maggie was silent for a moment as she tried to work out best how to convey what would undoubtedly be bad news to McKean and his younger lover. But the fact was, there was no easy way to say it. Luckily, Jimmy stepped in to say it for her.

'Nice offer Dougie,' he said, adding, 'You don't mind if I call you Dougie do you?' Without waiting for an answer he continued, 'But unfortunately, I don't think you'll be living at Inverbeck after the legal separation I'm afraid. I mean, we're in the era of no-fault divorce these days, but a court will still take into account parental behaviour when deciding on custody. The thing is, they're still a bit conservative in outlook, and they probably won't look too favourably on your well-publicised rock-star lifestyle, you know, all that drugs and booze and stuff. They see that kind of thing as a bad influence on kids, quite understandably. And even if that wasn't the case, nine times out of ten custody is awarded to the mum anyway.' He shrugged and gave an apologetic smile. 'That's just the way it is I'm afraid. Nothing we men can do about it.'

'I want that bloody house,' McKean said, the smile now gone. 'It's my place and it was bought with my money. I thought I made that clear to my bloody lawyers. I pay them enough, that's for sure.'

Maggie nodded, slipping once more into her sympathetic tone. 'I fully understand that Mr McKean, but you see, the court will always put the welfare of the children first. And Ryan and Grace are settled at Inverbeck and they go to schools nearby. The court won't want to see any of that disrupted.'

'It's my bloody house,' he repeated, his voice raised, 'and I want it, understand? Oh and by the way, I'll be asking for custody of my kids too. I mean, their mother, she's a right piece of work. Spends most of the day pissed out of her head on the chardonnay.'

Maggie gave him a sharp look. 'That's a serious accusation Mr McKean, one that of course you would be asked to provide evidence of if this goes to court. I presume you can do that?' she added provocatively.

'Aye whatever,' he said, avoiding eye contact. 'My lawyers will tie you two in knots if you try that one.'

Jimmy smiled. 'If this goes to court, it will be our gaffer Asvina Rani who your lawyers will be facing. And she never loses. *Fact*. She's bloody scary in a wig and gown, believe me. And as far as you getting Inverbeck is concerned, well that's not going to happen either, I'm afraid.' He paused for a moment. 'You see, there's enough assets in the marriage such that they can be split fifty-fifty without having to sell the family home. That's what any family court will support, and so that's what we've written into this agreement. It's fair to everybody, that's what the courts will judge, no question.'

'It's not bloody fair to me and I won't have it,' he exploded. He stood up and shot his girlfriend a look. 'You know what Tamara doll, I think we're done here. These guys are wasting our time.'

Maggie frowned. 'Mr McKean, I'm afraid there's quite a lot we have still to go through with you. Cassie has made some generous proposals with regard to your access to your kids, and we need to look at your forecasted future earnings too, because there's one or two points we aren't in agreement with.'

He gave her a look full of malice. 'Do you think I give a shit about any of that crap?' Reaching forward, he shot out a hand and slammed shut the lid of her laptop. 'You two can take your fancy wee agreement and shove it up your arses. I told you, we're finished here.'

***

'So that went well,' Maggie laughed, as they made their way back to the car.

Jimmy nodded. 'Aye, he's such a lovely guy isn't he? But I don't suppose we really expected it to go any better. Mind you, that big punch-up at the start was great entertainment, wasn't it?'

She laughed again. 'Yeah, I think McKean is going to be spending the next twelve months buried in lawyers. Because you know who these two guys were, don't you?'

'I'm guessing the American was from the film company and the other guy was Orla's boyfriend, the record company executive she told us about.'

'I think so. And it looks like our Dougie has done exactly what Orla said he *wouldn't* do.'

'Which is?'

'He's refusing to give them the rights to use the song in their film,' Maggie said.

Jimmy nodded. 'But the David guy said they had a deal, that was his exact words. No wonder he was going mad at McKean.'

'And not just because they've wasted a ton of cash on that Balvenie, ' Maggie said with a wry smile. 'I guess that was what Dougie meant when he said it was a bribe. It was to get him to change his mind back again, if that make sense.' She paused for a moment. 'But it just confirms what we already know.'

'Aye, that McKean's about as untrustworthy as a....' He broke off, evidently struggling for an apt comparison. '....as a thing that really can't be trusted very much,' he finished, giving a wry smile.

She frowned. 'The problem is, we promised Cassie we would get an agreement. Because we *really* don't want to have to go to court with this one.'

'Our pal Asvina might,' he grinned. 'The fees will be enormous.'

'Her fees are already enormous. But I don't see how we can avoid it, going to court I mean. He's not going to sign anything voluntarily is he? He's going to fight it all the way. Everything.'

He shrugged. 'Unless there's something we can give him that he really wants, something he might be prepared to trade everything else to get.'

'But we already know what that is, don't we? He wants Inverbeck. And that's not on the table.'

'Aye, that's true. But we need to try again. And if we can't give him a carrot, maybe there's a stick we could use.'

'Like what?'

'No idea. But there must be *something*.'

But nothing came immediately to mind, and now she worried that their latest assignment would fizzle out before it had even started. Yes, carrot or stick, that's what they needed.

But what, that was the unanswered question.

Chapter 6

Frank had been hoping he could get an interview with Orla McCarthy right away, but then, bizarrely, he'd had a call from his Maggie telling him the pop singer was actually up in the Highlands and was helping her latest client - the wife of Dougie McKean no less - with her divorce case. Obviously not wanting to conduct such a sensitive interview with the singer over an impersonal Zoom link, he had decided, with some disappointment, that it would have to wait until she returned to London. The fact was, there wasn't much to get stuck into until they found out what this new evidence was all about, and, embarrassingly, that would be after the singer's accusations of sexual assault aired in the coming Sunday's *Chronicle*. Which, he had discovered as a result of a call from his journo pal Yash Patel, was to be supported by a mid-morning press conference on the day of publishing, an event that as SIO he really had to be at, ballsing up any opportunity he would have had to nip up to Scotland for a lovely weekend with his Maggie. Still, next weekend he would definitely be up there for the big concert. Assuming Dougie McKean's career hadn't totally exploded by then of course.

But now it was the Sunday in question, and in about fifteen minutes' time, Orla McCarthy was going to step up onto the platform and put the knife into the aforementioned McKean, one of his all-time musical heroes, the consequences of which were unpredictable but unlikely to be good news for the Scottish rock star. The *Chronicle's* PR gurus had already been trailing the sensational story, leaking out tit-bits the previous evening to their rival media outlets, such that this Sunday morning every newspaper was leading with the story, whilst no doubt frustrated that they had missed the sensational scoop themselves. He picked up a discarded copy of the *Sunday Globe* and took a quick glance at the headline. *Accuser Set to be Named as Orla McCarthy.* This was in response to the Met's press conference a day or two earlier, where they had revealed they were now working on a historic case of alleged sexual assault, but had named neither the accuser nor the accused. Somehow, after more than forty-eight hours since he had sat on that platform with the Commissioner, the identity of the accused had still not leaked, although there had been plenty of speculation in the regular press and on social media. Now, in about ten minutes' time, it would all be out in the open.

They were in the Hilton on Park Lane, a venue that seemed to be favoured by the Chronicle for this type of shindig. The event room was packed, with over a hundred or so hacks eager to get their stories filed for the lunchtime web editions, and hoping that their legal guys had sorted out syndication rights with their Chronicle opposite numbers. He was accompanied on this occasion by DS Gemma James, the first time they had worked together since she had been involuntarily transferred to his Department 12B. It was a rule in the force that interviews with victims of sexual assault should be ideally conducted by a female officer, or one should be at least in attendance should a male officer be leading the session, on the grounds that female officers were more likely to display empathy for the victim. Today, Frank hadn't quite made up his mind whether he should let the borderline-insane DS James take the lead when they sat down with Orla later. Undoubtedly the DS was female, but whether she was equipped with empathy was still to be proven. But before all of that, he wanted to find Patel. Scanning the room, Frank soon spotted him, raising his hand to grab the reporter's attention before wandering over to engage him in conversation.

'So Yash my boy,' he said, proffering a hand which the reporter accepted and shook warmly. 'I should have guessed you were behind all this. Another scoop for Britain's number one investigative scribe? As you would describe yourself.'

Yash Patel laughed. 'I'd like to claim the credit Frank, and actually I will come award season. But the truth is, Orla came to us with the story. It's just that the editor has very kindly given it to me to run with.'

'Same as me,' Frank said, giving him a wry look. 'The Met just cottoned on to this story a day or two ago and my gaffer's made me Senior Investigating Officer. So I'm here in an official capacity. I'm hoping to do my initial formal interview with Miss McCarthy afterwards. And by the way, this is DS James. Jessie to her friends.'

Patel gave her a thumbs-up. 'Good to meet you DS James. Although you have my sympathies, working for this cowboy.'

Frank gave an ironic smile. 'Aye, so one day I'll tell you why they call her Jessie. Anyway, as I said, I'm the SIO on the case.'

He'd been vaguely aware of a guy standing next to them, a man in baseball cap, dark jeans and leather jerkin, with one of those steady-cam TV cameras mounted on his shoulder.

His presence was routine in a media event like this, so he hadn't given the bloke a moment's thought. That was, until the cameraman turned and addressed Patel.

'So Yash, is Orla going to do a to-camera piece before she steps up on the platform?'

Patel shrugged. 'Not sure we've got time for that Rupert. We'll just start with her speech, and then maybe we can get her to add a voice-over in post-production. With a bit of nice background music. Maybe one of her songs actually might be quite good.'

'So what's going on here?' Frank asked, intrigued.

'I don't think I told you Frank, but they've given me a job on *Chronicle TV*.' He nodded towards the cameraman. 'This is Rupert, by the way. We're doing a fly-on-the-wall documentary on Orla's situation, and they've made me the lead presenter and producer too. Great, eh? It's what I've always wanted.'

Frank laughed. Yash Patel was a man not short of ego, but he was so unapologetic about it that somehow it didn't grate. And there was no denying he was a good-looking guy, with what many people would believe was the perfect face for television.

'Well congratulations Yash, I'm pleased for you.' But then he hesitated for a moment. 'But just make sure this doesn't get in the way of our investigation, okay? I don't want this to become any more of a media circus than it already is.'

'Are *we* going to be in it Yash?' DS James asked eagerly.

'What, do you fancy a second career as one of these reality telly stars?' Frank said, not hiding his scorn. 'So Yash, before you say anything, the answer to DS James' question is no, we're not going to be in it. Got that?'

'But the public will want to put faces to the investigation team,' Patel said, grinning.

Frank gave him a scathing look. 'Well you can keep *my* face out of it, okay?' Glancing round, he saw that Rupert now had his camera squarely pointing at DS Jessie James, who was responding with a goofy smile. 'And you can bloody stop that too mate,' he said, 'or I'll have you arrested for obstruction.'

'I wasn't recording,' Rupert said, a mild note of defiance in his tone. 'But she's quite telegenic.'

Frank shook his head but said nothing.

'Well anyway, I'm glad they've made you SIO,' Patel said, and Frank knew exactly what the smooth journalist meant by that. *Excellent that I'll have an inside track on how the investigation is going, so I can keep this sensational story in the headlines for as long as humanly possible.*

'This is a serious business Yash,' Frank said, deadpan. 'So I'll not be sharing anything with cheap tabloid hacks.'

Patel laughed again. 'Ooh, that's cruel. But you know how it works Frank. You scratch my back, I'll scratch yours. And don't forget, Orla's contracted to us right now. We'll be learning new stuff from her every day. Stuff that might be useful to your investigation.'

Frank shrugged. 'No doubt. But I'm surprised you're not going to be up on that platform with her this morning. Or are you strictly behind the camera now that you're the big TV producer?'

'Not this time,' Patel said, shaking his head. 'Susan Jeffries, the paper's deputy editor, is going to be alongside her. It looks better that way I think. This is one for the sisterhood. And we're being genuine on this one, it's not just a PR exercise for the paper. It's not appropriate to have her surrounded by stale white males. Or any other sort of male either.

But they still gave the story to a man, Frank thought ironically, but decided against making any comment. Then, looking across to the platform, he saw there was activity. 'Here they are,' he said to James, as two woman stepped up onto the low stage.

'Gosh, she's beautiful, isn't she?' the DS said. Yes, thought Frank, she is, and Orla would have made special efforts this morning with her dress and grooming such that her natural beauty was accentuated. The platform was equipped with a slim lectern, and Orla McCarthy stood behind it, a faint smile on her face as she surveyed the room. She looks nervous, he thought, but more than that, there was a vulnerability that seemed to knock years off her age, such that one could easily picture her as the shy teenager, alone and scared in that recording studio all these years earlier. That, he decided slightly cynically, was probably the idea. Susan Jeffries introduced the singer with a minimum of ceremony, a diffident *good morning ladies and gentlemen, and thank you for coming,* and then a simple *so Orla, over to you.*

The soft Irish lilt was instantly familiar, hers being one of those voices that had exactly the same timbre whether the possessor was speaking or singing.

'What I have to say today, I should have said years ago,' she started with. 'But I've been on a journey, and finally, after many twists and turns, I've arrived at a place that I'm comfortable with.' She paused for several seconds, as if composing herself, before continuing. 'So now is the right time, for me and more importantly, for my mental health.' *Aye, you need to get that one in nowadays, it's mandatory,* Frank thought, then chided himself for what he recognised as weary cynicism. It was unfair, and he should have known better, given his own brother Jimmy's struggles with his demons.

Orla paused again, then said. 'Guys, twenty years ago, when I was only fifteen years old, I was the victim of a horrendous sexual assault whilst I was recording at Advance Studios, in St John's Wood here in London. I was forced, against my will, to perform a sickening sex act on a man I trusted, a man who was old enough to be my father.' There was an audible gasp around the room, seasoned hacks exchanging glances as they feverishly tapped into their iPads or scribbled into notebooks. 'Afterwards, I was disgusted with myself, as if it was *my* fault. So it took me weeks and weeks to have the courage to tell my mum and dad. And when I did, dad went mad of course and came straight over to London and reported it, as any father would.' She paused once again. 'But the police did nothing. *Nothing.* They thought *I* was lying. And now, the detective inspector in charge of my case is an Assistant Commissioner no less. But of course, what else should I have expected from a corrupt, incompetent police force? Screw up and they promote you. It happens all the time.'

'Bloody hell James,' Frank said, shocked. 'The AC's right in the brown stuff now, poor guy.' Looking round, he recognised one or two faces that had been at Thursday's press conference with the Commissioner, and it was clear from their expressions that they were relishing the occasion. But now, Orla was holding something up, an object that he struggled to recognise at first. And then, as he saw it glint under the room's overhead lights, he realised what it was.

'But now I have new evidence. It's all *right* here,' she added dramatically, 'so incontrovertible that not even the useless Metropolitan Police will be able to ignore it.'

Frank shrugged at the jibe, in response to an amused look from a nearby journalist who had recognised him. It was a bit unfair, he thought, tarring every cop with the same brush. But what was on that CD she was brandishing, that's what he was now desperate to find out.

'Twenty years ago, a studio engineer pressed *record* but then forgot to turn it off. And now twenty years later, another engineer has discovered this masterpiece hidden away at the end of one of the tracks on *Oran na Mara.*' She paused for a moment to allow the significance of the revelation to sink in before continuing. 'And believe me ladies and gentlemen, this masterpiece will never find its way on to a Claymore Warriors album.'

'What is it?' one of the journalists shouted.

'Clear and irrefutable evidence that I was sexually assaulted,' the singer said. 'Clear and irrefutable.'

'And can we hear it?' another hack asked.

Orla shook her head. 'I've been advised by the Chronicle's legal team that such a course of action would not be wise. So later this morning we will hand the recording over to the police.'

'Ah come on Orla, let's hear it,' a male TV reporter shouted. 'Our viewers would want to hear it.'

She smiled at him but didn't reply.

'So now,' she continued, ' I'm sure you will want to know the identity of the man who did this to me. The man who shamefully used his power to abuse a young schoolgirl, simply to satisfy his evil desires. Yes, he will deny it, and yes, he and his team of lawyers will threaten to sue me for libel, and yes, his legion of fans will abuse me on social media and call me a liar and a tart and worse. Guys, I'm prepared for all of that and more.' She took a sip from the glass of water that had been resting on the lectern, then said quietly,

'Ladies and gentlemen, that man is Dougie McKean of the Claymore Warriors.'

***

Afterwards, Frank was surrounded by a scrum of journalists, all wanting some quotable words from himself in his role as SIO, but it wasn't too difficult to fend them off for now. *'We've opened the formal investigation and we'll be conducting interviews and examining the new evidence over the next few weeks. Obviously as soon as we have something to report, you guys will be the first to know.'* He had it almost off pat, having used it or something very like it many times in the past, and it seemed to satisfy them for now. He didn't tell them that he was about to sit down with the alleged victim and get her to run through her story again for the record, nor did he mentioned that if this recording was as dynamite as Orla claimed it was, then he expected to be arresting Dougie McKean within a matter of days.

'So are we going to see Orla now guv?' DS James asked him.

'Aye, we are,' he said, pursing his lips. 'And you know what, I think you should take the lead in this one.'

But to their frustration, it didn't prove possible to get an audience with the singer that morning, she citing a constant stream of media commitments, no doubt carefully choreographed by the Chronicle's commercial team. In the end, Frank had to have a few sharp words with her, telling her that if all this media bollocks was more important to her than sitting down with the police and telling her side of the story, then *he* would conclude that the allegation itself was simply a big publicity stunt, and that he would recommend to the acting Commissioner that they closed down the case before it even got started. He'd said all of this with force, and he might have thrown in a couple of mild expletives too, so wound up was he about the situation.

It was only afterwards he noticed that Rupert had captured the whole scene on his bloody steady-cam.

Chapter 7

It was Saturday, and the *Thunder in the Mountains* climate festival was getting up to full speed, with so-called delegates - or revellers, which Maggie thought might be a more apt description - pouring into the riverside site from all points far and wide. Today's star attraction was to be a headline speech by the climate activist and rebel-rouser Freja Portman. As a teenager, Portman had been maimed in a hideous acid attack by a global warming denier, her features being expertly rebuilt by a noted cosmetic surgeon, who by coincidence, had heavily featured in one of Maggie's earlier cases. Now Portman, a sculpted if somewhat artificial beauty, was in her early twenties, and attracted the kind of superstar following normally reserved for pop stars - pop stars like Orla McCarthy, who Maggie had learnt was today flying down to London to front an early Sunday morning press conference. Annoyingly, Frank was going to be attending that conference too, it apparently being related to the new top-priority investigation which had whisked him off to London earlier in the week. He'd phoned that morning, apologetic, promising he would be back in Scotland on Tuesday at the latest, and before that he would explain exactly what this new case was all about. But as a teaser, he'd dropped the bombshell that Dougie McKean, husband of her new client Cassie, was at the centre of it.

Yes, Cassie. She and Jimmy had scheduled a follow-up meeting with her that morning, and given their disastrous attempt to get her husband to sign the divorce agreement, she wasn't looking forward to it at all. They'd arranged to meet once more in the reception of Cassie's hotel, Maggie having taken a taxi down from the festival site, he having driven over the Lecht pass from his rented Braemar flat. He was already there when she arrived.

'Where's wee Ollie this morning?' he grinned. 'Abseiling off a big rock-face up on Ben Macdui? White-water rafting?'

'Not far off,' she laughed. 'He's on some sort of nature trek along the River Spey. I think they might even be fishing, but from the banks, not on a boat, thank goodness,' she added. 'He was really looking forward to it.'

'Sounds great. Actually, I wouldn't mind a wee trek along the river myself, although I'd be stopping off at all the distilleries along the way to sample their wares. You can't go five minutes before you bump into one up here. But anyway, to Cassie. What are we going to be recommending Maggie? Does she go to court, or is there some sort of negotiated settlement still possible?'

'I don't know, to be honest,' she said gloomily. 'It depends what Cassie wants the most I think. To be with her children, or to have Inverbeck. Because to have the former, she might have to give up the latter.'

'That's no contest,' Jimmy said. 'She wants her kids to live with her, obviously.'

'Yes I agree. So let's go and talk to her, shall we?'

Mrs McKean was in the same plush and comfortable room they had met her in the day before, but this time she had selected a table in one of the bay windows that overlooked the rear garden. Today she was wearing a dress, a navy calf-length design that was both sober and classy at the same time. Seeing their approach, she got to her feet and gave a half-smile. 'Hello again,' she said. 'Please, take a seat. Some coffee should be along in a few minutes'.

Maggie smiled back, but there was something about the demeanour of her client that made her wonder if something had happened in the last twenty-four hours. 'Coffee would be lovely thanks,' she said. 'So Cassie, I'm afraid it didn't go too well with your husband yesterday. I know it's what you and I both expected, but it's disappointing nonetheless.' Whilst she was speaking, the woman was delving into her handbag, obviously distracted. A few seconds later, Maggie learned why.

'This came this morning. My cleaner's been forwarding my mail whilst I'm up here. Please, read it.'

It was a letter, on headed notepaper. *Shore McPhail & Robertson, Family Law Specialists.* The subject line read *Re: The Last Will and Testament of Douglas Robert McKean.*

'He's changed his will,' Cassie said, pre-empting what Maggie had already discerned from a quick scan of the letter. 'He's leaving everything to that *woman*. Nothing for me of course. But nothing for his own kids either. *Nothing*.'

'Goodness,' Maggie said, the word just slipping out involuntarily with the surprise of the revelation. 'That must be *so* upsetting for you Cassie. I really don't know what to say.'

She gave them a sad smile. 'He told me a couple of months ago that he was going to do it. But I just closed my eyes and ears to it all. Now it seems it's coming true.'

'It must be really hard to take,' Jimmy said. He was silent for a moment. 'But you know, it's only a will, and he's probably got at least another twenty-five or thirty years left on this earth. We can get the divorce sorted and then you can make a new will taking care of your kids. And then he can do what he likes.'

'But he drinks like a fish,' Cassie countered, 'and he doesn't look after himself either. I'm always expecting him to drop dead of a heart attack.'

Maggie nodded sympathetically, but didn't say anything. Perhaps Dougie McKean was keen on a drink or two, but on the evidence of their meeting with him the other day, he seemed in robust health. But then something came to her.

'But what this *does* do,' she said quietly, 'is give us some powerful ammunition. Distasteful and upsetting I know, but it does, definitely.'

'What do you mean?' their client asked.

Maggie paused. 'I think it shows unarguably what he really feels about his children. Because what father would disinherit his kids if he really cared about them? Cassie, we can use this letter.'

Jimmy gave her a knowing look. 'Aye, I can see what you're getting at Maggie. This is definitely one for the courts isn't it? Yeah, I can see how this might play out.'

'That scares me,' Cassie said. 'Because I don't suppose you can ever predict what the magistrate or whoever it is will decide.'

'Family courts don't like it when parents can't agree on the parenting arrangements, I can tell you that for a fact,' Maggie said. 'So we'll still have to try very hard to agree an access arrangement with your husband before we go in front of the Sheriff. But we'll only give Mr McKean one more chance, then we go straight to legal process.'

'But what if the court decides that the kids should stay with him?' their client said, evidently still frightened. 'Because I would die if that happened.'

Maggie shook her head firmly. 'No no, that would never happen. We'll be going into the proceedings making it clear that we offered your husband reasonable access to the kids from the start, but he wouldn't agree. His demand to have full custody will come across as vindictive, and the courts will see through that immediately.'

'And then we can produce this new will, which will expose his true feelings about his children,' Jimmy said. 'And remember, it'll be Asvina Rani who will be representing you in court. She's the best, believe me.' He smiled. 'I know it's a worry, but honestly, you'll be in the very best of hands.'

Cassie gave an uncertain nod. 'I suppose I have to trust your judgement. I really have no other option, do I?'

'There *is* an option, obviously,' Maggie said, then paused for a second before continuing. 'Honestly, I think it's Inverbeck that your husband really wants more than anything.'

'So he and his little American tart can pretend to be part of the landed gentry?' Cassie said, not hiding her bitterness. 'No way.'

'Thing is,' Jimmy said, 'and don't take this the wrong way, but it *is* only a house. A special house, granted, but it's still only bricks and mortar at the end of the day.'

Maggie gave him a quizzical look. 'You're going somewhere with this, aren't you?'

He nodded. 'All I was thinking is how hard it is to value a place like that, because they don't come on the market that often. So perhaps if you were to quietly mention to two or three big London estate agents that you were thinking of putting the place on the market, and that it would be perfect for a seriously rich foreign investor who wanted to buy a unique little piece of Scotland....'

'You'd get an astronomical valuation, and then if your husband wanted it, he would have to accept that's what it's worth,' Maggie interjected. 'He'd have to pay that price and give up his bid for full-time custody of his kids too.'

'But then I would lose the house,' Cassie said, looking puzzled.

'I did an online search before we got here,' Jimmy said, 'Around the Braemar area and in and around Speyside too. And I'll tell you what, there are some properties available that I would absolutely die for, and with the money you've got to spend, you could buy one of them and have a big chunk of change left over as well. Just saying.'

Their client broke out a wide smile. 'You're really trying to make me feel better, aren't you? And thank you, because it's actually working, I do feel a bit better now. And after all, a home is all about who's in it, not the building itself.'

'That's true,' Maggie said, relieved that somehow, they seemed to have arrived at a way forward with their lovely client. 'But look, nothing's finally decided. Why don't you sleep on it and I'll give you a call on Monday? Then we'll take it from there.'

'And I'll tell you what Cassie,' Jimmy added, 'if you do decide you want to get the house valued, I'd love to be your representative. I'd go round the agents and give the place the big sell.'

She laughed. 'Yes, I'd like that Jimmy.' Maggie wasn't sure if her client was serious or not, but glancing at her colleague, he saw that *he* was.

'Well that's all settled then,' she said finally. 'And just to let you know, I'm heading back to Glasgow tomorrow for an important engagement on Monday. Because I've got to pick a dress for my wedding and I've only got six weeks until the big day.'

***

'I didn't know you were a property buff,' Maggie said, struggling not to laugh as they made their way back to Jimmy's car.

'I'm not, not really,' he said. 'But the thing is, I really love it up here and I'd like to buy a wee place sooner rather than later. So I've been looking, but you know what it's like on these property websites,' he added ruefully. 'You go on to look at the two-bedroom places and it's the big fancy palaces that catch your eye. And I didn't make it up, there's always a few beautiful places up for grabs in the Highlands. If you've got a couple of million to spend of course.'

'Which Cassie has.'

'Exactly,' Jimmy said. 'And what's been going round in my mind in the last couple of minutes is that if she can somehow break her emotional ties to Inverbeck, but keeps that well-hidden from Dougie...'

'...then it puts her in an amazing bargaining position,' Maggie cut in. 'Jimmy, it's absolutely brilliant, it really is. They get into a bidding war over its value, when she doesn't actually care if she gets it or not.'

He nodded. 'It's a kind of reverse psychology I suppose, not that I know anything about *that* subject.'

'You'd better get on to these agents then,' she said. 'And don't forget to mention the fishing rights.'

Chapter 8

Frank was gutted he hadn't been able to get back to Scotland the previous weekend, so desperate was he to see Maggie again, but work was work, and today looked like being one of the most interesting days in what had already been a pretty long and interesting career. It wasn't every day that you got a chance to visit the famous Advance Studios in St. John's Wood, the very location where the Claymore Warrior's epic Oran na Mara album had been recorded all those years previously. Not that that fact seemed to be impressing his companion DC Ronnie French.

'I don't like any of that folky-rock crap myself guv,' he said, insensitively, shouting above the roar of traffic as they waited for the pedestrian crossing in front of the studios to turn green. 'Me, I love the old ska and reggae stuff. That's the London sound, ain't it? *One Step Beyond.*' He sung the latter phrase *fortissimo*, giving a surprisingly tuneful rendition of the iconic Madness hit.

'If you say so Frenchie,' Frank said. 'And I suppose it's everyone to his own when it comes to taste in music. But really, you should give the Claymore's album another listen. It's bloody brilliant.'

An insistent beeping from the crossing signified that it was now safe to cross, and also drowned out the DC's reply, which Frank doubted was favourable. An automatic sliding glass door swished open on detecting their arrival, welcoming them into an airy glass-ceilinged foyer, the walls adorned with gold records and blown-up photographs of musical artists who had presumably once recorded here.

'Hey look Frenchie,' Frank said, pointing up at one of the photos. 'There's your Madness boys. They look about fifteen in that picture.'

'Yeah, that's my boys,' he grinned. 'Proper band that is. Proper Londoners too.'

'I wouldn't argue with that,' Frank conceded. The reception desk was staffed by a middle-aged woman of pleasant but unprepossessing appearance, which surprised him, since he held a vague stereotype of the recording business being the preserve of the young, beautiful and glamorous. But then again, he thought reproachfully, this nice lady would certainly have been young once, and she might very well have been beautiful and glamorous too. He smiled at her as he introduced himself. 'DCI Frank Stewart with the Met and this is DC French. We're here to see Damian Hammond.'

'Ah yes, we have you on the visitor's register,' she said, glancing down. 'And do you have some ID? I'm Kelly by the way.'

'Sorry, yes I do Kelly,' Frank said, scrambling in a pocket for his warrant card. 'Should have got it out at the start.'

'We get a lot of fans here you see,' she explained as she peered over her glasses at the proffered card. 'We have to be very careful. They'll do anything to get in, especially if one of these boy-bands is in the building. Mind you,' she continued, her voice dropping to a conspiratorial whisper, 'most of them don't do much singing themselves. We have session singers for that. Saves the producers a lot of time and money. But don't tell anybody I told you.'

Frank laughed. 'Aye, I've heard that before and no, I won't tell anybody.'

'Thank you. So if you would like to follow me, I'll take you along to Damian. He's in the control room of Studio One doing some rough mixes. He'll have his cans on so I can't ring him.'

'So is he recording someone at the moment? Someone I would know?'

'Goodness no,' she laughed. 'It's only ten-thirty in the morning. Our musician friends rarely surface before noon. And Damian's a sound engineer, not a producer. It's all digital these days so they spend much of their time working on post-production. You know, equalization and compression and things like that.'

'I'll have to take your word for that Kelly. But it sounds very clever stuff.'

The control room was surprisingly spacious, but dimly lit, one wall dominated by a giant mixing desk with a bank of computer monitors suspended on ceiling-mounted hinged brackets. Everywhere you looked there was electronic kit, all flashing lights and bright digital displays. A full-length glass panel afforded a panoramic view of the iconic Studio One, and Frank took a moment to imagine the scene eighteen years previously, when the Claymore Warriors in their pomp were blasting out the opening bars of Oran na Mara, to be committed to tape and to posterity. He wondered if they knew then that it would become their masterpiece, a body of work still revered in the present day, and destined to continue to be so for as long as folks listened to music. Yes, he thought ruefully, the music was timeless, but he doubted very much if the band would survive the scandalous tsunami that was about to engulf its leader.

A young man sat on a stool, hunched over the desk, headphones clamped to his head, eyes glued to a waveform display that stretched across one of the monitors, whilst he manipulated a mouse with his left hand. Seemingly oblivious to their arrival, it took a gentle tap on the shoulder from Kelly the receptionist to interrupt him. Spinning round, he removed his headphones and said, 'Oh yeah, hi. The police. Sorry, I'll be with you in one second. Just need to save my work.' He spun round again to face the monitor and with a few clicks of the mouse, the screen went blank.

'Grab a pew, ' he said, pointing to a bank of swivel chairs along the back wall of the control room. 'There's some famous arses sat in them I can tell you. Rod Stewart was in that one just last week,' he said, as Frank selected the nearest one.

'My namesake,' he said, 'although he's definitely a better singer. I'm DCI Frank Stewart and this is DC Ronnie French.'

'Great,' he mumbled. 'I'm Damian.' As much as Kelly had broken Frank's faith in music-biz stereotypes, then the appearance of Damian Hammond served to re-establish it. He was probably late twenties or early thirties, with a pock-marked complexion and wearing faded jeans, dirty baseball boots and a black *Guns 'n' Roses* t-shirt. His mousy brown hair was long enough to almost touch his waist, and he was unshaven, although there wasn't quite enough facial growth to describe it as a beard. And he was seriously overweight, a condition Frank attributed to lack of exercise and a diet comprising ordered-in junk food.

'Working on anything interesting?' Frank asked him.

The young man shrugged. 'Depends what you call interesting. The process itself is a bit dull, but the outcome can be quite cool. I'm doing some autotune tweaking at the moment. On some stuff we recorded yesterday.'

'So what's that when it's at home?'

'We can use some awesome software to correct problems with any vocal track. Basically, we can get the computer to fix any flat notes.'

'I think I've heard of that,' Frank grinned. 'It's what you use to make a crap singer sound great, isn't it?'

'Like *no way*,' Hammond shot back. 'That's like an urban myth perpetuated by the right-wing tabloid press. It might surprise you to hear this, but you can't make a long-term career in this business if you can't sing.'

Frank gave him an apologetic smile. 'Sorry Damian, I didn't mean to cause offence.'

The man gave him a chiding look. 'Well okay. But just so you know, all we're doing is saving time and money. Yesterday for example - and I can't tell you who we were working with, but it was somebody like *massive* - the singer gave us the most *unbelievable* vocal performance, totally spine-tingling, one of her best-ever. But there was one note she didn't quite reach. So what are we going to do? Get her to go for another full take, which might not capture the magic, or just use the tech to make a little correction? It's a no-brainer, isn't it?'

'I get that now,' Frank said, suitably chided, 'and thanks for explaining it to me.' He paused for a moment. 'So anyway, to the reason we're here. You're the guy that discovered some... well, call it some very *interesting* stuff on the Oran na Mara master tapes, if that's the correct term. Am I right, and if so, how did that come about?'

'You're *nearly* right,' Hammond said with a hint of a smile, Frank relieved that he seemed to have caused no permanent offence. 'The album was actually a digital recording, one of the first on the new 128-channel desk they'd just had installed. I was still in nappies back then, but I curate the master recording archive now as part of my duties here.'

'So what made you dig it out again after twenty years or however long it is? Is that something that often happens?'

He shrugged. 'Not that often, but it does happen. Sometimes the artist or the record company might do a re-mix to freshen up an old recording, but generally-speaking no-one wants to mess with the original soundscape in case they inadvertently lose some magic.'

'That old magic thing again?' Frank said.

'Exactly,' Hammond said. 'It's intangible, but all I know is if you could bottle it, you would make a fortune.'

'So what caused you to dig out the Oran na Mara masters again?' Frank repeated.

'It was that new recording for the movie that Orla McCarthy's going to be in. They're re-recording the song for the title sequence, and the new producer wanted to sample some of the original backing track, because there's an incredible string section that plays the main theme. It was actually multi-tracked by Jamie Cooper's guitar using a massive bank of effects, but when they tried to reproduce it on the new version they just couldn't nail the sound. So they decided the best solution was actually to sample the original. That's quite common practice nowadays,' he added.

'Jamie's a brilliant guitarist,' Frank said, the observation directed mainly at Ronnie French. 'And this sampling you speak of, you're basically copying the original, right?'

He shrugged. 'Well there's a bit more to it than that, but in essence that's what it is, yes.'

'Aye, I thought so. So you pulled the masters from your archives or whatever it is you do, so you could copy Jamie's fancy guitar bits for the new record. Sorry not copy, *sample*,' he added.

'That's right. Orla came in one day and sat right here,' he said, nodding at the desk, 'and we worked through the master recordings and she showed me the passages she wanted.'

'And it was Orla McCarthy herself who was doing this?' Frank asked, surprised. 'Not the producer?'

'That's right,' he said. 'Lots of people think she's only been successful because she's beautiful, but she's an incredible musician, and massively technically savvy too. She knew exactly what she wanted.' It was said with the passion of a devoted fan, which Frank somehow found surprising in a guy who looked like central casting's rock geek.

'You like her then?' Frank said. 'Rate her as an artist I mean?'

'She's awesome,' he gushed.

'Good-looking bird too,' French said, with a music-hall leer.

Frank gave his colleague a disapproving look. 'DC Ronnie French, always the king of political correctness.'

'Sorry guv,' French replied. 'But she is.'

Frank shook his head before continuing. 'So Damian, somehow McKean's assault on poor Orla made it on to the recording, to lie undiscovered for all this time. Until you found it. Tell me how that happened.'

He shrugged. 'Not much to tell really. I was working on cleaning up the sample because there was a ton of overspill on it.'

'What's that?'

'Unwanted sounds spilling over from other tracks on the song. The Warriors obviously liked to capture a live vibe on their records, so they weren't too fussy about that kind of thing. But if you want to re-use a bit of a track somewhere else, then you need to get rid of the unwanted stuff.'

'It's like what they did on that new Beatles track ain't it?' French cut in. 'They had a dodgy Lennon vocal and piano bit, and they used some fancy AI gizmos to clean it all up.'

'That's right,' Hammond said. 'I had to do multiple passes through the AI filters and on one occasion I was thinking about something else and I let the sample run right through to the end of the original recording. And that's how I found it. It blew my mind to be honest. Crazy.'

'I can understand your reaction Damian,' Frank said, 'Although I didn't understand any of the technical explanation. But what gets me is how come it wasn't found before? And how did it get there in the first place?'

The engineer nodded. 'The answer's the same actually. If I answer your second question first, it got there because the recording engineer at the time forgot to stop the recording on a track they were working on. So after the artists had finished laying down their piece of music, the engineer just omitted to press the stop button. Simple as that. To be honest, it happens all the time in the studio. An easy oversight to make. Done it myself plenty of times.'

'So anything that happened in the studio afterwards would have been caught on tape? And aye, I know it's not actually tape, but you know what I mean.'

'Yes it would,' Hammond agreed. 'As to why it wasn't found before now, well it was captured a good six or seven minutes after the end of the music itself. Anyone who was subsequently using the master recordings for mixing or the like would have no reason to go beyond where the actual music stopped.'

'But you *did* find it sir,' French interjected. This time the look he got from Frank was one of approval, as once again he reflected how easy it was to underestimated his corpulent DC.

Hammond nodded. 'As I said. I was thinking about something else and I let the sample run right through to the end of the original recording. And there it was.'

'Okay, I think we get that,' Frank said, then paused for a moment. 'So Ronnie, are we ready to hear this stuff?'

French nodded his assent.

'Okay,' Hammond said, 'Just give me a minute to load it up.' The engineer wheeled his chair over to the recording desk, and hammered some instructions into a keyboard. A few seconds later, one of the monitors sprang into life, displaying a complex graph pattern that stretched all the way across the screen.

'This is the waveform of the recording. I'll route it through the studio monitor speakers so you can hear it. But I should say in advance, it's fairly indistinct.'

'Why's that?' Frank asked.

'There was just one vocal microphone switched on, and I guess they must have been a fair distance away from it.'

'Alright, play it for us Damian. Not that I'm exactly looking forward to it.'

The engineer took an audible breath. 'If you say so. But it's quite disturbing.'

'We'll cope,' Frank said, indicating with a nod towards the screen that the playback should start.

'Okay, I'll run it from about two minutes before.... before the incident starts.' He clicked on his mouse, then leaned back on his chair, throwing his hair back until it nearly touched the floor. As he had trailed, the recording was indistinct, Frank straining to make sense of the snippets of conversation that could just about be made out. First, he heard a female voice saying what might have been *that was a great take*, followed by a girlish giggle. Then a man's voice, definitely Scottish, responding. *Aye, bloody brilliant doll* and then, in a louder voice, easier to make out, he said, *I hope you got that Nicky.*

'He would have been talking to the control room, to make sure the engineer had got a decent recording,' Hammond suggested. 'No cock-ups with the levels or anything like that.'

'And that's definitely Dougie McKean's voice?' Frank asked. 'I've heard him sing obviously, but I don't think I've heard him speak that often.'

The engineer nodded. 'Yeah, must be. I checked what was on that track, and it was him and Orla overdubbing some vocal harmonies on the choruses.'

'And Nicky? Are we talking about Nicky Nicholson? *The* Nicky Nicholson?'

Nicholson was the veteran record producer who'd worked on a string of classic rock albums in the sixties and seventies, and whose name adorned the sleeve of the iconic Claymore Warrior's album. At the time, it had been a great coup for the band to secure his services, and Frank remembered the proud tagline from the sleeve of his own CD copy. *This album produced and engineered by Nicky Nicholson.*

'So this Nicky geezer must have witnessed whatever happened then?' French asked perceptively.

'Listen on,' Hammond said, 'and you'll get your answer.'

For thirty seconds or more, all that could be heard were a series of unidentifiable shuffles and mumbles, Frank speculating that perhaps the engineer had gone back into the studio and was tiding up some of the equipment. And then suddenly, McKean's voice broke through the background hiss. *So Orla doll, how about a wee kiss for your Uncle Dougie?*

There was a laugh, a girl's laugh, followed by a *that's gross*. And then McKean spoke again. *I'm not asking you, I'm telling you.*

No way, the girl responded, her tone now signalling fear and revulsion in equal measure. *You're older than my dad.*

Once again, McKean spoke, this time in a pleading voice. *Ach come on Orla, it'll be nice.* There was a moment's pause and then he continued, *Here, look at this big beauty. Actually, you'll want to get your nice wee lips around it doll.*'

'Bloody hell,' Frank said quietly, feeling a wave of revulsion sweeping over him.

Hammond sighed. 'Yeah, it's horrible isn't it? But I'm afraid it gets worse.' He paused for a moment. 'Do you really want to hear it?'

Frank shook his head. 'No, we don't *want* to. But we *need* to, unfortunately.'

The engineer nodded, then clicked on the *play* button, restarting the audio. This time, another voice had appeared, male, with a distinct London accent. *Get a move on Dougie, because I want a go after you.*

'Oh God, is that Nicholson?' Frank asked, aghast.

Hammond clicked his mouse again, pausing the playback. 'I'm pretty sure it was. I looked at the old diaries and it was him that was booked to engineer the session.'

Now it was McKean speaking again. *Come on Nicky, grab her. Get her on her knees.*

'Right, enough,' Frank said suddenly, jumping up from his seat. 'We don't need to hear the gory details. So Damian, you've got this all secured and backed up, have you?'

'We were given an mp3 file after Orla's press conference, remember guv?' French said. 'On that CD. It's been stored away now by our digital evidence guys. Safe and sound.'

'Good to know.' Frank gave a long sigh, hands on hips, then turned to address the engineer. 'Okay mate, I appreciate the time you've given us.' But then he paused, his face taking on a serious expression. 'But why didn't you report this to the police immediately Damian?'

The engineer shuffled uncomfortably, avoiding eye contact. 'I just thought I should tell Orla first.' Aye, thought Frank, you wanted the chance to hobnob again with the big star, grab your fifteen minutes of fame whilst you could, have something to tell your grandkids when you were old and past it. It was understandable if not exactly commendable. But the thing that was still pissing him off was the fact that Orla McCarthy had gone to the newspapers before she had come to them. Why had she done that, he wondered? Surely it wasn't just so she could post it all on her YouTube channel.

***

'I've glad you got him to stop that playback guv,' French said as they made their way back to the car-park. 'Bloody ghastly, wasn't it? It was as if we were in the room, watching it.'

'Aye, not pleasant,' Frank agreed. 'But it had to be done.' He paused for a moment. 'What do you make of our boy Hammond then?'

French grinned. 'I didn't expect him to be an Orla McCarthy fan-boy.

'I've seen her in the flesh,' Frank said. 'She is bloody beautiful. But I don't think poor Damian's got much chance with her if I'm being honest.

'Or with nobody else either,' French said. 'He ain't no Brad Pitt.'

Frank laughed. 'That's cruel. But I think we need to get our minds back to the job on hand.'

'Sure guv,' his DC said, grinning. He paused for a moment then said, 'Well at least we can go and round up that Nicholson bloke. He's going to have some explaining to do and make no mistake.'

Frank shot him a wry smile. 'That's going to be a bit problematic Frenchie.'

'Why's that guv?'

He sighed. 'Because if I'm not mistaken, Nicky Nicholson died two or three months ago. At eighty-three. Not a bad innings.'

And it was true, even if that life might not have been something to be proud of.

Chapter 9

Maggie and Ollie had got back to Milngavie mid-afternoon on the Sunday of Orla McCarthy's astounding press conference, and although she had learned in advance that Dougie McKean was to be accused of sexual assault, courtesy of an early-morning phone call with Frank, it made the revelation no less shocking or disturbing. The rolling news channels had been all over the story, and she had caught up with the wall of speculation disguised as analysis whilst she prepared dinner for herself and her son. The question of course, was how this sensational development would affect the Cassie McKean divorce case. Whatever the outcome, it wasn't going to show Mr McKean in the best light, and that probably would favour her client, which she supposed, rather guiltily given the circumstances, was good.

But this Monday morning, for a couple of hours at least, she would be parking all of that whilst she tackled the thorny but pleasurable problem of what she should wear to her upcoming wedding. The truth was, she had been putting it off to the last possible moment, in a brave attempt to get her weight down below nine stone and her size down to a waif-like ten, but had admitted to herself several weeks ago that at the rate of progress she had been achieving - the weekly weight-loss measured in ounces, not pounds - that it simply wasn't going to happen. And in any case, her spirits had been buoyed by the encouragement of her recently-employed assistant Lori Logan, a straight-talking twenty-something, who had contended, with some uncorroborated but nonetheless convincing authority, that men didn't want to share their beds with stick insects, and that in any case

Maggie looked lovely as she was. So now the pair of them were striding purposefully down Byres Road on route to Elle McAndrews Bridal Wear, one of Glasgow's pre-eminent wedding outfitters and conveniently located a mere half a mile from their office, Lori bouncing with visible excitement at being appointed trusted advisor for this critically-important event.

'I'm really sorry your friend Asvina couldn't make the trip up from London Maggie,' she said, and then laughed. 'Actually, I'm not. That's horrible isn't it? But I'm *so* excited that it's me that's going to be with you in that big shop when you're trying on all these dresses.'

Maggie grinned. 'No it's not horrible. Unfortunately, Asvina had to be in court for a big case this afternoon. But we'll get her on a video call this morning. She's really looking forward to it.'

'And is she not getting her bridesmaid's dress from McAndrews too?' Lori asked. 'By the way, I looked her up on Google. She's gorgeous, isn't she?'

'Yes she is, and she's a very lovely person too,' Maggie said. 'And as to the dress, well Asvina has already got about a hundred designer outfits in her wardrobe. So she told me to pick my wedding dress first and then she would look out something that complimented it.' She knew too that Asvina's outfit would be carefully selected so as not to outshine her own dress. That was the kind of friend Asvina Rani was, and Maggie loved her with every fibre of her being.

They were greeted by Elle McAndrews herself, an immaculately-groomed woman who Maggie estimated to be in her mid-to-late-sixties, and exceptionally well-preserved for her age. She wore a knitted two-piece suit in a salmon-pink shade, with matching high-heeled formal shoes that clearly had been picked for style and not comfort. But the effect was classy, understated and professional.

'So Maggie, welcome to my little establishment,' McAndrews said, smiling warmly. 'I know how incredibly difficult it is to find that perfect dress or outfit, but we'll do everything we can to help you. And of course you can take as long as you like over your choice.' She laughed. 'Even if that means trying on every outfit in the shop.'

'Does that often happen?' Maggie asked, grinning.

The woman gave a mock-rueful smile. 'More than you'd think. But really, we don't mind. So before we get started, there's just three little questions to ask you. Firstly, I'd say you're about a twelve, is that right?'

Maggie nodded. 'Yes, I'm afraid it is.'

'Not at all, twelve is the perfect size. After all, men don't like skinny little things these days, do they?' she added, chuckling.

'See, *told* you,' Lori burst out, her tone triumphant.

'The second question,' McAndrews continued, 'is, are we looking at a formal white wedding gown, or are we going for a more informal outfit?'

'White wedding gown,' Lori burst out again. 'You'd look amazing in one Maggie, really you would.'

Maggie shook her head. 'No,' she said quietly. 'You see, my previous marriage just has too many awful memories, and I've been trying so hard to erase everything about it from my mind. So, no a white wedding gown would just bring it all flooding back. I can't go there.'

'Oh god Maggie, I didn't know,' Lori said, a hand shooting up to cover her mouth. 'I'm sorry.'

'Don't worry about it Lori, it's not something I like to talk about,' Maggie said. 'So yes Elle, I'd like something a little less formal. Oh, and there is one important thing. You see, my groom and his brother are going to be wearing kilts. So I'd like something with a Scottish theme to match them.' She grinned. 'Even though I'm getting married in Yorkshire. But I'm sure you'll have plenty of choice in that regard.'

McAndrews nodded enthusiastically. 'Oh my *goodness*, we have so many *lovely* dresses like that, and many that brides choose even when they were originally thinking of a traditional white wedding gown. You are going to look *so* amazing Maggie, believe me.' She paused for a moment, then said, 'So to my third question, and always the most delicate.'

'No limit Mrs McAndrews,' Lori butted in, anticipating the question. 'It's your wedding Maggie, and you want to look incredible for your lovely Frank. And I'll take a wages cut if it's too expensive. Only for a week, mind.'

Maggie laughed. 'I'm pleased you're so enthusiastic about spending my money Lori, and thank you for your kind offer too. But yes Elle, she's right. Getting the right dress is more important than the price. *Within reason*,' she added, rather fearfully.

***

But in the end, she needn't have worried, Elle McAndrews justifying her stellar reputation by instantly producing four beautiful contenders, any one of which Maggie would have happily chosen. She tried on each one in turn, video-consulting each time with Asvina, who liked them all, but in her typical decisive fashion, her friend was prepared to express a slight preference. Lori evidently concurred with Asvina's choice.

'Maggie, you look flipping *incredible* in that one,' she said, her eyes shining. 'Look, here's what it says about it,' she continued, holding up the glossy leaflet that had been in its box, then reading out loud. *'This Fiona Ingleton classic wedding dress is the perfect choice for those of you who seek a traditional yet romantic and eye-catching effect. The tartan upper garment is tailored with the tartan of your choice, so you don't have to worry about whether it will match your groom's Highland outfit or not. The dress can be worn with an additional petticoat for a structured shape, or without for a more flowing style. This gorgeous dress features a beautifully tiered underskirt, in natural white silk, corset-style cinching on the top, silk-lined for soft comfort, and romantic ruffled silk and beading to the bust.'*

'It's a Fiona Ingleton is it?' Maggie asked, with some apprehension.

'Surprisingly affordable,' Elle McAndrews cut in smoothly, answering Maggie's unspoken question. When the price was revealed, it was certainly a surprise, although describing it as affordable was perhaps stretching a point. But it looked and felt absolutely right, and now all that was required was for her to share her choice with her lovely mum, who was waiting patiently at home in Yorkshire for the photographs from her daughter.

'This is the one Elle,' she said, beaming. 'This is the *one*.'

'An excellent choice,' the shopkeeper said. 'Now, shall we look at shoes? I have a very nice matching pair right here. Navy blue.'

Lori cut in in her best Glasgow vernacular, an eyebrow raised. 'Aye, and are they ones surprisingly affordable as well?'

***

It had been such a relief to have all of *that* out of the way, and it had been lovely to share the photographs with her little son, who *of course* said his mummy looked like a fairy princess and *of course*, promised not to tell his Uncle Frank anything about it. On the Tuesday, her mum had arrived from Yorkshire to take on school-holiday child-care duties, not that Mrs Bainbridge regarded spending time with her adored grandson anything other than a wonderful pleasure. On Wednesday it was time to get back to work, which meant travelling back up to the Highlands too. The only problem was, their big McKean divorce case had hit what could only be described as severe turbulence after the sensational events of the last weekend, where Orla McCarthy had accused Dougie McKean of a horrible sexual assault back when she was a teenager. Not surprisingly, the revelation continued to generate a media storm, and McKean, though issuing furious denials, had shut himself away with his band in a secluded farm not too far from Grantown-On-Spey, where they had taken over a capacious barn in order to complete rehearsals for their upcoming headline slot at the *Thunder in the Mountains* festival. She and Lori had chosen to drive up this time, mainly because her assistant, who would also be attending the festival, had insisted on bringing her own tent and associated gear - of which there was quite a lot - rather than taking up the offer of the compartment of the glamping accommodation previously occupied by Ollie. 'I want the full-on festival experience,' Lori had declared, which evidently included getting blind drunk and returning to your tent at three o'clock in the morning with a boy with whom you intended to have relations, whilst singing tunelessly at the top of your lungs. In truth, Maggie was quite pleased with this development, since perhaps Frank, who was also travelling northwards in pursuit of Dougie McKean, might be able to desert his hotel at least once in order to spend the night with her.

Now it was Thursday morning, and they were temporarily camped up in an Aviemore cafe having breakfast, Lori having earlier lost the argument with the small gas stove on which she had promised to make them eggs and bacon.

'So what's the plan boss?' she asked, taking a slurp of tea. 'Have we got one?'

Maggie shrugged. 'We've got one, but it's not much of one. We'll just drive up to the farm and force our way in, and tell Dougie that unless he takes the time to look at our proposal, Cassie's definitely going to court. Full stop.'

'And that's not likely to turn out well for him given his current predicament, is it?' her assistant said. 'I mean, the court's not going to grant custody to someone who's assaulted an underage girl in the past, are they?'

'Remember, that's only an allegation,' Maggie cautioned. 'But no, they're not. So hopefully, he'll see sense.'

But in truth she *wasn't* hopeful, and the dilemma of what they would do if he refused to have anything to do with them fully occupied her mind as they drove in silence northwards along the sweeping A95, the majestic River Spey never out of sight for long. Frank of course would not have that problem, he having the option of arresting McKean and carting him away to a police station for questioning, which she imagined was exactly what he was going to do as soon as he got here. But the two of them took great care to keep their respective jobs properly separated, so she couldn't and wouldn't ask for any special favours as far as access to McKean was concerned. The fact was, she thought rather gloomily, if the singer told them to sling their hook then the only response would be *okay then, see you in court.* She could see it being a very short meeting indeed.

The farm was located on the eastern side of the river about three miles north of the town, approached via a narrow rutted lane of nearly a quarter of a mile in length, bounded by moss-covered dry-stone walls on either side. Turning a bend in the lane, they saw it opened up into a large concreted yard, which, to their surprise, was packed with vehicles. But then, thought Maggie, maybe that shouldn't have come as a surprise, given the amount of gear a major rock band must have to cart around with them. And as confirmation, she noticed the huge articulated truck parked in the corner, its side bearing the slogan *Claymore Warriors on Tour*. A bunch of expensive cars and SUVs were dotted about the yard too, which she presumed belonged to members of the band. But then, something much more interesting caught her eye.

'Lori, is that Orla McCarthy over there?' she said with a note of surprise. 'Wearing the short red puffer jacket?'

'Aye, it is,' she said, peering ahead. 'Definitely. And I recognise that skinny wee guy who's with her. That's your pal Yash Patel, isn't it?'

'Yeah it is, you're right. I wonder what the hell he's doing here?' she said. The question was mainly rhetorical, since there was always only one reason why Yash went anywhere, and that was in pursuit of a story. And then she remembered what Frank had told her, in scathing terms, about the *Chronicle's* fly-on-the-wall documentary.

'Hey Yash,' she shouted. 'What's going on here, as if I don't already know?'

Patel swivelled round on hearing his name. 'Maggie, it's you,' he said, sounding pleased to see her, or at least faking it very well if he wasn't. 'What the hell are you doing here?'

'Same as you, I expect. We're here to see Dougie McKean.'

'Yup, you're right,' he said, smiling. 'We're doing a documentary for Chronicle TV, and I'm the presenter and producer.' He nodded towards the man in a leather jacket who stood a few paces away from them, with what was evidently a TV camera mounted on one shoulder. 'And that's Rupert, our camera guy.'

'Yeah, Frank told me all about Rupert and your little documentary, ' she said sardonically. 'He's not very pleased about it.'

Patel smiled. 'Maybe, but it's very important to Orla that her story is told properly.' *Especially if she gets to write the script herself*, Maggie thought rather unkindly.

'Maggie, hello again,' Orla said, slightly warily. 'Are you up here to see Cassie again?'

She nodded, 'Yes, and her husband.' She paused for a moment. 'And obviously I've read all about your situation Orla. It's really terrible. I was *so* sorry to hear about it.'

The singer shrugged. 'I had to bring it all out into the open, because it was really messing with my mental health. It was my duty, don't you think? Because it happens to so many young women nowadays, and I just hope that what I've done inspires some of them to speak out.' It sounded like a prepared speech, Maggie thought, causing her to remind herself once again of the fact that Dougie McKean should be regarded as innocent until proven guilty. A hint of movement caused her to glance over her shoulder, to see that Rupert had evidently been filming the encounter.

'It's fly-on-the-wall,' Patel said, with a hint of apology. 'It does what is says on the tin.'

'Well just make sure Rupert gets my best side,' she said wryly. 'So what's happening now Yash? What's the big plan?'

He gave an expansive smile. 'We're going for the big action shot. Orla's going to run into that barn, talking to camera as she goes, and then she's going to go right up to McKean and confront him. It's going to be TV gold, I guarantee it.'

'What, is she going to punch him or something? Because that wouldn't be the smartest thing to do.'

'Nah,' Patel said, 'She's going to ask him to *confess*. To tell the world what he's done, and repent for his sins.'

Maggie shook her head. 'Well if his lawyers are any good, then he'll have been told to answer with a brisk *no comment*.' And then she recalled the name of Tamara Gray, the lawyer who was his lover too. She was no doubt a smart and savvy woman, and she would definitely have made sure that McKean was properly briefed. But that didn't seem to be worrying Patel.

'Exactly,' he smirked, 'and can you imagine how that's going to look on camera? Like I said, it's going to be TV gold.'

Enjoy it whilst you can, Maggie thought, because she knew exactly what Frank was going to say when he found out about this vigilante operation. They'd be warned off in no uncertain terms, and if that didn't work, they'd find themselves facing a perverting the course of justice charge. But for now, she was happy to go along with it.

'Well you'd better go first,' she said, 'but Lori and I will follow you in, if you don't mind.'

'Sure,' he grinned. 'I just hope we don't have to boot the door open.' He paused for a moment, looking pensive. 'Actually, that wouldn't be such a bad idea,' he continued, evidently serious. 'Maybe I'll just go and pull it shut before we go in. It'll make great telly. Just hang on a minute Rupert,' he added, nodding in the direction of the barn door. 'And Orla, if you could just do a little introduction to camera before we go in.'

She watched the singer turn to address Rupert's camera and then give her spiel, pointing over her shoulder in the direction of the barn, looking rather like a war correspondent reporting on some third-world insurgency. But a very beautiful and charismatic one, Maggie thought, having no difficulty in understanding why the Irishwoman was about to become a big movie star.

'Right, let's go,' Orla shouted. 'We're going in.'

She set off towards the barn at a fast trot, but not so fast as to prevent Rupert keeping up and capturing the action. The door was kicked open as choreographed by Patel, the group emerging into a large high-roofed space that was carpeted with a thin bed of straw, presumably testimony to its normal use as a cow byre. The band had set up stage along one wall, an enormous drum-kit mounted on a wooden plinth and huge banks of loudspeakers on either side of it. Three musicians stood on a low platform, a guitarist, a keyboard player and a drummer, each doodling quietly on their instruments. But Dougie McKean, lead singer and occasional bass player, was not amongst those present.

'Oh hi Orla,' the guitarist shouted out as he noticed her approach, muting the strings of his instrument. 'I suppose you're here to see Dougie? He's not around, as you've no doubt noticed.'

'Hi Orla,' the other two said, almost in unison. Wracking her brains, Maggie struggled to recall the names of these lesser-known musicians, names that Frank revered and had been keen to make sure she recognised. Yes, that was it. Jamie Cooper was the guitarist - a seriously awesome player according to her lovely fiancé - and his younger brother Rab was the keyboard player. Completing the line up was Geordie Fisher on drums and percussion. They'd been together more than twenty years without a single change in line-up, a situation which she knew was highly-unusual if not unique in the music business.

'So where is he Jamie?' Orla asked sternly.

'He came in half-pissed this morning. He'd been hitting the bottle, which isn't exactly remarkable to be fair.' Cooper gave a judgemental nod towards a cardboard box printed with a familiar logo that sat in the corner of the room. 'The film company and your bloody boyfriend David sent him these cases of Balvenie, to try and get him to agree to using Oran na Mara in the movie. I've no idea why they thought *that* was a good idea.'

Orla shrugged into the camera, but didn't say anything.

'There's only about half a dozen bottles left now,' the guitarist continued. 'He's been battering through it at a great rate of knots. But anyway, he was all over the bloody place this morning, couldn't remember what day of the week it was, never mind how to play any of our numbers. So we told him to bugger off and sober himself up. Him and his girlfriend have rented a lodge over at Glengarnet to try and get away from the paparazzi. I've been picking him up most mornings to make sure he bloody got here.' He paused and gave her a disdainful smile. 'In fact yesterday he was still in bed with that woman and I had to hang about for an hour before he got his arse moving. Anyway, I'll give you the address if you want.'

She smiled. 'Yeah Jamie, that would be like *awesome*.' As she said it, she looked into the camera, gave a thumbs up, and said, with a dramatic flourish, 'The quest continues guys. *Game on.*'

Maggie gave Lori a quiet nudge. 'Just make sure we get that address too,' she whispered.

'Affirmative boss. But where's this Glengarnet place exactly?'

She shrugged. 'Don't know exactly, but we passed some signs for it on the way here, so it can't be too far away.'

'So I guess the rehearsals have been a bit of a car-crash then?' Orla asked Jamie Cooper.

He sighed. 'You could say that. We got nothing done yesterday or today either, obviously. We're going to sound like a pub band on Saturday. Or worse.'

'Hey, maybe we could have a wee jam, now that you're here,' the drummer shouted out. 'This place is costing us enough so we might as well use it.'

Orla exchanged a questioning look with Patel, then smiled once more into the camera. 'Yeah, like why not?' she told her invisible audience. 'It's only rock and roll but I *like* it.'

'What shall we do?' Jamie Cooper asked, then paused for a moment. 'Actually, do you know *Mountain Dew* from the Oran na Mara album? It's the second or third track. Bit of a power ballad.'

'I know it a wee bit,' she said, 'but I won't remember all the words.'

'Don't worry,' Cooper said, laughing. 'Just go *do do do* if you don't know them. It'll sound way better than Dougie's awful bloody wailing no matter what you sing. And Rab will bung on some bass on his keyboard, so we won't miss that either.'

'Okay, let's try it,' she said. She looked into the camera and smiled again at her audience. 'And don't worry you guys, if this is god-damn awful, you won't ever hear it. *Promise*,' she added, signing off by blowing them a kiss.

But it wasn't awful, it was magical, and for the first time, Maggie could understand why Frank and his brother loved this band so much. The music was powerful and vibrant, Orla's vocals soaring crystal-clear above the intricate interlinked melodies of the Cooper brothers, the band driven along by the hypnotic back-beat provided by Geordie Fisher's dynamic drumming. Then all too soon the number was over, concluding with a dramatic guitar power-chord, a crash of the cymbals and an impossibly-high falsetto note from Orla's unbelievable voice.

'Bloody hell,' she heard Lori exclaim alongside her. 'That was *bloody* amazing. I mean, how can they do that, without even having played together before?'

'They're professionals,' Maggie said, equally awestruck. 'It's what they do. Together with natural talent of course.'

And, she reflected, the wonderful Orla McCarthy hadn't screwed up a single word of the song either, despite her prior apologies. *Interesting, that*.

Chapter 10

Frank was looking forward very much to his trip up to Scotland, not so much because of the necessity to interview Dougie McKean in connection with Orla McCarthy's allegations, but because he would get to see Maggie again after what was it? - aye, nearly ten days, and that was ten days too long in his opinion. But work came first, and with McCarthy's case now in the public eye, he needed to continue to pick up the pace of his investigation. Ordinarily his first priority would be to haul in the accused and go through all the formalities, top of the list being to collect fingerprint and DNA samples. But the Commissioner had made it clear to him and DCI Jill Smart that this case had two priorities. The first, sure, was to investigate Orla McCarthy's claims and bring Dougie McKean to justice should the claims be substantiated. But the second priority - of equal importance to the brass, Frank knew - was to dive into the historic investigation conducted by the now-Assistant Commissioner Ian Archibald and see what had happened, or more specifically, to see what had gone wrong. So as a simple matter of logistics, Frank had decided he had to see Archibald first before heading north. There was a risk in this of course, a small one admittedly, but one that had the potential of causing a serious shit-hitting-the-fan scenario should it transpire. What if Dougie McKean was guilty and decided that he wouldn't wait around to see justice dispensed, and so decided to go into hiding? Or more practically, what if he decided to leg it to the United States with his American girlfriend? He could be extradited of course, but that could take years, and in the meantime the public would be asking why McKean hadn't been arrested as soon as Orla's allegations had surfaced.

Still, he would leave the brass to worry about that if and when it happened. This Wednesday morning, Archibald was turning up at Kensington police station for a formal interview, which would be conducted in the presence of a senior officer from the Association of Chief Constables, which was basically his trade union, although they didn't call it that. Because of the respect that needed to be shown to someone of Archibald's rank, Frank wasn't going to be accompanied on this occasion by DC Ronnie French - which would have been his preference - or DS Gemma James, but by his gaffer DCI Smart. They'd picked the biggest of the interview rooms rather than one of the dungeon-like ones down in the basement, and Frank wouldn't have been surprised to have seen a wee vase of flowers on the formica table that would separate interviewers with interviewee. He'd been involved in one of these cases before, a very similar one in fact involving a former Chief Constable of Police Scotland, and he remembered only too well the excruciating awkwardness of the affair. But he would just have to put up with that, much as he didn't like it.

On Monday they'd finally got to Orla McCarthy, inviting her in to Atlee House to recount her story, which was pretty much as Frank had expected, although he could have done without the tearful interludes that interrupted the session every five minutes. Yesterday, he had set DS James and Eleanor Campbell the task of digging into the case files on the old police computer, and he'd come armed with a few summaries of the interview notes from back then. On arrival he'd swung by Jill's office to pick her up, and together they wandered down to the interview room, notebooks in hand. They found AC Archibald already there, sitting at the table alongside another uniformed senior officer with whom he was exchanging a few words.

'Good morning sir,' Smart said to him, pulling out a chair opposite and sitting down. 'This is DCI Frank Stewart, who's been appointed SIO on the McCarthy case, and is also conducting our little cold-case review as you know.'

'Morning sir,' Frank said pleasantly, taking his seat and placing his notebook and pen on the table.

'Good morning,' Archibald said, his tone stiff and formal. 'And this is ACC Jane Lennon from Merseyside Constabulary. Jane's my association representative,' he added.

'Good morning both,' she said, a trace of Liverpool accent discernible. 'And before you ask, no, I'm no relation to the famous Beatle.'

'I bet you get asked that eight days a week ma'am,' Frank said, deadpan.

'Very droll DCI Stewart,' she said, raising an eyebrow. 'So, let's get down to it shall we? And before we start, let me remind you that this isn't a criminal enquiry. It's a meeting, no more or no less, where we will have a discussion about events that happened nearly twenty years ago.' She nodded in the direction of the recording device that sat at one end of the table. 'So we won't be needing that today.'

'No ma'am it wasn't my intention to use it,' Frank lied. 'But you won't mind if I take notes?' he added, holding his pen aloft. She nodded her assent.

'So sir,' he began, looking at Archibald and giving a faint smile, 'you know the background to this. There was an investigation way way back that you were in charge of, one that came to nothing at the time. And now some new evidence seems to have emerged and we have to take another look at what happened back then. That's it in a nutshell, isn't it sir?'

'That's it,' Archibald agreed. He looked nervous, Frank thought, as well he might, because they both knew the tricky situation he found himself in. If the probe discovered that the original investigation was flawed, the AC and the AC alone was going to take the blame, thrown to the lions or the dogs or whatever the expression was. Afterwards, the Force would blandly assert that lessons would be learnt so that it couldn't happen again, these lessons remaining unspecified, and Archibald would be consigned to the annals of easily-forgotten history. Frank felt a bit sorry for him in truth, because every cop had cases in their back-catalogues that hadn't gone exactly the way they would have wanted. The AC was a good-looking guy, reminding Frank a bit of Richard Gere in his *Pretty Woman* prime. Late forties, and with well-founded expectations of making it all the way to Chief Constable, he was also openly gay and proud of it. It was a stance that Frank admired and respected very much, given that culturally, the Met was still stuck in the nineteen-seventies. But this affair could ruin his reputation in a stroke, and as the AC continued, he made it clear he wasn't intending to go down without a fight.

'Obviously DCI Stewart, I've thought long and hard in the last few days about how myself and my team conducted that investigation, and I don't think there's anything I would change if we were to do it again. So please, feel free to dig into any aspect of our original case. We've got nothing to hide, believe me. You'll have my full cooperation.'

'Good to know that sir,' Frank said. 'So maybe you could just take us through it from your recollection? I appreciate it was all a long time ago now, but give us as much detail as you can remember.'

'I can remember it very clearly. Obviously with such well-known musicians being involved, it wasn't your ordinary case.'

'You were a fan of the Warriors, weren't you sir?' Frank said. 'I'm a massive fan myself as it happens. In fact, I'm off up to Aviemore to see them this weekend at that Thunder in the Mountains festival. If I don't have to arrest Dougie McKean first, that is.'

Archibald gave a wry smile. 'The tickets. I know what you're thinking, and I admit from a distance how bad it looks. But I accepted them several weeks after the investigation was completed. And yes, in retrospect, I know it was a mistake. But it had absolutely no influence on how I or my team conducted the investigation. None whatsoever.'

It was his Achilles' heel, they both knew it, and they both knew too that if it ever got into the press, he would be toast, irrespective of the outcome of the investigation. But it was good to get it on the table right at the start.

'I'm working on that assumption sir,' Frank said, speaking slowly. 'Let's just say we're looking for cock-ups, not corruption. Initially at least,' he added, recognising the need to hedge his bets at this early stage.

'You'll find neither, I can assure you.'

Frank shrugged. 'Aye, well let's hope so. But anyway, we got distracted sir, sorry, my fault. Take me through your investigation, and I'll just dive in from time to time if I need any clarification. Is that okay?'

Archibald nodded. 'Fine.' He hesitated for a moment before continuing. 'So the first thing to recognise was there was a considerable gap between when the allegation was reported to us and when it was purported to have actually happened. Almost eight weeks in fact. The second thing was, the garbled and incoherent nature of the accusation itself.'

'Okay, so explain please.'

'It was Orla McCarthy's father who brought the complaint to us. Paddy McCarthy was his name, and he was a difficult man to make sense of if I'm being honest. I don't know Ireland at all,' Archibald continued, 'but he was from County Cork, and he had a pretty impenetrable accent. And he wasn't an educated man either, not that there's a problem with that, obviously,' he added, somewhat apologetically. 'But as I said, it wasn't easy to understand what he was talking about, and that wasn't just the accent. He spoke at about a hundred miles an hour and his thoughts were all over the place. So at first, we thought his complaint was just about a song that he was accusing the Warriors of stealing from his daughter - Oran na Mara, as it turned out.'

Frank nodded. 'Yep, Orla maintains she came up with that whole iconic passage in the middle - you know, the slow bit - but Dougie refused to give her a writing credit.'

'Exactly, that was it,' Archibald said. 'So as you'll understand, we told Paddy McCarthy that whether his daughter's assertion was true or not, it wasn't a criminal matter, and that he'd have to get himself a lawyer and take it up with the civil courts if he wanted to pursue it. And I'm ninety-nine percent certain that it was only after *that* that he brought up the sexual assault allegation against Dougie McKean. It was as if Plan A had failed and so they were moving on to Plan B. That's how it felt at the time.'

Frank hesitated for a moment then said, 'So I'm already getting the feeling, even twenty years on and after just five minutes listening to you, that you were sceptical about Orla's claims right from the beginning. Which if you don't mind me saying, isn't exactly a brilliant way to approach a serious accusation like this. What do you say to that, AC Archibald? Do you see where I'm coming from? It doesn't look great, does it?'

'Look,' Archibald said sharply, 'it's easy to be a smart-arse with the benefit of twenty-twenty hindsight. But I'm telling you, that's how it felt to me at the time.'

'Appreciate that sir,' Frank said, 'but what I said is just how it feels to *me* right now. Anyway, despite your reservations, you did push on with the investigation, we know that from the files. So tell me how that went.'

'Okay. Obviously we had only heard the story from the father, so we had to hear it again directly from Orla, who, I remind you, was only fifteen at the time.'

Frank glanced down at his notebook. 'Right. So it says here you brought in a DS Anne Clark to conduct the face-to-face interviews with Orla. Clark, I assume, had been trained to know how to handle this sort of sensitive stuff.'

'That's correct,' Archibald agreed. 'It was handled with great care, and DS Clark did eventually manage to get to the detail of the allegation.'

'Which was?'

Archibald looked at Lennon, as if seeking guidance. 'But you know all this already,' he said, nodding at Frank's notebook. 'I can see you've looked at the file.'

'I want to hear it in your own words sir, if you don't mind. Please, continue.'

'There was an allegation of oral sex. That Dougie McKean took out his penis and made her… well, I'm sure you can fill in the blanks.'

'Charming,' Frank said, glancing at his notes again. 'And as to who held her so that his foul act could take place, that was never properly established in your investigation, was it?'

'No it wasn't,' Archibald conceded. 'Orla maintained that she went faint when she saw his *thing* - that's what she called it at the time - and that everything was a blur to her afterwards, and so she didn't know who had held her.'

'Aye, understandable,' Frank said, chewing his ballpoint pensively. 'And what did your DS Clark make of all of that?'

'She was unconvinced,' Archibald said. 'Definitely.'

'That's *your* opinion sir, or would she say the same if we spoke to her? And by the way, is she still with the force?'

'No, she left several years ago,' the AC said sharply. 'And yes, it was her opinion too.'

'And why was that do you think? Why did she form that opinion?'

Archibald hesitated for a moment. 'It was the mechanics. It's not easy to force someone to perform that act, is it? The victim has to be kneeling for a start, and you wouldn't do that voluntarily if you were trying to avoid it. DS Clark challenged Orla on that aspect, and it was only then that she remembered that she had been held. Or said she had been.'

'Okay,' Frank said slowly. 'So after DS Clark's interview with Orla, I'm getting the feeling that you were minded to disbelieve her.'

'Look, it wasn't *just* that,' the AC said. 'Obviously, we interviewed all the other parties too. McKean, the band, the studio guys, even the receptionists. And there was an *incident*, which you no doubt will have seen in the files.'

'Aye, this incident. Tell us about that, will you?'

He nodded. 'McKean was drunk nearly every day of the Oran na Mara sessions, according to everybody. He was never seen without a bottle of Johnny Walker in his hand.'

'It's his trade-mark, isn't it?' Frank said. 'Although he seems to have moved a bit upmarket since then in his choice of whisky.'

'But apparently he'd been slipping Orla a dram or two all the way through the sessions as well. The band in particular were quite open about this and said it was her that had always been asking for some. Nobody had forced it on her, according to them.'

'Hardly a surprise,' Frank said, giving a shrug. 'She was a teenager after all.'

'Indeed. So on one occasion the band had been in the studio adding some vocal overdubs, and they were all a bit merry, and McKean had been particularly inebriated, even by his standards. This was according to Jamie Cooper the guitarist.'

'Aye, we saw that in the file,' Frank said. 'Go on.'

'So everybody was in good spirits on account of it having been a great session, that's according to Jamie Cooper again, when out of the blue, McKean asks Orla for a kiss. She laughs and tells him that she finds the idea disgusting because he's old enough to be her father.'

'Which he is.'

'Yes he is. But then, he takes out his penis and says something like *one day you'll learn how fantastic it is to have one of these inside you*, or something equally tasteless. Everybody's laughing their heads off except Orla, who bursts into tears. Jamie Cooper realises McKean's gone too far this time, and pushes him out of the studio and along the corridor to the reception area, where he tells the reception girl to get McKean a taxi and get him back home.'

Frank nodded thoughtfully. 'And you believed this version of events sir did you? Because it all sounds a bit too neat and tidy to me, if you want my honest opinion.'

Archibald gave him a cold look. 'It was as plausible as any other version.' Softening a little, he continued, 'And you know what these kind of cases are like. It often comes down to one person's word against another's. And this one was the same, unfortunately.'

'And yet you didn't seem to look too hard for corroborating forensic evidence, did you? As far as I can see from the files, Orla was never examined by a doctor.'

'There was no vaginal penetration,' Archibald said matter-of-factly. 'So we were given the advice that a physical examination would cause the victim distress but wouldn't yield anything useful.'

'Aye, I suppose that's fair enough,' Frank conceded. 'And the docs ruled against an oral examination too, did they?'

'Yes. It was their opinion that even if there had been ejaculation, Orla's saliva would have destroyed any trace of DNA in the weeks between the alleged incident and when she reported it.'

Frank nodded. 'And *was* there ejaculation? Because Orla says there was.'

Archibald gave what looked like a regretful shrug. 'That was never established. But as far as I can recall, it was thought to be unprovable.'

'So nobody asked then, I suppose?' Frank said quietly, the question intending to be rhetorical. That, in a nutshell, was the problem with this investigation, he thought. No-one had asked the right questions or enough of them either, a major failing in what was looking like a sloppy, second-rate piece of detective work. He paused for a moment, closed his notebook, then sighed. 'So I'm kind of thinking we're done here, unless there's anything else you can think of sir?'

***

It had been a stressful session, and Frank was pleased to accept Jill Smart's offer of a coffee down the canteen, an offer he had cheekily augmented by adding a jam doughnut on the side. They ordered the comestibles at the serving counter and carried them back to a small table that sat against one wall of the room.

'So what do you think Frank?' Jill asked. 'Because you heard Orla's side of the story on Monday, didn't you?'

'Aye, I did, and to be honest, there's no glaring inconsistencies to call out. Different interpretations, sure, but nothing that jumps out at you.'

'So what am I going to be reporting back to the Commissioner? Actually I'm surprised he's not been on the phone already.'

He laughed. 'Tell him enquiries are on-going and you'll report back when you've more to say. That's what he always says to the media, isn't it?'

'No, seriously,' she said, not laughing. 'Where are we on this?'

'Okay. So Orla's story is that they were in the studio one day, and yes they had been drinking - and you can see here how easy it is spin two different stories for the same event. *They'll* say she was begging for some booze, *she'll* say they were shamelessly plying an under-age girl with the stuff.'

'Yes, I can see that.'

'Orla says McKean asked for a kiss and then took out his penis. So far, both accounts square up. But Jamie Cooper contends he was there during the incident, and that he ushered McKean away before he could do any more damage. She, on the other hand, says she was a bit drunk and woozy and that she was forced to... well, perform a sex act, I think that's how it's often described. And apologies in advance if this is even more distasteful, but she says that he came in her mouth too.'

'Something that was and is impossible to prove.' Smart pointed out.

'Aye, exactly, 'Frank agreed. 'Now look at it from Archibald's point of view. Right from the start, he's suspicious that these allegations might have been fabricated by the McCarthy family to hurt McKean, whom the father has accused of stealing Orla's song. The AC thinks that maybe Orla has latched on to the penis incident - which no-one is denying actually took place, by the way - and has woven a spiced-up tale around it to accuse Dougie McKean of sexual assault. There's no forensic evidence to support her story, and given it's just going to be Orla's word against everybody else's, Archibald and the CPS decide this one is best filed in the drawer labelled *too difficult.*' He paused for a moment. 'I mean, you can see both sides of it, can't you?'

'Sure. But what do I tell the Commissioner?' Smart asked again.

Frank shrugged. 'No real evidence of corruption, which is good, although accepting these free tickets was seriously dumb and might come back and bite him on the arse if it gets out. If there was any fault, it's perhaps that the investigation was guilty of making up its mind too early, and then closing it to anything that might challenge its assumptions. Let's just say it doesn't look like the AC's finest piece of work.'

And with that recording now in the hands of the Maida Vale forensic guys, it had every prospect of getting a whole lot worse.

Chapter 11

It was Thursday evening, which had always been a special one for Maggie and her precious little gang, stretching back almost three years, back to when she barely knew the Stewart brothers and when they all used to meet up for an after-work drink at the Old King's Head in Shoreditch -which, she had subsequently discovered, wasn't actually in Shoreditch at all, but more in Finsbury, being close to the Barbican, not that that was important to know. Since then, Frank and Jimmy Stewart had become the most precious people in her life, apart obviously from her amazing little son and her mum and ailing dad. When they'd all moved up to Scotland about a year ago, they'd kept up the tradition, moving location to the welcoming Horseshoe Bar on Glasgow's Great Western Road. But this time they were back in Aviemore, in a newly-opened establishment called *The Infamous Grouse*, a name that though undoubtedly amusing, was unlikely to last long once the multi-national drinks company that owned the trademark to the *famous* Grouse brand got to hear of it.

They were five in all - herself, lovely Frank, his brother Jimmy, her associate Lori Logan and a colleague of Frank's - a woman who was new to her - officially named Detective-Sergeant Gemma James, but who apparently went by the nickname Jessie. Since falling in love with Frank, Maggie had found herself casting a critical eye over any woman who came into her fiancé's sphere, and this Jessie creature was now undergoing the same covert examination. And to be honest, she didn't very much like what she saw, assessing James as one of these women whose carefully-curated appearance was overtly designed to attract the attention of men. The woman's hair, long, thick and wavy, was jet-black - dyed, obviously, given her age, which Maggie estimated as late thirties - and her eyes were surrounded by a deep ring of navy liner. She wore skinny denim jeans and a short check-patterned jacket which struggled to cover a full bosom squeezed into a dazzling white T-shirt. And most importantly, the third finger of her left hand was bereft of a ring. Moreover, in the few minutes since they had met, Maggie had already discovered that the woman's favourite subject of conversation was herself, although she conceded that might be because she was nervous in new company. Luckily though, and not unexpectedly, DS Jessie James' attention was focussed not on Frank but on Jimmy, a fact that pleased Maggie but was visibly annoying Miss Lori Logan, who wore an expression like thunder.

'I'm like you Jimmy, I'm into all that outside adventure stuff myself,' Maggie overheard Jessie saying to him. 'One of my old boyfriends had a souped-up Land-Rover and we used to go battering down the green lanes in Surrey. It was an absolute blast, and it upset the eco-mentalists too, which was a bonus.' *One* of my old boyfriends? *Yes, exactly*.

'Hey Frank, I've seen Maggie's dress,' Lori said, evidently keen to steer the conversation in a new direction, and with more than a hint of mischief in her eye. 'And she looks absolutely amazing in it. I've got pictures.'

'Don't you *dare*,' Maggie said, laughing.

'Can I see it Lori?' Jimmy asked. 'I'm the best man after all.'

'Nah, you're not allowed,' she answered. 'You'll just have to wait until the big day, like Frank.' She took a theatrical pause. 'But maybe, just maybe, I'll let you have a wee peek.'

Maggie laughed again. 'Don't, or I'll kill you. Not literally, of course,' she added quickly, to everyone's amusement.

'I was a bridesmaid once,' Jessie said. 'Best maid actually. But the marriage didn't last. She obviously wasn't right for him, I said that to him at the time. He should have married me instead.'

'Interesting,' Frank said, exchanging a raised-eyebrow look with Maggie. 'So, I don't like to talk about work in these wee get-togethers,' he continued, 'but hasn't the brown stuff really hit the fan for our pal Dougie McKean? Given the allegations against him, I'm not sure I can feel sorry for him, but there's so much trial by media these days. It's supposed to be that a person is innocent until they're proved guilty, but now it's the complete opposite.'

'Well it's certainly messed up our case,' Maggie said. 'We've got a revised divorce agreement we need him to sign, but I don't think that we'll be on his priority list now.'

'Pity,' Frank said, 'but maybe all of this will come to nothing. That recording that emerged is with the tech geeks at our Maida Vale labs, and they should have it processed in a day or two after they get McKean's voice sample. In fact, I'm going to get it onto Eleanor Campbell's radar, just to make sure it gets the priority it needs.' He reached over to the bar and took a swig from his pint, draining the glass with an audible *aah*. 'Well, that's me done I think,' he said, getting up from his stool. 'Big day ahead of us tomorrow DS James. Oh and by the way, I'm not staying at the hotel tonight, I'm going to risk a night under canvas. I'll pick you up in the morning, eight-thirty sharp.'

'Fair enough guv,' she shrugged, then looked at Jimmy. 'And where are *you* staying tonight?'

'I'll be driving back to my wee flat in Braemar,' he said hurriedly, holding up his glass. 'That's why I've been on the low-alcohol beers. It'll be a nice drive over the pass on a nice summer's evening.'

'But Frank's not using his room now,' James said shamelessly. 'So we could stay here and have a couple more drinks, make a night of it. It's only half-eight.'

'He's driving back to Braemar,' Lori cut in. 'And you can bugger off back to your hotel. *Alone*.'

****

It had been great to be with Maggie again, although Frank hadn't managed to get much sleep - not because of any carnal activity, because that had been ruled out by Lori Logan's occupancy of the wee tent next door - but because of the bloody rain that had started at about one o'clock and continued relentlessly through the night, the rhythmic pitter-pattering of raindrops on canvas extinguishing any hope of dropping off. As a result, he looked a bit less than his best when he swung by DS James' hotel at the agreed hour, to find her already waiting outside, smoking a cigarette and looking a whole lot worse than he did.

'Thought we were all having an early night?' he said, after she had crushed her cigarette with a heel and stepped into the car.

'Yeah guv, I met a couple of guys in the bar after you all left,' she said. 'They were telling me all about single malts and how many come from around here and how they're made and stuff like that. I tried a few, actually. Very nice.'

He gave a wry smile. 'Well, as long as they don't appear on your expense claim. Anyway, it should be an interesting morning I think. A nice drive....' An incoming call stopped him in his tracks, and glancing at the screen, he saw it was from Eleanor Campbell.

'How's it going Eleanor?' he said brightly. 'Plenty of geeky things on your plate to keep you occupied?'

'I've been given the McKean recording to look at,' she said, slightly sourly. *'Because everybody thinks I always work with you.'* By everybody, he assumed she meant her colleagues in the Forensic service, and the way she said it, it didn't sound like a badge of honour.

'What do you mean, look at?'

'It's evidence,' she said. *'Jeremy said it had to be authenticated.'* Jeremy, he knew, was her immediate boss, although like almost all of Eleanor's work contacts, his surname, assuming he had one, remained a mystery.

'And how do you do that?' he asked.

'Fourier wave-form analysis. We compare the waveform of the recording with authenticated samples of the voices. It's like routine.'

'Ah, I *get* it, ' he said, simultaneously surprising himself and failing to disguise the resultant note of triumph in his voice. 'You grab a recording of Dougie McKean speaking and compare it with what's on this recording. And then if you get called as an expert witness, you can tell the court that it's definitely him on the tape.'

'Something like that,' she agreed. There was a pause at the end of the line, and for a second he thought she might have hung up. But then she continued, *'That's why I'm calling you. I need you to get me vocal samples from...'* There was another pause, and he realised she must be reading from a list. *'...from Douglas McKean, Orla McCarthy and Nicholas Nicholson, and they must be of digital CD quality and be of seventy seconds in length minimum. I've sent you a link to an app you can use, it's called Voice Record.'*

'Does what it says on the tin I suppose,' he said, knowing the remark would go right over her head. 'Well okay. McKean and McCarthy I can definitely get you. Nicholson's dead, so that will be more difficult. But I seem to remember him doing an interview on the Old Grey Whistle Test in the late eighties, when I was just a wee boy.' He knew she wouldn't have heard of the show either. 'I'll give it a Google. I might find a clip you can use.'

'Okay,' she said. *'So when will I get them? Because Jeremy has allocated next Wednesday for me to look at them.'*

'I'm on my way to see McKean now, so you'll have that tomorrow latest. The others I'll get as quickly as I can.'

'Awesome,' she replied, then hung up without saying goodbye. But her sign-off made him laugh out loud, since it was the first time in their long working relationship he could recall her using a word of such positivity, making him wonder if the Forensic Service had recently forced all their geeks to take a *working with colleagues* training course.

'That was wee Eleanor,' he said to James needlessly, because she no doubt had overheard the whole conversation.

'Crazy girl,' James remarked, 'but nice.' Takes one to know one, Frank was about to say, before thinking better of it, although not saying it didn't make it any less true.

'Aye, a bit, ' he said. 'Anyway, we've got a nice drive up to the Glengarnet estate and then we'll need to haul McKean up to Inverness for the formalities.'

'Do you think he'll come quietly?' James asked.

He shrugged. 'Who knows, but we'll soon find out. Anyway, sit back and enjoy the scenery. It's about three-quarter of an hour's drive.'

She groaned. 'Actually guv if you don't mind, I'll just shut my eyes. Let me know when we get there.'

Glengarnet Lodge was easy enough to find, located on the edge of the eponymous country estate on the western side of the Spey. They had travelled up on a narrow B-road equipped with passing places, but that facility only had to be used a couple of times on the trip, such was the remoteness of the location. For most of the journey, the river had been about half-a-mile away and to the right of them, but as the sat-nav heralded their imminent arrival at their destination, the road took a sharp turn and equally sharp descent, and soon they were driving along its banks, the grey and brooding water almost within touching distance. The lodge sat alongside the main entrance gates to the estate, its location heralded by a brown tourist sign advertising tours of the distillery which was located in its grounds. But even without that assistance, the place wouldn't have been hard to locate, due to the presence of a dozen or more vehicles parked haphazardly along the riverside, a number of which were vans sporting roof-mounted satellite transmitters. Frank had fully expected the media to be out in force, and he hadn't been disappointed. Equally expected too, but less welcome, was the presence of Orla McCarthy and Yash Patel with their Chronicle TV cameraman. And they were in recording mode the minute he stepped out of his car.

'Here's DCI Frank Stewart and DS Jessie James,' the singer shouted excitedly, speaking to camera. 'And the question we all must ask is, have they come here to arrest Dougie McKean? I guess we'll soon know.' She stepped away and Rupert swung the camera round to face the two police officers. DS James smiled and looked as if she was going to say something, but Frank stepped in front of her, addressing the camera directly. 'Bugger off. Please excuse my French, but you're interfering with official police business.'

'It's a free press in this country Frank,' Patel protested from the sidelines, somewhat half-heartedly. 'We're not breaking any law.'

Frank gave him a look of exasperation. 'Okay Yash my boy, you can explain that to the sheriff after I've arrested you for obstruction.'

Patel laughed uncertainly. 'And I thought we were mates.'

'Aye, so did I,' Frank said wryly. He then turned to Orla. 'And I've told you once before Miss McCarthy, this.. this bloody *circus* isn't going to help your case. So if you'd like to take my advice, you should switch of that bloody camera and try a wee period of silence, so that us cops can do our job without interference.'

She returned a sullen look, before turning once again to face the camera. But whatever she was going to say, she evidently thought better of it.

'Good,' Frank said. 'So we're off in to see Mr McKean now. Come on Detective Sergeant, let's go.'

The door was opened by an attractive woman who he assumed was the rock singer's manager and recently-acquired girlfriend.

'Miss Gray?' he enquired. 'I'm DCI Stewart of the Metropolitan Police and this is my colleague DS James. We're here to speak to Dougie and just so you know, we might have to be scooting him up to Inverness police station so he can further help us with our enquiries. I assume he's in?'

She nodded. 'Dougie?' she shouted. 'It's the police.' She lowered her voice, presumably so McKean couldn't hear. 'He's had a few drinks I'm afraid. It's been a terrible few days.'

'Aye, no doubt.' They followed her through the hall into the kitchen, where Dougie McKean was sitting at a breakfast bar, a half-full tumbler of whisky in front of him.

'Cheers,' he said, raising his glass. 'I like a nice snifter for breakfast.' His voice was slurred and his eyes were bloodshot, rather like DS James's, Frank thought, stifling a grin. 'This is Balvenie. I got given a few cases for free by some American gob-shite and I've really taken a liking to the stuff. Can I get you two a wee dram yourselves?'

'No thanks sir,' Frank said. 'I assume you know why we're here?'

He shrugged. 'Aye I do. It's because of that wee Irish bitch. So what are you going to do then? Arrest me? Because it's all bollocks, every word of it.'

'It is indeed these historic allegations we are investigating sir,' Frank said in an even tone. 'We need to ask you a few questions, which we are happy to do here, and then we need you to take a voluntary trip to Inverness so that we can take a DNA swab and make a recording of your voice. Just routine, and you don't need to agree to this, but it would be better if you did. Because if you don't, we will have to arrest you under caution and take you to the police station, where we would have the right to hold you in detention for up to twenty-four hours. You would also of course have the right to have a lawyer or other representative present if and when we question you.' He paused for a moment. 'Do you understand that sir?'

'So what sort of a bloody choice is that?' he complained. 'I can't afford to be locked up. I've got a big show tomorrow, in case you didn't know, and I need to be rehearsing.'

'I *do* know sir,' Frank said, smiling. 'In actual fact I've got tickets myself and I'm looking forward to it.'

'And what about you doll?' McKean asked James, unscrewing the top of the bottle and filling his glass to the brim. 'Have you got a ticket my darling?'

'Not my scene sir,' the DS answered. 'I'm into techno and grime.'

'Electronic crap,' McKean said. 'You should learn to appreciate real music.'

'I'll bear that in mind sir.'

'Make sure you do,' McKean slurred genially. 'But we can get you a wee executive ticket if you like, so you can start your education. And a backstage pass as well, then you can meet the other three arseholes that I call my band.' He gave a short laugh, then stopped and took a large swig from his glass, which he just about succeeded in emptying. 'Now are you sure you don't want a ticket my darling? We have a right bloody party backstage, and everything you've heard about rock and roll? It's true, and a lot worse besides.' He gave a cackle. 'Sex, drugs and rock-and-roll, you'll get all of that.

Mainly sex and drugs actually, because we don't really give a shit about the music.'

Frank could appreciate how it might have played out eighteen years back, the throwaway invitation to the show, the offer of a post-gig drink with the big rock star, DI Ian Archibald succumbing to temptation even although he knew deep down that it was dodgy. But that wasn't going to happen here.

'Mr McKean,' he said, in a serious tone, 'we need you to answer a few questions if you don't mind.'

'Well I do mind, so you pair can sod off,' he replied, still slurring. 'I'm a busy man, and an important one too. So why don't you grab your wee tart here and bugger off back to wherever it is you both came from.' He paused, then leered at James. 'Or maybe take her back to your hotel and shag the arse off her. Because she looks as if she might be up for it, big-time. I wouldn't mind a go myself actually. What do you think my wee darling?'

Frank was just about to reply when DS James stepped forward, wrenching McKean's arm up his back and slamming his head downwards against the worktop with a sickening crack that drew a spurt of blood from his shattering nose. 'Douglas McKean, I'm arresting you on suspicion of assault under the Sexual Offences Scotland act. You do not have to say anything, but anything you do say...'

He listened with a mixture of alarm and amusement as Jessie James reeled off the standard arrest spiel, lines he had heard a thousand times before. But on this occasion the suspect wasn't going to be saying anything, speech being a bit difficult when your head was pinned down against a marble-topped breakfast bar.

***

Obviously they had to exit Glengarnet Lodge through a sea of media, and there were gasps of astonishment as McKean was led handcuffed to their car, Tamara Gray tagging alongside, dabbing away the blood from her boyfriend's nose with a now badly-stained handkerchief. They got him cleaned up as soon as they arrived at Inverness police station, Frank brushing off enquiries by the desk sergeant about what had happened to their charge, and feeling bad about the half-true story he had to make up to explain it. The DNA, fingerprint and mug-shot formalities over, they sat McKean down in an interview room with a surprisingly-decent mug of coffee, with Gray, apparently a qualified US attorney, acting as his solicitor. Of course, McKean denied Orla McCarthy's allegations, as Frank knew he would. *Sure, there had been loads of drinking so most of the time we had no idea what we were doing, and yeah, maybe the chat might have been a bit close to the knuckle sometimes, but you had to realise that Orla was a manipulative wee bitch even back then, and a bit of a cock-teaser too if you wanted to know the truth. But assaulting a wee schoolgirl? No way. It's mature women that do it for me, it was then and it is now, no offence to my wee baby doll Tamara here of course.* That was the gist of McKean's story, which, Frank had to reluctantly admit, was not a million miles away from the one Assistant Commissioner Archibald had related to him just the other day. But when Frank brought up the subject of the recording, currently with Eleanor Campbell awaiting the arrival of a voice sample with which to compare it, McKean's bravado seemed to evaporate. His initial reaction was to refuse to allow a section of the interview to be recorded by Frank's app, to be told that he had no choice in the matter. Was he suddenly recalling some sepia-tinted incident that had occurred during these legendary alcohol-fuelled Oran na Mara sessions, something that his brain had buried deep in its vaults and hoped would never resurface? Whatever the truth of the allegation, technical analysis of that recording was going to prove it one way or another.

Time would tell, and in the meantime, Frank was going to have to have a few strong words with DS Jessie-bloody-James.

Chapter 12

For Maggie, it had been a very unsettling day and a bit of a worrying one too. Dougie McKean had been all over the media, particularly the clip of him emerging from his rented lodge, hand-cuffed and bloodied, in the custody of two officers from the Metropolitan Police, and pursued by a crowing Orla McCarthy and her TV cameraman. Speculation had been rife of course, the bland statement put out by the police - that Mr McKean was simply helping them with their enquiries - only succeeding in fuelling the frenzy. On the unregulated badlands of social media, his sexual assault of McCarthy had already transitioned from allegation to fact, his bloodied nose had become the result of a violent attempt to resist arrest. The net result was that it had pretty much stuffed any hope she and Lori had of getting to see McKean and putting the new and heavily-revised divorce settlement in front of him. But she owed it to her client Cassie to at least try, so even although it was Saturday and the day of the Claymore Warriors' big show, she had attempted to get him on the phone to let him know a new deal was waiting in his email in-box. Instead, the call to his phone had been intercepted by Tamara Gray, who had given her a frosty reception but had at least committed to look at the document. But then, just as Maggie had been about to hang up, the woman had dropped a bombshell. *Of course, the agreement will need a re-draft anyway, because Dougie signed a new will yesterday.* It was news that she had anticipated, but that wouldn't be welcomed by Cassie McKean. No doubt her client would get a letter from the solicitors informing her of the fact. Maggie hoped she would, because she definitely didn't fancy having to tell her herself.

And as for Frank, he had spent the day fretting that DS James' over-enthusiastic arrest would result in a formal complaint from the rock singer, egged on by his legally-savvy girlfriend Tamara Gray. That would have been a disaster, threatening to throw a spanner in the works of his investigation before it had even properly started. Before flying back down south, James had been given the bollocking of all bollockings, a reprimand which she had taken with an irritating insouciance, Frank suspecting - no, *knowing* - that she'd faced plenty of the same in the past, and so was well-practiced on how to react. But the day wore on and no complaint arrived. Maggie had given the matter some consideration, and suspected that the lewd remark which had triggered James' over-reaction wasn't something that a man accused of sexual assault would want to have made public. She had shared this opinion with Frank, which had succeeded in lifting his gloomy mood a little, so much so that the two of them had been able to enjoy a nice lunch in the Infamous Grouse before heading back to the festival site to meet up with Jimmy.

But now it was nine-thirty on a beautiful late-August evening, the sun only just having dropped below the horizon as the large festival crowd awaited the arrival on stage of the Claymore Warriors, an appearance that was now almost half-an-hour overdue. Jimmy and Frank were especially looking forward to it, being big fans of the band. Lori was politely non-committal although she seemed to be enjoying the atmosphere, but Maggie found that she herself was quite keen to see them too, having come to appreciate if not love the Warriors' music in the few weeks since she had become exposed to it. But looking around, it seemed that not everyone in the crowd was feeling the same way.

'Do you see them?' Jimmy said to her, pointing at a group who had jostled their way through the crowd to assemble near the stage. 'And do you see what it says on their banners?'

'I do,' Maggie said, nodding. *'Hash-tag me too. Respect for women. We are not sex objects.* I don't suppose it's a surprise, given all the negative attention McKean has been getting all week. And him getting arrested yesterday just threw petrol on the fire.'

'And I don't think it's just them,' Frank said. 'I'm sensing the vibe isn't exactly positive everywhere.'

'Wonder why they're so late on stage?' Maggie said, and as if responding to her speculation, a section of the audience unconnected to the protestors began a slow handclap.

'Yash told me that he and Orla and her tame cameraman had wangled a back-stage pass somehow,' Frank said, 'so I expect it's all kicking off big-time back there. But hang on, looks like something's happening now,' he added, nodding towards the stage.

At last the lights were slowly dimming, and the stirring and familiar melody of Ravel's *Bolero* began to fill the public-address speakers, the piece the band had adopted many years' earlier as their introductory theme music. Half a minute later, the stage was in total darkness, Ravel's masterpiece gradually fading into silence, a silence that was also being respected by the anticipatory audience, even the *me too* protestors temporarily suspending their sloganeering. And then with a crash of drums and a dramatic minor chord played in unison by guitar and keyboard, the lights went up, blinding white searchlights merging with a rainbow of coloured spots that flashed across the massive screen at the back of the stage, onto which a windswept island landscape had been projected. Under the lights the band were now revealed, McKean and lead guitarist Jamie Cooper wearing kilts and flowing tartan capes, the singer taking copious swigs from a bottle of Balvenie as he awaited his cue at the conclusion of the long instrumental opening passage. But the reaction from the audience would not have been what the band expected. Starting with the banner-carrying group of women at the front, a chorus of hisses and boos began to spread through the crowd, until Maggie estimated that more than half of the audience were taking part. Dougie McKean, now well into the second verse of Oran na Mara, reacted by striding to the front of the stage and giving a series of one-fingered salutes in all directions, which only succeeded in increasing the volume of the heckling. As the song came to its spectacular instrumental conclusion, McKean leered, raised his microphone to his lips and slurred disparagingly *thanks for frigging nothing folks*, before taking another guzzle from the whisky bottle, then propelling the evidently-empty receptacle across the stage. Almost instantly, a member of the crew appeared from backstage with a replacement, pulling out the cork before handing it to the singer. In the crowd, sporadic scuffling had broken out as groups of Warriors die-hards made clear to the dissidents how they felt about having their evening's much-anticipated entertainment disrupted. The band had already started the second number, a song that Maggie recognised as the one they had played a day or two back when they did that impromptu performance with Orla McCarthy in the rehearsal barn. Mountain Dew, that was it. She remembered its name just as she recognised the memorable opening melody.

'Bloody great song this,' Frank mouthed inaudibly, smiling and giving a thumbs up. But whatever the merits of the song, it didn't succeed in changing the mood of large swathes of the audience, who continued to boo and heckle as the number reached the part where Dougie McKean's vocals came in. And McKean did come in on cue, except that the lyrics that he sung weren't the ones that had featured on the album. Instead he blasted out a string of expletives, wearing a malevolent sneer and giving another single-finger salute to the crowd. A few seconds later, he threw his wireless microphone violently across the stage, and then with a sweep of his cape but without another word, he marched off, still swigging from the second bottle of Balvenie. Maggie thought she saw Jamie Cooper exchange a grin with his brother Rob, the band continuing to play to the end of the number, the guitarist then handing his instrument to a scurrying member of the crew before shrugging apologetically and shuffling off stage. The boos and slow hand-claps grew to a crescendo before tailing off, the crowd evidently angry that their show of virtue-signalling self-righteousness had been prematurely ended.

'That's what it must have been like in Roman days at the Coliseum,' Frank said. 'When the lion ate the gladiator before they'd even got properly started. These folks here were out for blood, and now they're all in a bad mood because they got what they wanted.'

'Well it's a bloody shame,' Jimmy said, giving a resigned sigh. 'We came here to hear the whole album and we didn't even manage two songs.'

'I didn't like it,' Lori said. 'The music was rubbish and the guy can't even sing.'

'To be fair, he was seriously pissed I think,' Frank said. 'But aye, I'm no musician, but his pitch seemed all over the place. I know it's the rock n' roll lifestyle, but folks paid a fortune for these tickets.'

'And then they stopped them performing, ' Jimmy said sourly. 'So it's their own fault.'

'Well at least there's a fridge in our tent,' Maggie said. 'Why don't we all come back to our place and we can crack open some beers and then listen to the album on my phone? And Jimmy, you can stay the night in the back compartment where Ollie slept if you like. It's small but perfectly-formed.'

'Or you could have my wee tent of course,' Lori said, then hesitated for a moment. 'But not to share with me, obviously,' she added, a tad wistfully. 'I'd be better in Ollie's den anyway, since I'm small and perfectly-formed too.'

Jimmy laughed. 'It's a deal Lori, and I'm very grateful.' The girl beamed with pleasure, and Maggie wondered for a moment if she was going to offer to go and tuck him in when they retired.

It was going to be a lovely evening despite Jimmy's disappointment over the abandoned concert, as for the umpteenth time she reflected how lucky she had been to meet the Stewart brothers.

Chapter 13

The early-morning call was as unwelcome as it had been unexpected, Frank uttering a groggy *bloody hell* as he fumbled to find his mobile. Eventually succeeding, he shot out another *bloody hell* as through bloodshot eyes he saw the time - five minutes to seven on a Sunday morning, for God's sake - and then clocked that the call was from an unknown number. Choosing to ignore it, he tossed the device onto the floor beside the upmarket camp-bed, groaned then rolled over to cuddle up to the still-sleeping Maggie. But the caller was persistent, ringing immediately after Frank's phone diverted to voicemail, and repeating the process four or five time such that he had no option to answer lest the call disturbed the whole blooming campsite. With another groan, he picked up the phone and jabbed the answer button.

'Who's this?' he barked, not hiding his annoyance.

'Stewart?' a disturbingly-familiar voice answered, the caller not hiding his annoyance either.

'Commissioner Naylor?' Frank said, jerked wide awake. 'Sorry sir, I was sleeping. We had a late night. I wasn't expecting your call. But aye, how can I....?'

'Have you seen the news?' the Commissioner said, cutting in.

'No sir,' Frank replied, alarmed. 'What's happened?'

'Dougie McKean is dead, that's what's happened.'

Frank gave a sharp intake of breath as the shock hit him in the stomach. 'Bloody hell, sir. How?'

'He collapsed at the lodge he was renting, just after he got back after the concert. His girlfriend dialled nine-nine-nine and they sent an ambulance, but he was dead by the time he got to hospital.'

'They would have taken him to Inverness,' Frank said, immediately wondering if this was something the Commissioner needed to know. 'It's at least forty minutes drive I would say.' He paused for a moment. 'So how did he die, do they know yet?'

'Cardiac arrest as a result of excess alcohol consumption. Apparently he had been drinking heavily all day.'

'It's tragic, but it doesn't surprise me sir. He was necking whisky all the way through the show. And there was a bit of a scene, I don't know if you heard. He walked off the stage half-way through the second song. A fair number of the audience had been protesting sir. I think there was a bit of a rent-a-mob on account of Orla McCarthy's allegations.'

He noticed that Maggie was now waking up, yawning then stretching extravagantly before pushing herself up on to her elbows and giving him a puzzled look. He smiled at her and raised a finger to his lips, then returned his attention to what the Commissioner was saying.

'My daughter showed me a YouTube video yesterday. You were in it Stewart, outside that lodge. And McKean was handcuffed and bleeding. It wasn't a good look.' There was silence at the end of the line, and Frank wasn't sure if his big boss was expecting a response or not.

'Yes sir, that was a bit unfortunate,' he said finally. He didn't really want to drop DS Jessie-bloody-James in it, but he was damn sure he wasn't going to take all the blame either. 'Mr McKean was very insulting towards DS James, and she got a bit over-enthusiastic when she arrested him, that's all. We've all been there sir,' he added, although he doubted whether the one-hundred-percent-play-it-by-the-book Commissioner ever had been. 'And there was no complaint made afterwards.'

For a moment, there was no response at the end of the line, which Frank suspected wasn't a good sign. Then the Commissioner continued, *'Our press office tell me the Globe is already running a story speculating whether McKean's excessive drinking was in response to police harassment.'*

Flipping heck, he thought, Naylor's had his press team on the phone before he even called me. He must be taking this seriously.

'But sir,' he responded, 'five minutes ago they were saying he was a sex-beast, now suddenly he's a victim of police brutality. I mean, you couldn't make it up.'

'We don't need to make it up,' his boss answered tartly. *'The media are perfectly capable of doing that for themselves.'*

It struck Frank that he hadn't yet actually worked out the reason for the Commissioner's call. Whatever it was, it had to be something way more important than simply telling him that Dougie McKean was dead.

'So where do we go from here sir?' he said cautiously. 'Are we going to shelf my investigation or...'

The Commissioner cut in before he could finish. *'No we're not going to shelf the investigation, the exact opposite in fact. Because the last thing we need is for McKean to become a tragic victim of injustice. Can you imagine the bad publicity for the force if that should happen? So we need to get this case expedited so that the public gets to learn what he was really like. Where are we with the forensics and the rest of the evidence?'*

But what if he's not guilty sir? The words had instantly popped into his head, and he was about to say them before thinking better of it. No, best to leave that one parked for a while, he thought. Instead he answered factually. 'The Police Scotland guys took his DNA yesterday sir and we took a voice sample too. And we've got a copy of that historic recording secured in the evidence files waiting to be authenticated, and I've got AC Archibald's statement too. So we're in good shape I think.'

'Good. So it's Monday tomorrow and we're going to have to make a statement to the media. I want you back down in London for that, okay?'

'I'm not sure if there's a flight on Sundays sir,' he said truthfully. 'We're up in the wilds here.'

'Get a train then,' Naylor said, *'I'll see you at Kensington Police Station tomorrow afternoon.'* And then, abruptly, he hung up.

'I heard most of that,' Maggie said, wide-eyed. 'McKean's dead? I can't believe it. It's just so weird when it's only a few hours since we saw him very much alive.'

'Weird it is,' Frank agreed. 'But I think you overheard where the Commissioner's coming from. The media are now saying it was Orla's accusations and the police investigation that caused McKean to drink himself to death, and he's not happy about it.'

'Will there be an inquest or a post-mortem or whatever, to prove that's what actually happened?'

He shrugged. 'I don't know. If the hospital doctors are satisfied that excessive alcohol was the cause of death, then they'll sign the death certificate and that will be it. Or I suppose they might have a quick word with the Coroner's office today, and close it down then. They don't like to drag out the process unduly, otherwise it's so much worse for the loved ones.'

'Yes, that's true,' she said, then paused for a moment. 'But I guess I'll need to phone Cassie. She loved him once and she wouldn't have wished this on him. And of course the kids will be absolutely devastated. But perhaps I shouldn't call today,' she added.

'Well, there'll be no need for a divorce now, will there?' he said. He saw her give a sudden concerned frown. 'What is it?'

'I've just remembered what Tamara Gray told me yesterday. Dougie McKean signed off his new will just a couple of days ago. And now he's dead and she inherits everything.'

Frank gave a wry smile. 'We're not in an old-school crime novel here. From what you told me, he'd been planning to change his will for a while now. So it seems unlikely that the new girlfriend got him to make a new one then bumped him off as soon as he'd done it, if that's what you're thinking. That only happens in books.'

'Yes, you're right,' she conceded. 'But it's really tough on Cassie, isn't it?' She paused again for a moment. 'But I somehow didn't get the impression that Tamara Gray was a gold-digger, so maybe Cassie and her might be able to come to some acceptable arrangement.'

'That's one of the many things I love about you,' he said, smiling fondly. 'Your blind determination to see the best in everyone, in obvious defiance of human nature.'

At that moment, they heard the zip on the door being opened, and a second later Jimmy stuck a tousled head through the gap.

'You guys are up early,' he said, grinning. 'Couldn't sleep?'

'Dougie McKean's dead,' Maggie said. 'Cardiac arrest as a result of excess alcohol consumption they're saying. Frank's boss called to tell him.'

'Crikey,' Jimmy said. 'But it's not exactly surprising is it? Although it's still a shock. Hard to believe actually.' He was silent for a moment then continued, 'So I suppose that's us done here, isn't it? We just need to give Cassie our condolences and that's it. End of mission.'

She nodded slowly. 'Yes it is. But I wouldn't have wanted it to end this way, obviously.'

No, me neither, Frank thought. Because the whole thing was now a bloody mess, and he'd just been landed with the job of clearing it all up so as not to stain the precious reputation of the Metropolitan Police. He needed to have a conversation with Eleanor Campbell to make sure the authentication of that recording proceeded at maximum pace. And he needed to have that conversation today. Which, unfortunately, was Sunday.

Now *that* was going to be interesting to say the least.

***

Frank had given Eleanor away at her wedding to the drippy Lloyd, and at the time he had been provided with her personal mobile number in order to ease the making of arrangements, a number that he had retained in his phone book. Now he glanced again at the time, and no matter which way you looked at it, it was early to be calling on what used to be called the Sabbath. *Eight minutes to nine.* He hesitated before jabbing the call button, wondering whether it might just be best to wait until after nine, which somehow didn't seem quite so bad. But no, it had to be done now, because he couldn't make a call of that confidentiality on a train. Best to get it over with, besides which, she probably wouldn't answer it anyway, especially when she saw the call was from him. Which got him thinking.

'Hey Jimmy,' he called. 'Any idea how to do that *hide caller ID* thing?'

'Nae problem,' his brother answered. 'Just chuck me your phone over and I'll sort it for you.'

Frank did as instructed, Jimmy catching the device in mid-air, then swiping up and down the screen a few times. 'There you go,' he said after a few seconds' work, tossing the phone back. 'Just go to *Show My Caller ID* in *Settings* if you want to turn it back on.'

'Cheers mate,' Frank said, giving a thumbs-up, although not having a clue what his brother was talking about. He pulled up Eleanor's number again and pressed *call*. After a dozen or so rings, it diverted to voicemail. The response was the network provider's default, the Forensic Officer evidently having not bothered to set up a personal greeting. Unsurprised, he ended the call then dialled again, instructed by his gaffer's persistence an hour earlier. Twelve rings later, he got the same response. Giving a shrug to himself, he repeated the process, getting the same result once again. The next one would work he thought, because she'll then realise it's something important.

This time, she let the phone ring five or six times before she answered, managing to make the *what* a whole lot more menacing than he had earlier.

'Hi Eleanor, it's Frank,' he said, speaking rapidly, 'and before you go mental, this is really important, otherwise I wouldn't have called you at home.'

'It's like Sunday,' she complained.

He nodded. 'I know, I wanted to catch you before you and Lloyd went to church.'

'Very funny,' she said, sounding anything but amused. *'What do you want?'*

'It's not what I want, it's what the brass want. I got a bloody quarter-to-seven wake-up call from the Commissioner this morning.'

'What, you like actually spoke to Dame Hermione?'

He laughed. 'Good to see you're keeping up with events Eleanor. We've got a new guy now, goes by the name of Naylor. Nice enough fella.'

'That McKean dude was found dead,' she said before he could explain any further. *'It was on my news app when I got up.'*

'Ah, so I didn't wake you, that's good,' he said. 'You're right, and that's why I've called you. We got that voice recording you wanted the day before yesterday and it's been emailed to Maida Vale. What I wanted to ask was if they have any sort of expediting process so that we can get it partly analysed today?'

'I would need to speak to my boss,' she said. *'And Jeremy doesn't like being called on Sundays.'*

'Nobody does. But nobody likes being called by the Commissioner either, and that's what it might come to if your Jeremy doesn't co-operate. He's standing in front of the media at three o'clock tomorrow afternoon, and he wants to be able to tell them that Dougie McKean was a horrible sexual predator.'

'But what if we don't find a vocal match?' she said. *'If he's like innocent?'*

He smiled. 'I was thinking along the same lines earlier. Let's just say the big boss sincerely hopes he's not innocent, because if he is, we're going to be battered in the press for hounding an innocent man to his death.' Although, he reflected, that would mean that AC Archibald's original investigation had come up with the right answer, so it wouldn't be all bad. But then another complication struck him.

'I haven't got the Orla McCarthy or Nicky Nicholson voice samples yet, so it would only be part verification I guess?

'There's plenty of her online,' Eleanor said. *'And the other guy is dead so we were having to find some old media recordings anyway. I think we can get enough for a reliable match.'*

'Well that's *very* helpful Eleanor,' he said, directing a wry smile at Maggie, who was listening in. 'So sorry for interrupting your Sunday, I won't take any more of your time. Just give your gaffer Jeremy a wee call and we'll catch up tomorrow when I'm back in London. Cheerio.'

'Successful?' Maggie asked him after he'd hung up.

He shrugged. 'I think so. She didn't go off in a big huff at least. Which I count as a win.'

'That's good,' she replied. 'Anyway, I've been exploring your transport logistics and actually, the best plan is for you to come back to Glasgow with me and Lori in the car this afternoon, and then you can get an early flight down to London in the morning.'

'And you've checked the timetable?' he asked, with some trepidation. 'So you now know how early *early* is?'

She nodded. 'Ten past six, which means you need to be at the airport for five. Or maybe half-four just to be on the safe side, since it's always really busy through security on Mondays. Poor you,' she added with a sympathetic smile.

He wasn't a man who normally employed the vile F-word, but on this occasion, he could see there was no adequate alternative. But out of respect to his love, he whispered it under his breath.

Chapter 14

It was Monday, and Maggie and Lori were back in their Glasgow office, and in truth finding themselves at a bit of a loss after the untimely death of Dougie McKean. They had one or two small matters to keep them busy for a week or so, but the sudden and unexpected curtailment of Cassie McKean's divorce case had knocked a serious hole in the schedule of Bainbridge Associates. Not that Maggie was particularly concerned about the loss of revenue that would result, although it was obviously a factor given she had Lori's salary to cover and the rent on their moderately-expensive Byres Road office too. Jimmy, now only an occasional consultant for her little firm, was busy that week with his Braemar outdoor adventure business, so at least she didn't have him to worry about as far as wages was concerned. No, her overriding concern was really the duty of care she felt to Cassie, who had been relying on Maggie and her team to absorb much of the stress of what was a very difficult life situation. Right now, the woman would be in turmoil, irrespective of her feelings for her late husband, with two suddenly-bereaved children to console and potentially facing an uncertain financial future. She wondered if her client had been informed about the recent finalisation of her dead husband's new will by his solicitors. Maggie expected she would have been, which would just have added to the agony of emotions she would be experiencing at this extraordinary time.

'What are you thinking about Maggie?' Lori asked. 'You've not said a word for about ten minutes.'

'Yes sorry,' she said, smiling. 'I was thinking about Cassie and what we could do to help her. I think professionally it's something we should do. And morally too I guess.'

Her associate nodded. 'Aye, definitely. But did you have anything in mind?'

'Yes, actually I do,' Maggie said. She punched a few characters into Google on her phone, then held it up so Lori could see the result. 'This is the website of Dougie McKean's solicitors.'

'Shore McPhail & Robertson,' Lori said, reading out loud. 'I've heard of them. They're quite big, aren't they?'

'They are. But look down here,' Maggie continued, pointing to the bottom of the screen. Do you see where their offices are?'

'Aye, I do. Edinburgh, Glasgow, Newcastle, Manchester, Leeds, Birmingham, Bristol, London. That's all the main places in the UK.'

'Exactly. But what's really important is that they have offices in both England and here in Scotland, which is in fact where their head office is. In Edinburgh actually.'

Lori gave her a puzzled look but didn't say anything.

'Come on,' Maggie continued, 'let's see if we can get Cassie on the phone. And remember, she's just lost her husband, and more to the point, her kids have just lost their father. So if I forget to tread gently, please give me a dig in the ribs.'

She swiped down to the number and after a few rings Cassie McKean, answered with a listless *hello.*

'Hi Cassie,' Maggie said softly. 'It's Maggie Bainbridge. I was so sorry to hear what happened. How are you and how are the kids?'

'Not great,' she answered, her sadness starkly audible. *'Ryan hasn't said a single word these last twenty-four hours and Grace can't stop crying. It's absolutely breaking my heart. But my sister's here and she's been amazing. I don't know what I'd do without her.'*

'That's good that you have someone to help you through this terrible time,' Maggie said, then paused for a moment. 'Obviously, the last thing I want to do is intrude on your grief, but I wondered if we might be able to offer some practical assistance with finances and so on, so you can concentrate on looking after your kids? There are a couple of things I have in mind which might help.'

There was silence at the end of the line, and Maggie wondered if Cassie was considering her offer, or was simply too stricken with grief to take anything in. But eventually her client responded.

'Yes, I'm sorry Maggie, my head's all over the place at the moment. What was it you had in mind?'

Maggie paused again before continuing. 'So, we had previously drawn up a very fair divorce settlement which I sent to your late husband just a few days ago. Obviously - and this is a very poignant thing to have to bring up - obviously the custody clauses for the kids are no longer relevant...'

She heard Cassie sob, unsurprisingly triggered by the mention of her children. Maggie gave her client a moment to compose herself then said, 'Yes, but the settlement we offered with regard to property was a fair one, and it occurred to me we might try to negotiate an inheritance settlement with Miss Gray along these lines. It's complicated, because I recall that three or perhaps four of the properties were held in joint names, and whilst your husband's share might be willed to Tamara Gray, she would not be able to do anything with them with you as joint owner. So you may have some leverage in the matter.' *But unfortunately not in the matter of Inverbeck*, Maggie thought. The deeds to that desirable property were held only in her husband's name, and his new will had purportedly left everything to his lover.

'He left everything to her, that's what the will says,' she confirmed. *'Nothing for me of course, but nothing for his children either. That's cruel, isn't it? Very cruel,'* she added, beginning to sob again.

'Now, there's something interesting to say about that will,' Maggie said. 'You see, it was drawn up by Shore McPhail & Robertson, who are a national firm, but their head office is in Edinburgh. Which means that the jurisdiction of the will is potentially a matter of debate. And what I mean by that is, it can be questioned whether it should fall under English law or Scottish law.'

'Does it matter?' Cassie said. *'I always thought you could draw up a will in Timbuktu and it would still be valid as long as it was properly witnessed.'*

'It matters very much,' Maggie said. 'Because under Scottish law, you cannot simply disinherit your children. They have a right to a share of the estate irrespective of what any will says.' She paused again for a moment. 'And with the family home being in Scotland and your kids born and brought up here, there is a strong argument to say that Scottish law should apply, irrespective of any fancy clauses the eminent family lawyers of Shore McPhail & Robertson may have stuffed into the document. Because obviously, they would have advised your late husband about the differences between the two jurisdictions, and the consequences for the inheritance of his estate.'

'I'm not sure I understand any of that,' Cassie said. *'Are you saying the will is invalid?'*

'No, not necessarily. But Scottish law gives offspring the right to challenge a parent's will if it deliberately excludes them. That's something we could use when we're trying to persuade Tamara to do a deal with us. We just tell her she has two choices. One, come to a fair and negotiated settlement. Two, risk going to court and getting a far worse deal.'

'Do you think that's what would happen?' her client asked. *'That the court would rule in our favour?'*

'They would look at it very carefully, let's put it that way,' Maggie said. 'Especially since your late husband's relationship with the main beneficiary is relatively recent. But you see, we don't actually want to go to court. We just use the threat of doing so as leverage. To try and get a negotiated settlement.'

'Makes sense,' Cassie said, sounding grateful. *'I'm happy to go along with that, thank you so much.'*

'No problem, we'll try and speak to her tomorrow. I know it's a difficult business but we will do our best for you Cassie.' She hesitated for a moment. 'So are you having to deal with the funeral arrangements, or is that... is that going to be Tamara?'

'No, it's me,' she answered sharply. *'In fact, it's all arranged. It's on Thursday afternoon, at Ballater Crematorium. It's the nearest to us.'*

'Gosh, that's quick,' Maggie said, surprised.

'I know. But I didn't want it hanging over the kids, them having to think about it for days and days. And I didn't want our family ceremony deluged with fans, no matter how well-meaning they might be. It's better this way. Much more private.'

Maggie nodded. 'Yes, I can understand that. It's hard to know what to say about funerals isn't it? But I hope it goes well. And thank you for talking to me.'

'That's okay,' Cassie said. *'I just want to get it over with so we can all move on. I know it's a cliché, but that's how I feel right now.'*

Discussing it afterwards, it was Lori who had made the throwaway comment about murderers in books being always very keen to get the body disposed of as quickly as possible.

Especially if the murder method was poison.

***

Frank arrived at Kensington police station a little after ten-thirty in the morning, after an unpleasant journey that had started with a taxi turning up outside the Milngavie bungalow at quarter-past-four in the morning, and a flight that took off an hour late, meaning he could have had an extra hour in bed had he known about the delay in advance. He immediately headed for the canteen for a further injection of caffeine, courtesy of a triple-shot espresso, then grabbed a table and pulled out his phone to dial Eleanor Campbell. Which resulted in news he didn't want to hear.

'What do you mean, *nothing's* happened?' he said, after she had dropped the bombshell. 'The Commissioner is going to do his nut when he hears.'

'It's not my fault,' she complained. *'Jeremy didn't answer his phone or text messages yesterday and I didn't know who else to phone.'*

'Flip,' he said. 'Look Eleanor, I'm sorry if I was sharp with you, I know it isn't your fault. But at least we've got McKean's voice sample now so I guess you can do it later today?'

'We haven't got it,' she said. *'I spoke to Maida Vale this morning. They've chased it up and it's still in some police station up in Scotland. I can't remember what it was called.'*

'Bloody marvellous,' he said again. 'I *told* these muppets in Inverness to get it emailed. I should have stuck it on a flash drive and brought it down myself.' And then he laughed. 'Tell you what Eleanor, if I give you his number, will you give the Commissioner a wee call and let him know all this? I think he'll be absolutely fine with it, these things happen.'

She hung up without bothering to answer. He'd only been joshing her of course, but that still left the dilemma about who was going to tell Naylor the bad news. Gulping down his coffee, he picked up his phone and set off to track down Jill Smart. A minute later, he was in her office and reciting the sorry tale, a suitably doleful expression on his face.

'So I think it needs a phone call ma'am, ' he concluded, noting the automatic and unthinking use of the term of respect. 'Jill, I mean,' he corrected, giving her a smile. The thing was, even although they were now technically the same rank since his recent semi-permanent promotion to DCI, he still couldn't help calling her *ma'am,* she having been his gaffer for so many years. 'Because the Commissioner was planning a wee press conference this afternoon to announce that McKean was an evil sexual predator, and that's obviously going to be a bit tricky now'.

'I knew about it,' Smart said ruefully. 'I've been invited.' She paused for a few seconds. 'And I can tell you, your phone call is going to be even more difficult than you think. Because have you seen this?' She swiped her phone and pushed the screen in his face. 'It's the Globe's website,' she continued, 'and they're breaking the story that Tamara Gray is going to raise a formal complaint of police brutality against us because of McKean's bloody nose. And when I say *us*, I actually mean *you*, or at least that nutcase DS James you've got working for you.'

He could have said, *aye, and it was you who sent her to me in the first place, wasn't it?* and he could have protested about him having to make that awkward phone call rather than her. But it wouldn't have done any good, so instead he said, 'Bugger, that's not good news,' which it wasn't.

He paused for a moment then gave a deep sigh. 'All right, I'll call him. Chances are I'll only get through to his PA anyway, and I'll just get her to pass on the message.'

'I thought you had his direct mobile number?' Smart said, raising a weary eyebrow.

He sighed again. 'I do. Okay then, I'll bloody phone him. But only if you help me write my resignation letter when I'm done.'

She laughed. 'It's a deal.'

Afterwards, he was able to reflect that the call had gone exactly as he'd expected, that was, very badly indeed. There was some mitigation, insofar as the Commissioner had quickly sussed the blame for the forensic foul-up fell squarely with the civilian Forensic Service and its inability to put proper out-of-hours procedures in place, resolving to call the head of that service immediately his call with Frank was over to raise the riot act. But that still left the matter of Dougie McKean's bent and bloodied nose to be dealt with, the outcome of which was that both Frank and DS James were to face an internal disciplinary hearing. In Frank's case, it was to be delayed until the end of the McKean investigation, whereas the likelihood was James would be suspended on full pay after a cursory review. *Bloody Jessie James*, he cursed. *Somebody should have sorted her out years ago, and now I'm left to take all the crap.* But then again, she had been severely provoked by McKean's misogynistic comment, and he had found his emotions switching from annoyance to a grudging sympathy. Still, she shouldn't have done it, that was the bottom line, and now they would both be facing the consequences.

Luckily, he'd managed to end the call without letting his bitter feelings of injustice spill out, but then he had vented for at least half an hour into the sympathetic ear of Jill Smart, after which he phoned Maggie and went through the whole story again. It was his own fault of course, because he could just as easily have taken Ronnie French up to Aviemore, and had only chosen James for the mission to help her to feel part of the team.

And now their new-season signing had been red-carded on her first proper outing.

Chapter 15

Maggie had been disappointed to hear that Frank was having to stay a few days longer in London on account of some unspecified foul-up on his McKean investigation. Still, it was now Thursday, and he had promised to fly back that evening as soon as his rescheduled press conference alongside the Commissioner was over. Fortunately, a new case had landed, giving her something to distract her and something for her assistant Lori Logan to get her teeth into too. The pair had temporarily decamped to the Bikini Baristas cafe, Lori's former place of work, located just two doors' down from their little Byres Road office. The objective, as well as enjoying the establishment's excellent coffee and delicious breakfast menu, was to discuss tactics and have a general chewing of the fat, case-wise. One of which had gone decidedly pear-shaped in the last few days.

'So Tamara told you to get stuffed, did she?' Lori asked through a mouthful of maple bacon roll. 'Because I knew she would actually. I would, if my lover left me millions. Anyone would in fact.'

Maggie gave a rueful smile. 'Yes, Frank said I was being crazily optimistic if I thought Tamara would agree to a negotiation over the will, and he was right. When I spoke to her on the phone, she said it was quite clear that everything had been left to her, and that was the end of the matter as far as she was concerned. But obviously she was very emotional so soon after Dougie's death. Maybe she'll have a re-think when it's all a bit less raw.'

'She won't. So what are we going to do? Challenge it?'

She shrugged. 'Cassie sent me a copy, and as I thought they would, Shore McPhail & Robertson included a clause that states any challenge to the document would be under English law.'

'Bummer.'

'Yes, but it's not the end of the story. I spoke to Asvina, who said a court might strike out the clause as unreasonable, given both the deceased and his family lived and continue to live in Scotland. But obviously, it's not an ideal situation.'

'I bet wee Tamara poured a gallon of whisky down his throat after that concert,' Lori said, sounding as if she was serious. 'Saw her chance and took it. Boom, he's dead, then boom, she's a multi-millionaire. A few weeks of fake mourning, and then she moves into that beautiful house as lady of the manor. And with no piss-head lord to cramp her style.'

Maggie laughed. 'I don't think Lord Dougie needed any help in drinking himself to death.' But fleetingly, it did occur to her that perhaps the cool Tamara might not have done much to stop him. 'Anyway, I've left it with Cassie to decide what to do next. Not that she's got much choice I suppose. Other than to go to court I mean.'

Lori made a face. 'Not much we can do now though, is there?' she said. 'We're kind of stuck in limbo.

'Yes, I suppose we are. Which means it's great that we've got a shiny new case to get our teeth into. And something a bit different from boring old divorces and property disputes, thank goodness.'

'And will I be involved in this new case?' her assistant asked eagerly.

'Intimately,' Maggie said, smiling. 'In fact, you'll be starting an undercover assignment this afternoon. In Lewis & Clark's department store down the Buchanan Galleries.'

'Ooh, that sound's exciting. And will I be one of those swishy shop assistants they have, selling all those fancy designer labels?'

'Not exactly,' Maggie said, and left it at that.

***

He'd waited until Wednesday before bringing up the matter of DS Gemma James' suspension from duty pending an enquiry into the circumstances surrounding the arrest of the now-late Dougie McKean, and unsurprisingly, she hadn't taken it well. He had been careful to break the bad news in Atlee House, where a meltdown by one of its inmates was unremarkable, and where he was usually the most senior officer on the premises and could thus brush away any nosey-parker enquiries as to what was going on. Still, her reaction had been quite spectacular by any standards, involving a stream of X-rated invective and the propulsion of several items of expensive IT equipment across the open-plan office, most of it aimed in his direction. He was just bloody glad she was no longer a member of the armed response squad. Eventually though he had succeeded in calming her down, making it clear that he would plead for mitigation on account of the outrageous provocation of McKean. Grudgingly satisfied, she slunk off and left him to contemplate the upcoming press conference in peace. Not that he had much to contemplate, because the Commissioner had made it clear that he himself planned to do all the talking. 'So you just want me to sit there and look pretty sir?' was what he had been tempted to say when informed of this in a phone call, but sensibly had decided against it, a sense of humour not being one of Naylor's qualities.

This time they had elected to keep it in-house rather than rent an expensive hotel event space, so next day they gathered at ten in the morning in one of the larger incident rooms at Kensington nick. The room was crammed to bursting point with hacks and TV crews, including, he noticed, Orla McCarthy, Yash Patel and their cameraman Rupert. The singer was wearing a short purple dress, black tights and a pair of leopard-skin ankle boots, her flame-red hair tied up in her normal bunches. There was no doubt about it, Frank thought, perfectly dispassionately, she was a very attractive woman, and as such, a goodly percentage of the assembled TV crews had their cameras focussed on her and not on the low platform onto which Naylor was about to step. He wondered if she was preparing to create a scene, irrespective of what the Commissioner's speech contained. Knowing Yash Patel -evidently now installed as her Svengali -and his constant thirst for sensational stories, she probably would be.

He saw his pal Patel give him a shifty look and then quickly look away. Aye, definitely, they've got something planned, he thought, and wondered whether he should have a word with them in advance. But no, whatever little stunt they were planning it might be quite entertaining to watch, especially since he knew that nothing could possibly be directed at his own very recent involvement in the investigation. At least, he hoped that was the case. But at that moment the atmosphere in the room perceptibly changed, the cameras doing a one-hundred-and-eighty-degree swivel as Metropolitan Police Commissioner Trevor Naylor strode into the room, closely trailed by DCI Jill Smart, who was wearing her dress uniform. Frank allowed himself a wry if slightly disrespectful smile. As long as you didn't have to listen to him for too long, Naylor cut a commanding figure. Six-foot two, broad-shouldered and quite handsome, his physical attributes went a long way towards offsetting his tendency for plodding worthiness. Still, given the aching woke-fest that had gone before, he was seen as a definite improvement in the eyes of most of the rank-and-file, and in most of the general public too. Today he had come with prepared notes, laying several sheets of neatly-typed A4 paper on the raised dais of the lectern as he took his place at the front of the room. Frank gave Yash Patel a warning look before taking the few steps forward to join Jill and the Commissioner.

'Good morning ladies and gentlemen, and thank you,' Naylor said, reading from his script. 'This session is to provide members of the written and broadcast media with an update into our investigations into certain allegations raised by the well-known pop singer Miss Orla McCarthy and concerning events that were said to have transpired on the twenty-third of October, two-thousand and-six. Joining me on the platform are DCI Jill Smart and the Senior Investigating Officer for this case, DCI Frank Stewart.'

Frank smiled to himself. That would be the same Orla McCarthy that's standing about ten feet in front of you then. All it needed was for Naylor to say *I was proceeding along the road in a westerly direction...* to complete the impression that he had been beamed down from a nineteen-fifties black and white B-movie. But now he was about to get to the nub of the matter.

'You will now know that the subject of our investigations, Mr Douglas McKean of the folk-rock group The Claymore Warriors, was found dead in his rented home in the Scottish Highlands just five days ago. That of course means that this investigation will not result in a perpetrator being charged with any offence.' He paused for a second and took a sip from his glass of water, during which Frank was sure he heard one of the assembled hacks whispering *no shit Sherlock,* an observation that was as apt as it was unoriginal. 'Nonetheless,' Naylor continued, 'it is important for the delivery of justice that this case is taken to a proper conclusion, irrespective of the guilt or otherwise of the accused.'

Orla McCarthy took a step forward towards the podium and shouted, 'So this is going to be another cover-up just like the first time is it?' The barb was directed at the Commissioner, but her head was half-turned towards Rupert's shoulder-mounted camera to ensure he got a good shot of her attractive profile.

'We have reviewed very carefully how the force conducted its investigations into the original very serious allegations,' Naylor said stiffly, 'and I'm satisfied that everything was done quite properly given the evidence we had available to us at that time.' That was the truth, but it didn't seem that was going to satisfy Orla McCarthy.

'Did you know,' she shouted again, 'that the Senior Investigating Officer was given VIP tickets to a Claymore Warriors concert in Munich and that him and his wife were flown there first class? With back-stage passes and everything? Did you know *that* Commissioner Naylor?'

Bloody hell, thought Frank, talk about a curve ball. Detecting Naylor's obvious discomfort, he stepped in. 'As you know Miss McCarthy, it is me who has been conducting the review of the original investigations,' he said. 'And they were *very* upsetting allegations, I fully understand that. But unfortunately, as Commissioner Naylor said, there was not enough concrete evidence to give any reasonable hope of a successful prosecution. Very unfortunate, but nonetheless, that was the fact of the matter at the time.'

'You haven't answered my question,' Orla persisted, her voice raised again. 'The cop in charge was bought. *Bought*. And now he's some big-time Assistant Commissioner, when it's an absolute scandal that he's still in a job.'

Looking at Naylor, it was clear he was hoping Frank would continue with the defence. The trouble was, it had now got a whole lot more difficult with the revelation that AC Archibald hadn't just accepted a couple of free tickets, but had benefited from a whole VIP shebang as well.

He smiled at her. 'Assistant Commissioner Archibald has been perfectly upfront about this issue during my investigation. He accepts now that it was a serious mistake to accept the tickets, but they were not presented to him until after the case had been closed, so had no influence on his conduct of the investigation.' Aye, that's when he *got* them, Frank thought, but that doesn't mean they weren't promised a whole lot earlier, and that was a matter the press was likely to be digging into pretty soon. But now another question came to him, and that was, how the hell did McCarthy find out about the tickets in the first place? As far as he knew, it had only been Archibald's dirty little secret, until he had wisely confessed to his boss Naylor at the start of the case. This was something he would need to look into, or more accurately, something to get DC Ronnie French to look into on his behalf. Looking up, he saw the assembled hacks furiously scribbling in their notebooks or banging text into their iPads. Tomorrow was going to be very uncomfortable indeed for Archibald, that was for sure, and it didn't look as if Naylor was going to offer any words in his defence either.

'Thank you DCI Stewart,' he said, shuffling his notes and picking up a second A4 sheet. 'Fortunately, new evidence has recently come to light which has put a different perspective on the case.' *Yup, not a word about Archibald.* 'With the benefit of audio analysis technology, we are now able to say with a high degree of certainty that Douglas McKean did indeed conduct a vile sexual assault on Miss McCarthy. And indeed we can conclude that were McKean still alive, he would be charged with the offence and we also believe that the Crown Prosecution Service would be happy for the matter to be put in front of a judge and jury.'

Frank nodded to himself, Eleanor having told him that she had found a positive match between the recording and McKean's voice sample that they had obtained during his interview at Inverness police station. However, she had also told him that she hadn't properly completed the authentication exercise of the other two voices on the recording, that of the producer Nicky Nicholson and of Orla McCarthy herself. Fair enough, he thought, because McKean's voice was probably enough, given that the case now would not have to go to court. It was a bit of a loose end, but maybe it didn't matter now that the guy was dead.

Unexpectedly, the door to the interview room was pushed open and a young female uniformed officer stepped in, holding a sheet of paper in her hand, showing her discomfort as a dozen hacks turned round to look at her. Hesitantly she approached the podium, scanning her eyes between Naylor, Frank and Jill Smart, evidently unsure as to who should be the recipient of her message. Finally, she opted for Smart, handing her the paper with a rushed *'I think this might be important ma'am'*, before hurrying away. Smart scanned it with an expression of surprise, and then touched Naylor's elbow to get his attention, before shielding her mouth with her hand and whispering something inaudible in his ear. The Commissioner gave a few nods of acknowledgement and then turned back to face his media audience.

'So ladies and gentlemen, that concludes today's conference,' he said abruptly. 'If there is anything further to add, we may schedule another session, but that's us for now. Thank you for your attendance. Good morning.' And with that, he gathered up his papers and strode purposefully towards the door. But Orla McCarthy had evidently anticipated his exit and now moved to block his departure.

'So is that it Naylor?' she said, her voice dripping with aggression. 'Is that it? No apology, no acknowledgment of the colossal mistakes that *your* police force had made? Haven't you a ton of questions to answer?'

The Commissioner stopped and looked her straight in the eye, but then hesitated before speaking, an action that seemed to unsettle McCarthy, who gave an uncertain look to camera. Then he smiled at her and said, 'Perhaps Miss McCarthy it may be *you* who soon has questions to answer,' before sweeping imperiously out of the room.

Chapter 16

Jimmy had been sitting in his pokey wee Braemar office, sorting out some dull administration for his outdoor adventure business, when the call had come in from his brother Frank. The message, short and succinct, left no room for misunderstanding. *Get your arse into your pal's swish new BMW and put your foot down too.* Which was the reason he was now powering eastwards along the A93 in his partner Stew Edward's big SUV, the picturesque route closely following the course of the River Dee and built on top of the Old Military Road that had been crafted some two hundred years earlier. The road also took him past the grounds of majestic Balmoral Castle, and according to a sign at the gate, today was one of a handful of days of the year that it was opened for visitors. But today, Jimmy had no time for leisure. Today, he was on a mission, and that mission was to prevent a cremation taking place.

The car's sat-nav had calculated a route distance of sixteen miles and a duration of twenty-six minutes from downtown Braemar to the crematorium at Ballater. That depended on the volume of traffic of course - not normally an issue in this neck of the woods - but also on how fast you were prepared to drive and how much you were prepared to risk coming across one of the speed-camera vans that were frequently deployed by the roadside. By ignoring the latter and maximising the former, Jimmy had worked out he could be there in nineteen minutes flat, and glancing at the car's clock, he saw that twelve of these minutes were already behind him. But what the hell was he going to do when he got there, that was the big question, especially since he only had a sketchy outline from Frank as to what was going on. *There's now reason to believe that Dougie McKean might have been poisoned*, that was all he'd been told. So sure, if that was the case, it meant that there ought to be a post-mortem, and you couldn't perform one of those on a pile of ashes. He'd also figured out why he had been given the task rather than the local police. That was because Frank could happily say to his brother *don't ask questions, just go and do it*, whereas the local police *would* ask questions, lots of them, and any request for assistance from these Fancy-Dans from the Met would have to be passed up the chain of command for approval by the brass. By which time, Dougie McKean would have already been turned into that aforementioned pile of ashes. But knowing why he'd been chosen wasn't going to make the task any less awkward once he got there.

The sat-nav took him straight to the wrought-iron gates of the crematorium, and as he had suspected, he pulled into a car-park crammed with vehicles, amongst which were a scrum of logo-emblazoned outside-broadcast vans belonging to the TV networks. The funeral was meant to be private, but there was no hope of that being respected, given McKean's fame in Scotland and the circumstances surrounding his death. Jimmy knew of course that Orla McCarthy and Yash Patel would not be amongst those present, having evidently decided that the YouTube footage to be gleaned from disrupting acting Commissioner Naylor's press conference in London was the priority. As well as the media, there was a scattering of what he guessed were fans, mainly guys in their forties or fifties, most wearing Claymore Warriors T-shirts, the majority sporting beards. It was a tight demographic, the

Claymore fan-base, and Jimmy reflected that he was probably an outlier, being too young to be a core fan, but he was no less keen for all that. He parked up and then strode towards the long canopy that covered the wide pathway into the crematorium building. From behind the double doors he could just about make out the strains of *Mountain Dew*, which apparently had been Dougie McKean's favourite Warrior's track. So that was good, it almost certainly meant that they hadn't yet committed his coffin to the furnace. Now the next thing he had to worry about was getting in. He expected there to be someone minding the entrance to make sure any intending mourners had been invited by the family, but he didn't suppose they'd have employed actual bouncers, capable of physically restraining any unauthorised attendees. In his army days, he'd been on plenty of raids, his bomb disposal guys following the hard-nut snatch teams into the den of some unsuspecting insurgents. The tactic back then had always been to use surprise, speed and a lot of shouting, the latter a deceptively simple technique that had been proven to cause maximum confusion and distraction. Ballater wasn't Helmand Province of course, but there was no reason why a similar strategy wouldn't work here. He waited until he heard the familiar final notes of *Mountain Dew* gently fading away, then, taking a preparatory deep breath, he kicked at the double doors of the chapel with all the force he could muster, causing them to fly open. The left-hand door smashed against an adjacent side wall with a loud crash, causing gasps of surprise amongst the assembled mourners, as they swivelled in their seats to find out what the hell was happening. A silver-haired elderly woman in a black knitted two-piece stood by the entrance, her hands covering her mouth in a gesture of shock and surprise.

'Stop the cremation!' Jimmy roared at the top of his voice, as he strode down the centre aisle. 'Stop the cremation! Stop it now!' A couple of seconds later he was at the front of the room, where the minister stood, bible in hand, in front of the platform on which lay Dougie McKean's coffin, draped in one of his trademark tartan capes.

'What *is* all this?' the minister asked irately. 'This is *highly* irregular.'

Jimmy ignored him, concentrating instead on the front row, where Cassie McKean was now on her feet, looking around in obvious confusion at the scene that was playing out in front of her eyes.

'Jimmy, what *is* this?' she asked, paraphrasing the minister's words. 'What the *hell* is going on?'

'I'm *so* sorry Cassie,' he said. 'I don't have the full details, but the police have come into some information that suggests that Dougie might have been poisoned. I don't know any more than that at the moment. It's just that I work in Braemar, so I was the nearest guy to the crematorium. Which is why I got the job.' He paused for a second. 'And obviously, I'm really really sorry to have to do this.'

'What's this all about pal?' a man's voice interjected, a voice that Jimmy recognised without having to look round.

'Mr Cooper, the police have reason to believe that Mr McKean may have been poisoned.'

'Bollocks,' Jamie Cooper said. 'Dougie was a piss-artist, and one of the finest on the planet at that. Unfortunately he took it just one step too far, and now here we all are, united in our grief.' He gave a smirk and nodded towards his band-mates who were seated two rows back, and seemingly in deep conversation about something. 'We're all gutted, every one of us.'

Cassie gave Cooper a reproachful look but made no comment. Instead she said to Jimmy, 'So are you - I mean the police - are they saying that Dougie was *murdered*?'

He shrugged. 'I honestly don't know. Maybe, or maybe they think it was accidental. But the police will be here soon, and they'll obviously be able to take you through what's going to happen.' He paused again for a moment then nodded in the direction of the mourners, most now on their feet and gathered in small huddles, whispering to one another. 'Perhaps we should ask the minister to explain that the cremation isn't going ahead.'

'I don't want that,' Cassie said, blurting out the words. 'I need closure. My family needs closure. We have to go ahead, we *must*.' And then she began to cry.

'See what you've done?' Jamie Cooper said. 'Now I don't see what authority you've got, but I'm with Cassie. We need to put the old bastard out of his misery. ' He gestured towards the minister. 'Hey pal, just press the button and let's get it over with, eh?'

'Don't do that,' Jimmy said sharply, addressing the minister. 'This is a serious matter.'

The minister looked at Jimmy, then at Cooper, and finally at Cassie before speaking.

'We haven't completed the ceremony in any case,' he said uncertainly. 'It wouldn't be right to send someone into eternity without asking God to forgive their sins.'

'Well that would be a bloody long list you'd have to go through,' Cooper said. 'But fair enough then. If Dougie's not going into the fire, then we might as well head to the wake and get started on the bevvy.' He turned and shouted over to his band-mates. 'Hey boys, the dead bastard's laid on a wee spread for us at the hotel across the road, and there's a free bar I've heard. Let's go and get stuck in.'

Jimmy waited until the Warriors had left the chapel before speaking to Cassie again, who was now being comforted by a woman whom he took to be her sister.

'Look Cassie,' he said. 'I don't know too much about how these things work, but obviously there'll have to be a post-mortem and then it'll depend on its findings as to what happens next. But the authorities are very sensitive to the feelings of the relatives in a matter like this, which means they always try to release the body as soon as they possibly can. I know it's not much of a consolation, but you'll probably be back in this chapel within the fortnight, maybe sooner.'

By which time, he reflected, the Dougie McKean murder enquiry will be very much up and running.

***

He struggled to get a hold of Frank on the drive back to Braemar, his brother's phone switching to voicemail on each of three attempts to call. But just as he was approaching the village, his brother phoned back.

'Brilliant work young Jimmy,' he said, launching straight into the conversation without preamble. *'And sorry I didn't pick up earlier. I was locked up in an interview room with the Commissioner to try and work out what we do next on the McKean situation. But I wish I had been at that crematorium. It must have been quite a show.'*

'That's not the words I would use to describe it. But it got the job done.'

'And did the local plod turn up eventually?'

Jimmy nodded. 'Yup. A detective-sergeant drove over from Aberdeen. Nice lass and very efficient too. I heard her on the phone to the police morgue before I left.'

'Aye, they'll get the body taken over there to await the post-mortem. Hopefully they'll be able to do it tomorrow.'

'So what's kicked all of this off?' Jimmy asked.

'A paramedic from Inverness took ill,' Frank answered. *'He called 999 last night, after retching and throwing up at his girlfriend's house. They rushed him into the Raigmore General Hospital, where a junior A&E doctor spotted right away that he had something called tachycardia and got worried. Went*

and fetched his consultant and she examined him and confirmed his findings.'

'Tachy-what?' Jimmy asked.

'It's abnormal heart rate apparently. And often symptomatic of poisoning it turns out. So they obviously needed to find out what he'd ate or drank. And then the story came out.'

'What's that?'

'The guy was one of the paramedic team that went to Dougie McKean's aid at Glengarnet Lodge. And afterwards, he swiped the singer's bottle of Balvenie as a wee souvenir.'

'Bloody hell,' Jimmy said, astonished. 'That'll get him the sack I imagine.'

'Aye, if he survives, because that's touch-and-go at the moment. The paramedic's girlfriend had come with him in the ambulance and when they asked her what he had eaten or drunk in the last twenty-four hours, she told them what he'd done. So the hospital called the police and a DC belted over to the girlfriend's place and retrieved the bottle and whizzed it in to the lab. Where they discovered it had been laced with a horrible substance called taxine. Bloody nasty stuff by all accounts. It comes from yew trees and there's no known antidote.'

'And so you think that's what killed McKean?'

'Got to be a high likelihood, isn't it?' his brother replied. *'Because that was the bottle he brought back from the concert.'*

'Well there's no shortage of suspects, that's for sure,' Jimmy mused. 'He wasn't exactly the most popular guy in the world.'

"Yeah, I thought that too. But that makes it harder for us, not easier.' Frank paused for a moment. *'Still, that'll be someone else's problem, thank god.'*

'So you won't be handling the case? If it turns out to be murder, I mean?'

'Nah, it's all about jurisdiction. His death was on Police Scotland's patch so they'll lead with it, and I'm not really a murder specialist to be fair. But I will be on the team, although maybe in name only, depending who they make SIO. A lot of guys and gals don't like someone second-guessing what they're doing.'

'Like you for instance,' Jimmy laughed. 'But you won't be able to stop poking your nose into it, will you? Because I know what you're like.'

'I'll be keeping a wee eye on proceedings, let's just put it that way.'

Chapter 17

As might have been expected, events moved at pace following Jimmy's dramatic interruption of the Dougie McKean cremation ceremony. Firstly, the post-mortem confirmed that McKean had died through cardiac arrest as a result not of excess alcohol consumption as originally thought, but by the action of a toxin introduced into his system, that toxin identified as taxine, a deadly substance found in abundance in the yew tree family. Secondly, analysis of the remains of the bottle of Balvenie single malt had shown the presence of the poison, its taste disguised by the addition of the sweetener aspartame. The concentration of the toxin was such that only two or three swigs of the whisky would be needed to cause death, and McKean had certainly imbibed a lot more than that on the night. There would be an inquest of course, as the formalities demanded, but already a murder file had been opened and Police Scotland had decided who would be leading the investigation. A name which caused a mixture of trepidation and indignation in the minds of the two early-evening drinkers presently gathered at the Horseshoe Bar on Glasgow's Great Western Road.

'So it's gone to Steph McNeil?' Maggie said, surprised. 'I thought she was only a DI, not a DCI?'

'Grade inflation,' Frank said sourly. 'She's just got promoted. And her sidekick DS Curran is now acting DI would you believe? I mean, they're scraping the barrel there, but it's everywhere, isn't it? You go on a wee three-day plumbing course and they give you a first-class honours degree afterwards. But the interesting thing actually is that they've allocated it to a Glasgow-based team. My jungle drums tell me that the boys and girls up in Grampian are seriously hacked off about that, because they never get to do any murders.' He paused and took a swallow from his pint. 'But our Steph's the golden girl at the moment, according to my mate DC Lexy McDonald.'

'But our Steph didn't exactly cover herself in glory on our last case, did she?'

He shrugged. 'Hardly, but that's never made any difference in the police service. And there is some logic for their decision I suppose. What I mean is, that although the murder happened up in Speyside, all the festival infrastructure's packed away now. No stage, no tents, no portal-loos, no nothing. And nobody who was involved is there anymore. It's just a big field again.'

'A very lovely one next to the beautiful river though.'

He nodded in agreement. 'There's no denying that. But another thing is, none of the suspects are likely to be local either. So it's not really a murder scene, except in the technical sense. They've parked one of these mobile incident rooms in the field just in case they need to interview any of the locals, but I think we'll be casting the net a lot wider than that for our murderer.'

'I've been thinking about that a *lot*, so I have,' said the unmistakable voice of Lori Logan, who had just sidled up to them, unobserved. 'Hi you two, by the way. I see you're on to your second drinks already, if these are your empty glasses.'

Maggie laughed. 'Oh hi Lori. How's your day been? Made any progress?'

Frank gave her an amused look. 'What's with the nice wee pink overall Lori? Not your usual style is it?'

She gave a dismissive harrumph. 'Maggie's got me working undercover. As a *stock girl*,' her tone of voice leaving no doubt as to what she thought about it. 'At Lewis & Clark's, down the Buchanan Galleries.'

'Very posh establishment,' Frank said. 'But bloody expensive too. I'd never buy anything in that place. In fact, I don't think they'd actually let me in.'

'They do Fiona Ingleton there,' Lori said. 'It's their biggest-selling line. Five hundred quid a dress minimum. Although they do look *amazing*.' Maggie gave the girl a sharp look, fearing she was about to spill the beans about her wedding dress, but the knowing smile she got back reassured her.

'And their most-shoplifted line too, which is why we've been asked to investigate,' Maggie explained.

'Shop-lifting eh?' Frank said. 'That's a crime which is about number a hundred and fifty on our priority list. We just don't have the resources.' He paused and smiled. 'That's me parroting the brass's party line by the way. It's not what I think myself.'

'Yeah, it costs the store about ten grand a month, so they would see it differently I think,' Maggie said.

'I think it's an inside job,' Lori said, 'I've got my suspicions on who and how, but I've not got any concrete evidence yet. But I'll get it. If I don't collapse and die first, with having to hump all those heavy boxes of stock around the place,' she added pointedly.

Maggie laughed. 'Well don't worry Lori, if you do drop dead, Bainbridge Associates will pay for the funeral, and I'll get Jimmy to read a nice eulogy at the service. But you said you've been thinking about the McKean case?' she asked, smoothly changing the subject. 'Bear in mind that we as an agency won't actually be having anything to do with it.'

'I made a list of suspects,' the girl said, taking her phone from a pocket. 'It's quite long.'

'Run it past us then,' Frank said, obviously amused. 'And maybe I'll write it down myself if you don't mind. Because I expect DCI McNeil will be looking for *my* list when I see her tomorrow morning.'

'There'll be a fee for that,' Maggie laughed. *'My darling.'*

He leant over and kissed her cheek. 'Consider that a down-payment.'

She giggled. 'I'd want more than just a *kiss*.'

'Get a *room*,' Lori said making an exaggerated grimace.

Frank laughed. 'We want to hear your list first. Then we'll get one.'

'Alright then.' She looked down at her phone and began to read. 'So the first thing you need to know is that I've approached this scientifically. I've started with all the possible motives you can have for murder, and then looked to see who I could fit into each category.' She paused for a moment before continuing. 'Right, motives. There's pure rage, that's when the murderer just loses it and lashes out. Then there's jealousy, there's financial gain, there's revenge, there's sexual rejection or uncontrollable lust. And then there's the cover-up motive, killing someone so they can't spill the beans about something. There's murder to escape an abusive situation, you know, when you've been pushed to breaking point and finally snap. And then there's when it's a mistake, when the wrong person has been killed.'

'Impressive list,' Maggie said.

'Very,' Frank agreed. 'So what are you thinking Lori?'

She smiled. 'Well let's start with what it's *not*. It's not rage, because our murder was pre-meditated, wasn't it? And McKean wasn't killed by mistake either, he was *definitely* the intended victim. And the motive wasn't sexual rejection, because that's normally only a factor when the victim is a woman. Besides which, Dougie wasn't exactly Brad Pitt was he? Plenty of woman might fancy his money, but not his body.'

'Someone else said that too,' Frank said, grinning. 'I mean that he's no Brad Pitt.'

'And he wasn't killed to shut him up or cover something up, at least I don't think so,' Lori continued, glancing at her list again. 'And I don't think his girlfriend Tamara Gray was in an abusive relationship with him, was she?' She paused before giving them a look of mild self-satisfaction. 'Which leaves jealousy, financial gain or revenge.'

'Which is more than enough to be going on with,' Maggie said. 'And the killer could have more than one of these motives of course,' she added.

'Right,' Lori agreed. 'But I think it's the ones driven by emotion that are the most powerful. Jealousy, and revenge - they could drive even the most unlikely person to murder. Financial gain is more of a spreadsheet thing, you weigh up the debits and credits before making your decision. Cold calculation really.'

'But there is another motive to add to your list, isn't there?' Maggie said thoughtfully. 'One that's related to that last one. Let's call it financial desperation. If you're in terrible financial trouble, you might see murder as your only way out. And that survival instinct is often the most powerful emotion of all.'

Frank nodded. 'Good point. But does *that* apply to anyone on your list Lori?'

She shrugged. 'I don't think we know enough to say. But probably not.'

'So getting down to basics, who benefits financially from his death?' he asked.

'That's a no-brainer,' Maggie said. 'Tamara Gray, his lover. He changed his will not so long ago and now she gets everything. Every penny.'

'Very nice for her,' he said. 'And does anyone else benefit?'

She shrugged. 'I don't think so. In actual fact, there's a bunch of people who are going to lose out by his death. His wife for a start. He died before we could agree a divorce settlement, and so she's in a very uncertain place at the moment, money-wise.'

'And all his ex-band-members are in the same boat too,' Frank added. 'Because to the die-hard fans, there's no Claymore Warriors without Dougie McKean. And his record company won't be too chuffed either by his demise.'

'Although they'll get a boost in sales of the back-catalogue,' Maggie mused.

Frank laughed. 'True, but he'd still be worth more to them alive than dead. The band had years of creativity ahead of them. And record companies don't have much of a history of being murderers to be fair.'

'So what about jealousy as a motive?' Maggie asked. 'Who might have been jealous of Dougie McKean, jealous enough to kill him I mean?'

'Everybody in his band, I suppose,' Lori said. 'If you asked any member of the public to name any of the Claymore Warriors, the only one they would come up with is Dougie McKean. It's a bit like Coldplay. Everybody knows Chris Martin's the singer but nobody knows any of the other members. So maybe one of the band was fed up with that, and decided to kill him.'

'It's *possible*,' Frank said, sounding dubious, 'but I refer you to my earlier point. Without Dougie, there's no Warriors. If you're a member of that band, it would be like cutting off your nose to spite your face, if you'll excuse the cliché. And why suddenly kill him now? Because they've been his backing band for nigh-on twenty years.'

'True,' Lori conceded.

'So what about revenge?' Frank asked. 'That's next on your wee list, isn't it?'

Lori nodded. 'There's a few possibilities on that one. Number one, his wife Cassie, seeking revenge for him dumping her. Number two, Orla McCarthy, for what McKean did to her all these years ago in that studio. Number three - and this is just a maybe - that American film producer and Orla's record-company boyfriend, because McKean reneged on the deal he'd done with them and they stood to lose a ton of money.'

'I'd agree with all of them, to some extent,' Maggie said. 'Although Orla, less so. She had been living with the mental consequences of the sexual assault for nearly twenty years, and she could have plotted to kill him any time during that period surely? I know they say revenge is a dish best served cold, but twenty years is stretching a point. Besides, I think she was totally focussed on having him face justice for what he did. She wanted to see him ruined, not dead.'

'I think you're right there,' Frank said.

Maggie nodded. 'Well, we'll see. So what about anybody else? Or any other motives?'

Frank laughed. 'How about everybody he ever met? But no, that's a decent list to be getting on with. So thank you Miss Logan. That's saved me a ton of work, and if DCI McNeil doesn't like it, I've got someone else to blame.'

'You know what? Maggie said, furrowing her brow. 'Everything we've ever learnt tells us it'll end up being something completely different. Different motive, different killer, something we've not even thought of as a possibility.'

Frank gave her a wry smile. 'Nothing like the power of positive thinking eh? On this occasion, I'm not sure I agree with you. I actually like Lori's short-list I must confess. Although I wish it was a wee bit shorter.'

'Well time will tell which one of us is right,' she said. But neither the firm of Bainbridge Associates nor its principal would have any further involvement in the drama, other than some prosaic toing-and-froing to try and persuade Tamara Gray into a more conciliatory approach with regard to McKean's inheritance. Not that *that* had much chance of success, she reflected bitterly. So she would be no more than an interested spectator, no less fascinated but no more involved than any other member of the public.

Which, as Lori observed in her inimitable fashion, was a bit of a bummer.

Chapter 18

It had been a while since Frank had been back at New Gorbals police station, and in a funny way he had missed the old place, in the same way that a hostage misses his prison cell after he's been freed. Now the unprepossessing concrete edifice was to be the headquarters of the Dougie McKean murder enquiry, under the leadership of newly-promoted Detective Chief Inspector Stephanie McNeil. A decent-sized incident room had been set up on the first floor, a bit far from the canteen and its coffee supply for Frank's liking, but functional enough. In a couple of minutes' time, McNeil would be launching the investigation, a small troop of about eight or so detectives having assembled in the room, sipping hot drinks and chatting away to each other. Pleased to see his old mate DC Lexy McDonald amongst the cohort, he sidled his way across the room to greet her.

'Hi Lexy,' he said brightly. 'Didn't know you were to be part of this exciting jamboree.'

'Yes sir,' she laughed. 'The Glasgow low-lifes are all away on their holidays so it's really quiet at the moment. We've not had a stabbing or anything for over a month.'

'And this is supposed to be the Gorbals? I'll tell you what, standards are slipping around here. But it's good you're on the case.'

'Central to it sir.' She nodded to an easel that sat at the front of the room. 'It was me that set up the whiteboard, and got the marker pens too. And I checked they were the rub-off ones.'

'We're about half-way there already then,' he laughed. 'But shoosh, I think Her Highness is about to honour us with a speech.'

McNeil had been in discussion with her right-hand woman, acting DI Curran, but now took a couple of steps towards the front of the room so that she stood just to the right of the whiteboard. The detective picked up a marker pen, waved it in the air, then said, 'Okay guys, let's get in the zone, shall we?'

The room fell quiet, the assembled detectives halting their conversations mid-flight to give their boss all their attention. Despite their run-in the last time they'd worked together, Frank still retained some respect for the recently-promoted DCI. She was one hundred-percent dedicated to the job, of that there was no doubt, and that was to her credit, but it came with an unconcealed ambitiousness that meant everything was calculated on how it was going to affect her career, for good or for bad. Above all, it was about getting a result, and getting one fast, which in Frank's long and jaundiced experience rarely delivered good police-work, nor much justice either. But here she was, her career powering ahead and probably no more than thirty-five or thirty-six, not far off ten years younger than himself, so who was he to judge? The brass rated her and that wasn't just because of the size of her breasts, no matter what the more cynical of her colleagues thought.

'Right guys, in case any of you missed the memo,' she began, 'this is the investigation into the murder of Dougie McKean on the twenty-fifth of August this year by poisoning. Many if not all of you will know that Mr McKean was the lead singer and main face of the Claymore Warriors, one of Scotland's finest musical exports. In that respect, his murder was a great loss to the arts if not to mankind.' She paused and surveyed the room with a critical air. 'Good to see everyone's awake,' she said. 'So we're very fortunate to have the services of DCI Frank Stewart to help us get the case up and running.' She nodded to where he stood. 'I assume most of you know Frank, since he's been seconded up here for a few months now and calls this station his home. Or at least, the canteen.'

'Aye, I've got a season ticket to that place Steph,' he said, garnering a few laughs from the assembly.

She held out the marker pen. 'So maybe Frank you could pop up here and get the ball rolling for us, before you move onto your next case?'

'Eh, sure,' he said, walking out to the front of the room. So he was moving on to his next case then, was he? That was news to him, but he didn't blame her if that was her game, because he would probably be trying to do the same if he was in her position. No-one wanted some smart-arse looking over their shoulder, second-guessing everything they were doing.

'Cheers Steph,' he said. 'So just before his untimely death, and as you will no doubt all have read in the papers, Mr McKean was the subject of a historical sexual assault allegation made by the Irish singer Orla McCarthy. At the same time, he was divorcing his wife, or more to the point, she was divorcing him, and that wee matter was being assisted by a firm of legal investigators called Bainbridge

Associates.' He smiled at McNeil. 'A firm that your DCI knows very well indeed.' To be fair to McNeil, she smiled back, even if it did look a bit forced. 'As a result,' he continued, 'we've already gathered a reasonable amount of information about the victim and some of the folks he was most closely associated with.' He paused and smiled again. 'For sharing this with you, there's no extra charge.' For the next half-hour he proceeded to tell them everything he knew, using Lori's list as a guide, scribbling names on the whiteboard as he reviewed them in turn, covering their relationship to McKean and possible reasons as to why they might want him dead. It wasn't an exhaustive list by any means, he realised as he wrote the names on the board, because there was a whole army of people who were backstage that night, any of whom might have had the opportunity to slip the lethal poison into the singer's bottle of Balvenie. Sound guys, guitar technicians, stage hands, even a make-up woman for goodness' sake, the Warriors travelled with a veritable army of support staff, and McNeil's investigation would have to track them all down and either stick them on the suspects' list or eliminate them. *Not* a task he envied much, that was for sure.

'So that's it,' he said finally. 'He wasn't the nicest guy in the world, and as DCI McNeil said, probably no great loss to mankind. But there's thousands of his fans who think differently, and he was a father, with two kids who loved him dearly. And I'll remind you too that there's a killer at large, and killers have got an awful track-record of striking again. So this matters.'

'Thank you Frank,' she said. 'That's been a fantastic help.' The tone was friendly enough, but there was no disguising the underlying message. *Thank you and goodbye.* In the next half-hour or so, she would be dishing out individual tasks to each member of her team, sending them scurrying across the country to interview suspects, but he wouldn't be getting one of them. *So what,* he thought, giving a mental shrug. He still had some stuff to do to properly close out the sexual assault allegation, including getting an official sample of Orla McCarthy's voice that Eleanor Campbell could use to complete her authentication of the accusatory recording. That would keep him busy for a few days, after which any involvement in the McKean murder case would be by invitation only, an invitation he expected to receive only if McNeil's investigation tumbled into a death spiral.

Which, feeling slightly ashamed with himself for thinking it, he hoped it would.

***

It had been a few days since Maggie had had anything to do with the McKean affair, the case giving every indication of being one of these unsatisfactory ones that just sort of fizzled out. The last formal discussion she'd had with Cassie McKean was more than two weeks ago now, where they had discussed her client's options for contesting the will in the face of Tamara Gray's unwillingness to compromise, and it had been left with Mrs McKean having to decide whether to go to court or not. Since then, Maggie had heard nothing, but that was hardly surprising given the tumult of the last week and a half, starting with Jimmy's gate-crashing of her late husband's cremation, which led to the post-mortem proving he had been murdered. Her client was now presumably a suspect too, which meant she'd probably been interviewed by the police, not a pleasant event even in the best of circumstances. Not wishing to push her at this difficult time, she had dropped Cassie a text, stark in its simplicity. *Hi Cassie, any thoughts yet about whether you want to take the matter to court?* So far, there had been no reply.

And then the phone call had come in, totally unexpectedly.

'Miss Bainbridge?' There was no mistaking the husky American voice. *'It's Tamara Gray here.'*

'Miss Gray,' Maggie said, temporarily nonplussed. 'Hi. How can I help you?'

'Please, call me Tamara,' she said, *'and you're Maggie, aren't you?'* Without waiting for a reply she continued, *'Look Maggie, I need your help. Badly.'*

Maggie paused for a moment. 'Okay Tamara...so what exactly is it you need my help with?' she asked, wondering if the woman was suddenly going to climb down from her unyielding position in respect of the will. But no, from her tone, it sounded more serious than that.

'I'm in trouble,' Gray answered. *'I had the police round here yesterday, and then they took me to a police station in Inverness for questioning. For hours.'*

'So are you still up in the Highlands?' Maggie asked. 'Because you were renting a lodge on Speyside I think?'

'That's right. My emotions are totally shot with everything that's happened and I've just been completely paralysed with

inaction. I can't bear to go back to the house I shared with Dougie, and with not being welcome at the funeral, I just can't come to terms with his death. So I'm just staying here a few days longer. I was going to fly back to the States to stay with my brother and his family, but now the police are saying I can't leave the country.'

'They can't stop you unless they charge you with something and then grant you bail with conditions,' Maggie said, automatically dropping into lawyer mode. 'I'm not quite as familiar as I should be with Scottish law, but I think that's how it works up here too.'

'They told me that. But you see, I'm really scared they're going to charge me very soon. I don't like the senior cop on the case, and I don't trust her either. I think she's already made up her mind that I did it.'

Maggie felt her heart sink as she began to suspect what might be coming next. In anticipation, she said, 'Tamara, if you are charged, then you need to have an experienced solicitor in the room when they interview you. Don't just take the duty one they offer you.' She paused for a moment then said, 'You're with Shore McPhail & Robertson, aren't you? They've got a big criminal practice, they should be able to help you.'

'It was them that got me into this position,' Gray said bitterly.

'How come?' Maggie asked, surprised.

'Two days ago the police talked to them about Dougie's will, and the stupid junior who was drafting it told them that I'd

been constantly on to Dougie to get him to sign it. Badgering him, that was the exact words she used.'

'And had you been?'

The woman hesitated for a moment. *'Well, I suppose so. But the will was just a part of it. All of his financial and commercial affairs were shambolic. Everything was a mess, and I mean everything. His property, all the contracts to do with the band, his personal finances, they were all over the place. He just didn't understand the potentially serious consequences of the position he was in. So I was just doing my job as his lawyer and manager to get it all sorted out.'*

'It wasn't something he was interested in then I take it?'

'He was interested in money alright,' she said. *'He wouldn't do anything unless he felt he was being paid properly. And I suppose you could say he was interested in managing his artistic reputation too. In fact, the only paperwork he had taken any interest in was the publishing contract for the Warriors material, which was written up years ago. Obviously the contribution of the whole band was important, but he wanted to make sure he got the lion's share of the money, and the artistic recognition too. That's really what was at the centre of all the arguments about allowing Oran na Mara to be used in that film. Because Dougie had 55% of the rights to the songs, so without his say-so, nothing could happen.'*

'Yes, Cassie told me about that arrangement,' Maggie said, recalling an earlier conversation with McKean's wife. 'By calculation, I think it means each of the remaining band members have 15% each.'

'That's right,' Tamara agreed. *'And each share is worth quite a lot of money. But not as much as Dougie's share, obviously.'* She paused for a moment. *'But that was as far as it went. He wasn't very good at managing his money once he'd earned it. And on top of that, his head had been all over the place after he found out about Cassie's affair. He was angry and wanted to make sure she lost out in any divorce settlement.'*

'Wait a minute,' Maggie blurted out. 'Are you telling me that Cassie was having an affair?' *This* was something that her client Mrs McKean had conveniently omitted to mention during their assignment. 'Who with?'

'He never found out. Cassie wouldn't tell Dougie who it was, but she swore to him that it was over by the time he'd found out about it. Some rather indiscreet text messages were what undid her.'

'And when was this exactly?'

'Eight, ten months ago maybe.' She paused again. *'I guess that was one of the things that brought Dougie and me together. He was really upset and well... one thing just led to another. You know how it can happen,'* she added.

Maggie wasn't sure that she *did* know, but she made no comment on the matter. Instead she said, 'So the police think you murdered Dougie to get your hands on his wealth? But what evidence do they have? They can't possibly prove you put the poison in his whisky bottle.'

'They say I had ample opportunity. The cases of Balvenie were delivered to the lodge. They've taken away what's left and

they're examining them in their forensics lab. And they've taken my phone and laptop too, I don't know why.'

'That's nuts,' Maggie said, thinking out loud, and recognising exactly what was happening. As DCI Steph McNeil saw it, Gray had the perfect motive, having engineered the rock singer into changing his will after just a few months of their relationship, a relationship he had entered into on the rebound, directly after he'd found out his wife had been cheating on him. With that background story, it would be so easy to cast Tamara as the calculating predator, taking advantage of an emotionally-vulnerable man, and now all the police had to do was to find some further slivers of supporting evidence to make the premise stick. She wondered if Frank already knew about this, or had it been kept from him as part of his exclusion from the investigation? Whatever the case, it didn't alter the awkwardness of the situation Maggie found herself facing.

'Look Tamara, I can fully understand why you're so worried,' she said, 'but I really don't think I'm going to be able to help you. There are just so many conflicts of interest for me. I'm already working for Cassie as you know. And you won't know this, but my fiancé Frank is a senior police detective and he's assigned to the case at the moment. So really, it's all very difficult.'

'But please, I really need you,' Gray pleaded. *'Please. There's no-one else I can turn to.'*

'That's not true, surely?' Maggie said, as gently as she could. 'I understand why you might not want to use Shore McPhail &

Robertson, but there are plenty of other law firms who could advise you. In fact, my best friend Asvina Rani is a senior partner at Addison Redburn, and they're a top firm. I could get her to recommend one of their criminal guys.'

'But that's not what I need,' the woman said, beginning to sound distraught. *'I need you to find out who did kill him. Because it wasn't me.'* She hesitated for a moment. *'I loved Dougie, I really did. I could never have done him any harm.'*

Maggie sighed. 'I'm sure that's true Tamara, but I can't help you. Honestly, I can't.'

Out of the blue Gray said, *'Okay then, she can have everything. His wife I mean. I don't need his money, it was never about that. Never.'* It was a massive about-turn, and Maggie couldn't help but distrust the reasoning behind this sudden change of heart.

'I don't think Cassie was asking for everything, just a fair settlement that recognised everything she had invested in the marriage over the years.' Except that story wasn't quite so straightforward, Maggie thought, her client having been less than truthful with her. That lack of truthfulness was something that would have to be dealt with in due course, but the question for now was, could she or should she help Tamara Gray? And then a thought came to her.

'Look Tamara, this is very difficult for me and my little firm, as I just said. But perhaps there might be *something* we could do to help, at least just a tiny little bit.' She paused for a moment. 'I've a part-time associate who works with me, Jimmy Stewart is his name, a really good guy. You remember, you met him when we came to see Dougie for the first time? He was an officer in the army, but before that he did a law degree, and he did his Scottish legal diploma too before he joined up. So perhaps we could get him to sit alongside you and make sure the police play by the rules. You're entitled to that representation, and you can choose who you like. And Jimmy's living in Braemar at the moment so he's pretty close to you.'

Almost as soon as she had made the offer, Maggie wondered if she had done the right thing. But she recognised the growing anger she was feeling towards her client Cassie McKean, for withholding what was surely such a material piece of information. For a start, the existence of the affair would have had a critical impact on the outcome of any court battle for the custody of their two children. Too late for that now of course, now that Dougie was dead, but that didn't make it any less serious. Had Cassie lied about anything else, or withheld any other significant information? Those were questions that needed urgent and truthful answers if their professional relationship was to be salvaged.

'Thank you for that,' Tamara said. *'And I'm really grateful for the offer, honestly. But will you find out who killed Dougie?'* she asked again.

Maggie grimaced, wishing now that she had just said *no* to the whole thing from the start. 'I'm sorry, but I can't take on an assignment with those terms of reference,' she said, 'for both of the reasons I mentioned. But look, if anything arises out of your questioning, or if you are actually arrested and charged, then as your lawyers, we would want to check the veracity of any police statements in the course of our professional duty to you. And obviously, if anything questionable came out of those investigations, we would follow their trail to wherever they led. That's the best I can do I'm afraid. And just so you know, I won't compromise the integrity of my firm nor do anything that would cause the integrity or professional competence of my fiancé to be called into question. At the slightest hint of any of that, I would have to pull out.'

'I understand, and I'm so so grateful,' Gray said again, her voice quivering with obvious emotion, *'And I'll pay you anything you want, money won't be a problem.'*

'It's not about the money,' Maggie said, rather more sharply than she had been intending. 'We'll charge our standard hourly rate for Jimmy's services, and I'll ask him to make contact and perhaps you could meet up at his office in Braemar. And then we'll just have to see where it goes from there.'

'I'm grateful,' Gray said for the third time in the space of a minute, *'and thank you.'* And then she hung up.

***

Afterwards, Maggie continued to harbour doubts as to whether she had done the right thing in accepting Tamara Gray's commission, albeit in such a heavily-caveated form. She wasn't exactly looking forward to telling Frank about it for a start, fearful as she was that he might see it as unwise meddling in an ongoing police enquiry, and a murder investigation at that. And despite her anger after discovering that Cassie McKean had been less than truthful with her, it was still difficult to see how she could work for Gray without bumping up against a massive conflict of interest. But the fact was, the question of who had murdered Dougie McKean was now really eating away at her, and she knew she wouldn't be able to rest until she found out what had happened to him.

Whether someone was paying her to do it or not.

Chapter 19

Frank wasn't exactly over the moon when Maggie told him, albeit rather tentatively, that she was planning to take on Tamara Gray as a client, her mission seemingly being to conduct a parallel investigation into the murder of Dougie McKean, in the event that Gray was charged with the crime. Admittedly there were caveats and a solemn undertaking that should her work get in the way of the official investigation then Bainbridge Associates would pull out immediately, and in any case, she had explained, the main element of the assignment was for Jimmy to act as the client's solicitor should Gray be brought in for further questioning. And the fact was, her business was entitled to take on any client that she wanted, and he knew she would respect the fact that he would now need to be very careful not to share with her any facts that DCI McNeil did not want in the public domain. But hopefully, with his own role in the investigation looking like being peripheral, maybe any conflicts would turn out to be few and far between.

So now he needed to concentrate on closing down the Orla McCarthy sexual allegation enquiry, which was still high on the acting Commissioner's priority list, despite the death of the accused. Actually, what Naylor wanted was for the Met to be exonerated from blame as far as the original enquiry was concerned, but that was looking a bit of a forlorn hope ever since that damning recording had been uncovered. Yes, what Commissioner Naylor wanted was clear, but what, Frank wondered, would Orla McCarthy now want, now that her alleged attacker had been murdered? In his experience of these type of cases, there was often a stain left on the character of the victim, no matter how unwarranted, as if they had somehow brought the attack on themselves by the way they acted or the way they dressed. In fact the unsavoury McKean had described McCarthy as a cock-teaser, a distasteful and un-evidenced description that had seriously angered Frank when he'd heard the rock singer say it. Maybe Orla would want to put it all behind her, now that the possibility of revenge or justice or whatever it was she had been seeking was impossible to satisfactorily attain. Hopefully he would find that out in the next ten minutes or so, since he was just about to call her. He picked up his phone and swiped to her number, smiling with wry amusement when he thought about just how many men would love to have the beautiful singer's number on their speed dial. She answered almost on the first ring, which he hadn't expected.

'Good morning Orla,' he said brightly. 'It's DCI Frank Stewart, from the Met. Is this a good time? I've just got a couple of small things to get sorted out on your assault case. Shouldn't take more than five minutes.'

'Yeah, sure,' she replied. *'Go ahead.'*

'First thing is, we need a recording of your speaking voice. It's just routine, so that our forensic boffins can say they've authenticated that recording before we put the whole thing to bed. I assume that's something you can get for us?'

'Sure, no problem,' she said. *'As long as you destroy it afterwards. I don't want it turning up for sale on eBay.'*

He wasn't sure if she was joking or not, but he moved to reassure her. 'It definitely won't. It'll go to the lab and then they'll delete it or whatever it is they do to get rid of it.' He paused for a moment then said, 'Well, that's about it actually. I mean, now that Dougie McKean's dead, it's just a matter of tidying up a couple of things and the we can close the file. And actually, that was something I wanted to ask you.'

'What was that?'

'Whether you want us to even go ahead with the authentication, now that he's dead. Because he's beyond justice now, sadly. I'm not sure if it serves any real purpose.'

'I want you to go ahead,' she said, spitting out the words. *'He might be beyond justice as you put it, but I want his legacy trashed. Whenever people think about McKean I want them to think about this, not Oran na Mara. Which he stole from me, by the way.'*

Frank was silent for a second, taken aback by her vehemence. Then he said, 'Look, I can understand how you feel, but I'd advise you to be very careful about making statements like that in public. Because it would be quite easy for people to surmise that you hated the guy enough to kill him.'

He heard her give a cold laugh. *'Oh, I hated him alright, but I wanted him humiliated in the public eye. I didn't want him dead, quite the opposite in fact. I wanted this to ruin him and to haunt him for the rest of his life.'*

As he was about to answer, some music struck up again in the background, and he gave a puzzled frown as he thought he recognised it. But then it stopped as quickly as it had started, and he heard muffled laughter followed by a loud crash on a snare drum.

'Aye okay,' he said finally. 'So, get me that recording and we'll get all this sorted as quickly as we can.'

'I will, I'll send it today if I can,' she said, in a softer tone that suggested her anger had evaporated as quickly as it had boiled over. *'And thank you.'*

'Nae bother,' he said. 'I'll be in touch.'

***

Maggie had put off the tricky phone call to Cassie McKean for a good two hours or more, waiting until Lori had returned to the office after a morning working undercover at Lewis & Clark's department store. The girl had got back just before twelve, and the pair of them had decided to shimmy along to the Bikini Baristas cafe for a spot of lunch and a cappuccino.

'How did you get on?' she asked her after they had got settled at a table.

'I saw how they do it,' her assistant said. 'Dead easy. But I'll tell you after I've got my food if that's alright. Because I'm dying for a sausage roll, so I am. In fact, I'm going to have two. *At least.*'

Maggie laughed. 'Of course, sustenance must always come first. Anyway, I need you for moral support. I want you listening in when I call Cassie.'

'I don't know what you're worried about,' Lori said, frowning. 'It was her that didn't tell you she was shagging someone else, and if we'd known that we would have taken a different approach to the divorce settlement with her husband. She's made us look right mugs.'

'I know, but I just hate confrontation. In fact, I've got a good mind to just text her and tell her we're not taking her engagement any further.'

'But then you would be a proper cowardy-custard,' Lori said, grinning. 'Anyway, here's Stevie. Let's get our order in.'

Stevie the proprietor noted down their order with his usual bonhomie, then scuttled off to the kitchen to prepare it. Finally accepting that she couldn't put it off any longer, Maggie took out her phone and swiped down to her client's number. Shooting Lori an apprehensive glance, she said, 'Here goes,' then jabbed the green telephone symbol to launch the call. To her relief, the call looked at as if it was going to ring out, and she just about to hang up when it was finally answered.

'Hi Maggie,' Cassie said, sounding out of breath. *'Sorry, I heard it ringing but I couldn't remember where I'd left it. Anyway, here I am now. How can I help you?'*

Maggie paused for a moment before answering. No, there was no question about it, she had to take the matter head-on.

'Look Cassie, I'll get straight to the point. You didn't tell me you were having an affair and that it was one of the reasons

Dougie left you. It wasn't just about his behaviour, was it? He found out about it, didn't he?'

There was silence at the end of the line and then her client said,' *Yes he did. The reason I didn't tell you was that it was a big mistake. It was over by the time I engaged you, and I just wanted to put the whole thing behind me.*'

Maggie sighed. 'I can understand that, but knowing about it would have made a huge difference to the way we approached the case. We wouldn't have risked a custody battle in court for instance.' She paused for a moment. 'The sad fact is, we've probably wasted much of the money you've spent with us.'

'And you're no' getting it back either,' she heard Lori say in a loud stage whisper, the girl evidently able to follow the conversation despite Maggie not having switched on speakerphone mode.

'What was that?' Cassie asked.

'Just my assistant concurring with what I said,' Maggie said hurriedly, shooting Lori a scolding look. 'Of course, custody is no longer an issue, sadly. But we still have the will to deal with of course.' She paused for a moment. 'And as far as that matter is concerned, there have been developments.'

'How do you mean?' her client shot back.

'So,' Maggie began, before inserting what she hoped was a tactful pause. 'Tamara Gray has been in touch with me. And before you say anything, I know she's not your favourite woman in the world.' *Although the picture you painted of her as a brazen husband-stealer is looking a bit less credible now*, she thought. And it seemed as if her client had understood this change in dynamic too, because when she answered, there was a discernible meekness in her tone.

'Really? That's a surprise. What did she want?'

'Good news I think,' Maggie said. 'She's been thinking about the will and now believes coming to some sort of amicable settlement is the right thing to do.'

'Yes, she's shit-scared that she'll be fingered for his murder because it was her that forced him to change it, and now he's dead.' So much for the outbreak of meekness, Maggie thought, allowing herself a wry smile. She wondered for a moment if it might be better to tell her client that her firm had been approached by Tamara to work for her should the woman indeed be charged with Dougie's murder, but then thought better of it. Gray hadn't been arrested and might never be, so no need to worry about any collateral issues until then. Instead she said,

'Well yes, she's probably a suspect, but so are a lot of people I guess.' She hesitated for a moment. 'As are you Cassie of course. Wives and lovers, they're always the number one suspect I'm afraid. Every time.'

'I didn't kill him,' Cassie said, quite quietly. *'Why would I kill him when he had left everything to that woman? It made much more sense for me to get a good divorce settlement. And when would I get the chance to put poison in his whisky? And even if I wanted to, what do I know about poisons?*

Absolutely nothing is the answer to that one. So you see, I had no motive and no opportunity and no means I either.' Her tone had a hint of triumph, reminding Maggie of one of her old school teachers, who used to scrawl an exultant *Q.E.D.* on the blackboard each time he solved some completely incomprehensible mathematical equation.

'Well look,' Maggie continued, choosing to make no comment about Cassie's passionate defence, 'I'll talk to Tamara and find out exactly what she's proposing. The good news is, I think she might have changed her mind about wanting Inverbeck. I suspect that was Dougie's doing, and now that he's gone, she probably realises she doesn't really have a connection to the place.'

'That would be good,' Cassie said. *'And again, I'm really sorry I didn't tell you about the affair. But it's not something you really want to talk about, is it?'*

'Did he know who it was?' Maggie said, realising it was a question she had omitted to ask. 'Did Dougie know?'

Once again, her client hesitated before answering. *'No, I don't think so. Or if he did, he didn't say.'*

Maggie noticed that Lori was furiously waving her arms in an attempt to get her attention. At the same time, she was able to make out the words she was mouthing. *Ask her who it was Maggie, go on, ask her.* So she did.

'Who was it you were having an affair with, can you tell me?'

'I'd rather not,' Cassie shot back. *'Besides, it's over now. So I don't see how it would be relevant to our matter.'*

'Yes, you're probably right,' Maggie said, thinking the exact opposite but electing not to press the matter for now. 'So let me get on with contacting Tamara and I'll get back to you as soon as I have anything to report. Speak to you later.'

***

'What did you think to all that?' Maggie asked Lori after she'd ended the call.

'She's a big suspect for her husband's killing,' Lori said. 'And I'll tell you why. Maybe the means and opportunity bit is problematic, but she's got a bloody huge motive, hasn't she?'

'The kids you mean?'

'Absolutely. You're always saying that you would do anything for wee Ollie, and every mother I've ever met says exactly the same about their children. So with big bad Dougie gone, Cassie gets the kids and then sails off to a smashing new life with her shiny new lover.'

'What, do you think she was *lying* about the relationship being over?'

Lori shrugged. 'You can't rule it out, can you? The way I see it, she commissioned us to try and get both custody of her kids and a decent chunk of the money through negotiation. But when that wasn't working and it seemed we would have to go to court, and that might expose her affair and make that custody less certain, she decides on a Plan B. That plan being cold-blooded and premeditated murder.'

'I'll tell you what,' Maggie said admiringly. 'There's something in what you say.'

And now, with Cassie McKean exposed as an unreliable witness, she began to realise that she wasn't going to be able to rest until she found out the truth about her client.

Smiling at Lori, she said, 'How would you fancy a couple of days' surveillance up in Braemar? I'll give Jimmy a call and maybe you can bunk down with him, or we can find you a little bed and breakfast up there. A couple of days watching the comings and goings at Inverbeck is what I'm thinking. Just to see if my hunch is right.'

The girl responded instantly, beaming a huge grin. 'I'll just get my coat.'

Chapter 20

He was a wee bit at a loose end work-wise, Frank couldn't deny it, being in one of these fallow periods between cases that he hated so much. The Orla McCarthy sexual assault business would now pretty much take care of itself, he fully expecting Eleanor's authentication of the recording to deliver a positive result, and given that the police couldn't possibly have known of the existence of it back when the crime was supposed to have happened -since *nobody* knew it existed - then both Assistant Commissioner Ian Archibald and his original investigation team were going to get exonerated from any real blame. There would be a press conference and then acting Commissioner Naylor would declare the case closed, smugly pleased with the outcome. Still, Frank had still headed for New Gorbals police station every morning, more from force of habit than anything, where he had been more or less banned from entering the McKean murder investigation room. But luckily, not banned from the canteen.

This morning he was having a coffee - but not, in a startling break from routine, accompanying it with a bacon roll - with his mate DC Lexy McDonald, who had just shared with him some rather astonishing breaking news.

'What, they're saying these bottles of Balvenie were *tampered* with?' he said, wide-eyed. 'So how did whoever did it manage *that*? Because they've all got that tough plasticy foil sealing stuff round the cork, and it's a bugger to get off, even in normal circumstances. And I speak from recent and bitter experience on that matter.'

Lexy laughed. 'Yes you're right sir. But they didn't take it off. What they did apparently was make a tiny wee nick in the seal right at the top, and then fold a little bit of the foil stuff back, just a little flap. If you can imagine, you could do that with a very sharp craft knife without too much problem.'

'Aye, I guess you could,' he admitted, after picturing the action in his mind.

'Then they drilled a tiny hole right through the middle of the cork. The forensic guys reckon the poison would then have been injected through the hole using a long syringe. Then whoever did it put a wee bit of glue under the flap and stuck it back down. It's bloody clever sir. You wouldn't see it unless you were looking really hard for it.'

'Devilishly clever,' he said. 'So how did they find this?'

'DCI McNeil was up at the lodge that Gray and McKean were renting, leading the evidence search. The team found a half-full case of the whisky in the larder and took it away for analysis. I think there was seven bottles left, and it turned out one had been tampered with in the way I just described. Although there wasn't any poison in it, strangely enough.'

'Crikey, this is mental. But clever too. Although you say no poison was found in the bottle?'

'No sir,' she said. 'But they're suggesting this was a practice one, to prove it could be done.'

'Right, get that, ' he nodded. 'So I guess our Steph is pursuing the motive and opportunity angles as far as the murder is concerned?'

Lexy nodded. 'Exactly sir. I was at this morning's eight o'clock catch-up, and she scribbled just three names up on the whiteboard. Tamara, obviously, but also these two guys that bought Dougie the cases of Balvenie as a present.'

He was silent for a moment, racking his brain for their names. 'Aye that's right. The American film executive, he's called Clay something-or-other, and then I think the other guy was a big cheese in Orla McCarthy's record company, and also her significant other, if my memory serves me correct.'

'That's right sir,' she said. 'David Gallagher's his name. Actually, Steph said she was going to ask you to follow these two up. I think the Gallagher guy is based in London you see, and the film guy spends a lot of time over in the UK as well.'

'Really, she's going to ask little old me?' he said, feigning surprise. 'Well I don't think I'll be making a special trip down there just for this. I can get Ronnie French to go and have a chat with him instead.' He paused again. 'So that's our Steph's short-list, is it? What about the five hundred other folks who had reason to see Dougie done away with?'

Lexy shrugged. 'She doesn't seem to be pursuing them too hard at the moment sir.' She gave him an uncertain look. 'But if you don't mind me saying so,' she continued, an apologetic note in her tone, 'I think I can see what she's doing. Because without opportunity, then there's no case to answer is there sir?' Lexy didn't wait for his reply. 'I think her plan is to apply maximum pressure to the three suspects that had the definite opportunity to poison the whisky, in the hope of getting a confession. Then if that doesn't work, then she'll move on to the other suspects.'

'I suppose that's one way to approach it,' he said grudgingly. 'But not the way I would do it.'

Lexy smiled but made no direct comment. Instead she said, 'Actually sir, I think she's already convinced it was Tamara. She's definitely her prime suspect at the moment, and in fact, Miss Gray's being hauled into Inverness police station tomorrow and McNeil and Acting DI Curran are flying up from Glasgow this evening so they can do the interview.'

'*Flying* up are they?' he said, amused. 'What, do they keep a private jet at the airport, all fuelled up and ready to go?'

She laughed. 'The DCI said time is money, when someone made a pointed comment in the room.'

'Wonderful,' he said, shaking his head. 'Anyway, are they planning to charge her today, do you know?'

'I don't know sir. Perhaps. They're certainly going to put some conditions on her movements I think. McNeil went off to see our tame legal wonk after the case conference to work out what they could or couldn't do.'

He shrugged. 'It all looks pretty thin to me, but really, it's got nothing to do with me anymore. But thanks for the update Lexy. I like to keep up with events.'

'Good to know sir. By the way, I was impressed that you said no to the bacon roll. It's not like you, if you don't mind me saying so. Are you not feeling too well?'

He gave her a wry look. 'Never felt better. But me and my brother Jimmy are having a final fitting for our wedding outfits tomorrow. It's at that fancy Lewis & Clark place in the Buchanan Galleries, and I need to be able to squeeze myself into that bloomin' kilt. Maggie's asked for a full report too, to make sure I don't try to slip up a size.'

But then suddenly something struck him, causing him to break into a seraphic smile. 'But actually, it's going to be postponed now, because my brother Jimmy is acting as Tamara's solicitor. He'll have to be in Inverness.' He smiled again. 'So Lexy, got time for another coffee? And I'll just wander up and get a bacon roll to go with it.'

***

Lexy had been right about McNeil wanting him to follow up on the two London-based suspects, a task that he had happily passed on to a reluctant DC Ronnie French. The job should have gone to DS Gemma James, on account of her sergeant rank if nothing else, but that was no longer an option following her suspension from duty. Going forward, he saw her as a liability, so was already trying to figure out how to shunt her out of his team. That, he thought ruefully, might not be so easy, given that Department 12B was already regarded as the last-chance saloon for hopeless cases as far as the force was concerned. But there was one angle he was keen on pursuing that might just deliver a result. He had been thinking about how it was that Orla McCarthy and Yash Patel had found out that AC Ian Archibald had accepted lavish hospitality from the Claymore Warriors, specifically that very nice all-expenses trip to a Munich concert. It had to be a leak, obviously, and with James being one of the few people who knew about Archibald's ill-advised action, she was the obvious suspect. So he'd asked French to take her down the pub and ply her with a few beers to see if she blabbed. It was on the edge of unethical of course, but Frank consoled himself with the thought that it was for the public good.

But what Lexy had said about DCI Steph McNeil's approach to the case had got him thinking. Sure, you needed to start with motive and opportunity, but you couldn't dismiss *means* either. Because whoever had committed this crime would have had to have done some careful research before coming to the conclusion that taxine should be the murder weapon. He took out his phone and swiped down to Eleanor Campbell's number. Usually she answered with a terse *what,* or in the rare occasions she was in a good mood, an equally-terse *hello.* Today, he got the former, which automatically slipped him into cautious mode.

'Hi Eleanor,' he said brightly. 'I won't take up too much of your time because I guess you must be busy. Just got something I want to quickly run past you.'

'What is it?' she harrumphed.

He paused for a moment, experiencing just a hint of trepidation. The thing was, what he was about to ask her was a bit complicated, and would take more than a few words to explain. But there was nothing for it but to push on, hopefully without interruption, although that was likely to be a matter of hope over experience.

'So am I right in thinking that the GCHQ guys in Cheltenham keep track of the whole country's internet search history, and store it on some big giant database and then they....'

'Like not all of it,' she said, already interrupting. *'Just if it triggers the anti-terrorism algorithms. And they're not in Cheltenham, the internet dudes are somewhere else, but they don't tell us where.'*

He just about managed to suppress a laugh at her pedantry. 'Well that's good to know. But wherever they are, they would store it if you searched how to make a bomb or something like that?'

'That would trigger it, defo.'

'And what about if you were searching for poisons? Because I guess you could be a terrorist planning to contaminate a food factory or something like that. Would that get picked up by these magical algorithms?'

'I don't know the whole list, but yeah, that might be one. Probably.'

Sensing that, unexpectedly, she sounded interested, he decided to go straight for it.

'And is it just these GCHQ dudes who can search it, or can you do it too Eleanor? On your laptop?'

'No way,' she shot back. *'That would be like treason or something.'*

'But you could if you had the proper authorisation,' he pressed.

'Only the security service can do that. It's because of civil liberties. They don't need to worry about that but the police do.'

It took him a second to work out what she meant.

'Aye, very important that we protect the civil liberties of our good citizens, I understand that. But that mate Zak you had in MI5...'

'It was MI6. And he's working in the private sector now.'

'Yes, I remember, he's one of these ethical hackers. But back when he was a spook, he was always giving you tons of beta software for you to test, wasn't he?' He didn't wait for her to answer. 'So I'm working under the assumption that *technically* you have access to the spooks' database, even if you aren't allowed to use it.'

She didn't immediately respond, which he took as a *yes*.

'So here's the way I see it Eleanor,' he continued, anxious to push home his advantage. 'I need this search information to fast-track the investigation of Dougie McKean's murder case, and I know I need to have special dispensation to do this kind of thing, given what you said about civil liberties and all that sort of stuff.'

'If it's not terrorist-related, you need to get it signed by like a home secretary or someone like that,' she intervened.

'Exactly, and quite right too. But Madam Home Secretary is a very busy and important woman, and we wouldn't want to waste her time if our search wasn't actually going to find anything. So really, we ought to do a test first before we go bothering her with all that tedious paperwork. And we wouldn't want to embarrass the acting Commissioner either, would we? So will you give it a go? Just a wee test search? Just for me?'

'No. Like absolutely no way,' Eleanor said, now sounding alarmed.

'Ach come *on*,' he pleaded. 'All I want you to do is a quick scan of the database to see if anyone's made a search related to something called taxine. That's T-A-X-I-N-E, just so you know. I mean, how many murderous poisonings are there in the UK each year? Just about zero, I would guess, so I doubt if you'll find much anyway. Just one little search, and if nothing turns up, that'll be the end of it.' He paused for a moment. 'What do you say Eleanor? Go on, be a pal.'

'No way,' she repeated, but this time her tone was discernibly softer. *'But I can set you up a one-time login under a proxy alias and you can do it yourself. But if anyone asks me, I'll totally deny I know anything about it.'*

'Understood, and that's brilliant Eleanor,' he said, but just as he began to wonder what he'd agreed to, she filled in the gap.

'And just so you know, GCHQ runs real-time login monitoring with IP location detection on that database,' she said darkly. *'And if they detect anyone using it, they send round the dudes with guns.'*

'I'll look out for them,' he said with mock seriousness. But of course they both knew he wouldn't be doing those searches. After a first aborted attempt, he would invent some technical obstacle he could blame on his incompetence, and she would make a pretence of being annoyed, but would sigh then take on the task herself. Grinning to himself, he hung up.

Chapter 21

It was raining again, biblically, which had really managed to screw up Jimmy's week. He and his business partner Stew had been scheduled to take a bunch of local government officers on a two-day Lairig Ghru trek, but that would have to be called off in this weather. Too dangerous, and none too pleasant either, given the real possibility that the precipitation would fall as snow at the top of the remote mountain pass, even though it was only early September. Even without that, the constant deluge would have rendered several of the streams they would need to cross virtually impassable, and he was hearing that the River Druie had burst its banks again where it joined up with the Spey just past Coylumbridge. And sadly, there had been another drowning, the body of an as-yet unidentified man in his twenties beaching at Speymouth, just under the old railway bridge. Aye, however you looked at it, you would be crazy to take a gang of inexperienced folks up in the mountains in this. Stew, though, hadn't seemed too bothered about the cancellation, the unexpected break in his schedule giving him the opportunity to book a cosy lunch date with the married school-teacher he had been seeing on-and-off for the past few months or so, one of several local women who managed to find slots in his busy diary. In defiance of the weather, Jimmy was just thinking about digging out his mountain bike for a wheeled assault on the steep pass, when his phone rang. Glancing down, he was pleased to see it was Maggie.

'Hi there,' he said brightly. 'How's things?'

'Wet,' she said. *'What about up there?'*

'The same or worse.'

'Something's come up,' she said. *'Are you available at short notice? I mean, like now?'* It wasn't like her to launch into the meat of a conversation without a pleasant preamble, so he guessed the *something* was important and urgent too.

He laughed. 'Well, by a strange serendipity, I am. What's the mission?'

'Tamara Gray's been hauled in to Inverness police station for questioning. DCI McNeil and her sidekick flew up from Glasgow last night, but they obviously won't start until she's got legal representation alongside her.'

'So you've decided to take the case then?' he asked, surprised. 'Because you were worried about conflict of interest.'

She paused before answering. *'I was Jimmy, and I still have my misgivings to be perfectly honest with you. But I've thought about it a lot, and I think we can keep the negotiations over Dougie's will separate from defending Tamara against a murder charge. And it's been made a bit easier by the fact that Cassie McKean wasn't straight with us. But yeah, it's still a bit tricky, to say the least.'*

'So you want me to drive up there now I guess?' he asked. 'That's not a problem, although it's a couple of hours from here. But what have they got on her, do you know?'

'Well, a massive motive for a start, given that she inherits everything under the terms of Dougie's new will. And

remember, witnesses from Shore McPhail & Robertson are saying she was pushing really hard to get him to sign the document. That's suspicious in itself.'

'Yes, I remember you told me that.'

'And then there's the opportunity bit,' Maggie continued. *'I don't know if Frank said, but police forensics have worked out how the taxine got into the whisky. Something about a sharp knife and a drill and a hypodermic syringe I think. But anyway, the cases of whisky were delivered to the lodge that Tamara and McKean were renting, giving her ample opportunity to tamper with it.'*

'Sounds thin,' Jimmy said.

Maggie nodded. *'That's exactly what Frank thinks too. But anyway, get up there as quickly as you can and tell me how it goes afterwards.'*

***

It hadn't been the most pleasant of drives in the incessant rain, but the traffic was light enough to allow decent progress, and he found himself pulling into the police station car-park just before two o'clock. A desk sergeant escorted him down to an interview room, swiped the reader to unlock the door and indicated that he should enter. Tamara Gray was sitting alone in the starkly-furnished room, wearing jeans and a pale yellow hooded fleece, the sleeves pulled down to almost cover her hands. It was the second or third time he had met her, but it was the first time he had seen her without the layer of carefully-applied makeup which seemed to be her favoured look. Her eyes were bloodshot and he guessed she had been crying, but that didn't take away from the fact that her face was a beautiful one, with flawless skin, a tiny turned-up nose and a wide mouth. He knew she was thirty-three, but unmade-up, she looked about five years younger.

'Hi Tamara,' he said quietly, pulling out the chair alongside her and sitting down. 'How are you? And what have they said to you?'

She gave a weak smile. 'I've been better. And they haven't said much, other than they want to question me about Dougie's death.'

'And did they bring you here under caution? Or are they saying you're just here voluntarily, to assist with their enquiries?'

'Under caution,' she said, her voice almost inaudible. 'They sent a patrol car to the lodge and brought me in. And they've taken my fingerprints and swabbed my saliva for a DNA sample.'

'Aye, well that's just routine.' He paused for a moment, thinking. 'Okay... so this is a formal session then, which actually, isn't totally a bad thing. Because it means they're bound by certain rules and regulations. Basically, they have to put up or shut up.'

She nodded uncertainly. 'I don't know what that means.'

'It means they're going to have to decide today whether to charge you or not, and they can only hold you for twenty-four hours in total, and if they *don't* charge you, they have to let you go. And to be honest, I don't think they've got a thing on you. It might be a bit uncomfortable today, but I don't think you've got anything to worry about.'

Not unless it was you who actually did it, he thought wryly, before giving a mental shrug. His dad had been a noted defence lawyer before he retired, and the old boy always maintained he didn't want to know whether any of his clients were guilty or not. It was all about facts and evidence, and the onus was on the prosecution to provide proof. As far as he was aware, Jimmy didn't think the police had that proof, but then why had they felt confident enough to caution their client? For the first time that day, he began to feel a little worried.

A second later, the door swung open and DCI Steph McNeil and Acting DI Curran entered the room, the latter carrying a transparent plastic folder. They sat down at the table opposite Tamara and Jimmy without saying a word. He had encountered both of them before and hadn't liked them much then, but on that particular occasion Maggie had been his client, the victim of a plainly ludicrous accusation of murder, so he hadn't been exactly well-disposed towards the pair. Today, he hadn't expected them to want to reminisce over old times, but a *good afternoon* wouldn't have gone amiss. Instead, McNeil gestured silently towards the recording device that sat on the table, Curran stretching out an arm to activate it. The DCI glanced at her watch and said, 'Right, it's seven minutes past two on the 6th of September, present in the room are....'

The formalities completed, she paused for a moment, then nodded again to Curran, who held up the plastic folder she had brought in so that they could see the contents. 'For the tape, Acting DI Curran is now holding up Exhibit A.' She paused again briefly then said, 'So tell me Tamara, do you recognise this object?'

Tamara gave Jimmy a confused look but didn't say anything.

'You need to answer,' McNeil pressed. 'I repeat, do you recognise this object?'

'It's.. it's a knife,' she said quietly. 'It looks like any old knife.' Again, she looked at Jimmy, her eyes betraying fear and uncertainty.

'Not just any old knife,' McNeil corrected. 'This knife was found in the drawer of the lodge you're renting on Speyside.'

'So *you* took that,' Tamara said. 'I wondered where it had gone. I used it to open my Amazon packages, but I couldn't find it the other day and thought I must have left it down somewhere.'

'So you're confirming it's your knife?' McNeil asked, narrowing her eyes.

'No no, I'm not saying that,' Tamara blurted out. 'It might be, but I don't know. It's just a *knife*.'

'It was found in a kitchen drawer at the lodge where you are currently residing,' the detective said. 'Later, a forensic officer will check the item for fingerprints, and I'm expecting to find a match to yours.'

'So where are we going with this?' Jimmy intervened, concerned. 'What is it you are implying?'

McNeil's lips curled into the faintest of smiles. 'Our forensic scientists have found traces of black plastic-coated foil on the tip of this knife. We have reason to believe it's the same material that is used to seal bottles of Balvenie whisky, and our team are currently in touch with the distiller's packaging specialists to confirm that.'

Her words momentarily stopped Jimmy in his tracks, his mind spinning as he processed the implications of what McNeil had just revealed. Maggie had believed that the DCI's case against Tamara was speculative, based solely on the existence of motive and opportunity, but this revelation changed that. This, potentially, was a piece of concrete evidence that might tip the balance should it be put in front of a jury. And more than that, it probably gave McNeil enough to charge Tamara with the crime, should she chose to do so.

'Of course you'll find my client's fingerprints on the knife,' Jimmy said, thinking fast. 'She's already said she used it to open her Amazon deliveries. That doesn't prove anything.'

McNeil smiled again. 'Tamara, we *know* you had a huge motive to murder your lover because of the terms of his will, and we *know* you had ample opportunity to tamper with these bottles of whisky, given they were delivered to your rented lodge two weeks before Mr McKean met his brutal end. We know *exactly* how the crime was committed and we believe fingerprints will confirm that the knife used to create the imperceptible flap in the packaging was handled by yourself.' She paused and looked Tamara in the eyes. 'And of course a jury are also bound to ask why a beautiful young woman like you would take up with a man almost twenty-five years your senior, and will I think, come to their own conclusions.'

'I loved him,' she spat out. 'I *loved* him. And I didn't kill him.' She slumped in her chair, raising an arm to wipe away an emerging tear.

'Come on guys,' Jimmy said. 'This is still bloody thin, and you know it. It seems to me you need to make up your mind whether you're brave or stupid enough to charge my client today. Because I'm afraid I don't share your confidence that any of this would convince a jury, or even your in-house procurator fiscal guys come to that.' He paused for a moment. 'So come on, what's it to be? Are you going to charge her or what? Because if not, we're out of here.'

McNeil gave him her thin smile again. 'We need to process the forensics first, you know that. So we'll be releasing you today Tamara, under conditions.' She nodded at Curran to stop the tape. 'But the next time we see you pair, you won't be so lucky. *Interview over*.'

***

Afterwards, he agreed to drive her back to the lodge, she understandably anxious to avoid the indignity of returning to her temporary home in the back of a police car. On the journey she had said virtually nothing, chewing on the sleeve of her fleece and staring out of the window of the car. He had seen the after-effects of shock plenty of times during his army service, the way dangerous and irrational thoughts crowded into your mind and stopped you thinking clearly. From time to time she asked him how long there was to go, even though she could see the ETA herself on his car's satellite navigation display. After an hour's driving they arrived. The rain had now reduced to a dampening drizzle, the sun making an effort to break through the greying clouds. He jumped out of the car and sprinted round to open the door for her. Fifty metres away, the Spey, in full spate, crashed and roared as it powered its way inexorably to the sea.

'Are you going to be okay?' he asked, as he escorted her to the front door, a guiding hand on her elbow.

She gave him a look of such heartbreak that he felt his own heart miss a beat. 'I'm really frightened Jimmy. I want to go back to the States and my family, but I can't do that now, can I?'

He shook his head. 'No, sadly not. That would just make the situation worse I'm afraid.'

'And I can't even go back to London, where all my friends are?' It was half-statement, half-question to which there was only one answer.

'No, you can't. The conditions say you can't travel more than fifty miles from your current place of residence.' He hesitated for a moment. 'We could always challenge that in court, but we wouldn't win. They hardly ever overturn bail conditions.' And this one, he thought, was perfectly reasonable from the police's point of view at least.

Unexpectedly she stopped and turned round, so that her lovely face was almost touching his, her huge eyes beseeching. Then she said softly, 'Could you stay with me tonight? Please Jimmy? Because I'm so scared.'

Suddenly, he felt a wave of uncontrolled desire pass through him, and for a desperate second he thought he would take her in his arms and kiss her and tell her it would be alright. But he couldn't. *He wouldn't.*

He shook his head again, taking a step back and holding out his hands in front of him, as if to push her away. 'Look, I'm sorry Tamara, I can't. But let me get you inside and settled.' It wasn't nearly enough, he knew that, but it was all he could allow himself to do.

***

In the aftermath of the terrible news, it was as if someone had plunged a knife into his heart, and he knew it would take a long time to get over the excruciating pain -the pain of knowing that had he said yes to an invitation a million men would have ravenously accepted, Tamara Gray would still be alive. Though he may have felt differently had he noticed the black executive saloon car lurking in a tree-shaded glade fifty metres along the riverside road, evidently awaiting her return.

Chapter 22

Frank could tell from Lexy's opening *hello sir* that something had happened, her tone betraying surprise and some excitement too. He was down in the canteen having a mid-afternoon cappuccino, and she had evidently come straight to the establishment to seek him out after hearing whatever this news was. Now she stood over where he was seated, her arms leaning on the table.

'You won't have heard sir, it's just come in from the Grampian boys,' she said breathlessly, 'but Tamara Gray was found dead first thing this morning, around half-past seven. Her body was washed up a few miles from the lodge she was renting. Seems like an angler spotted her floating downstream just before the Old Craigellachie Bridge, and he waded in and pulled her out, but obviously she was dead.'

'Bloody hell,' Frank said. 'That's a development, isn't it? *Crikey.*'

'Yes it is sir. The angler called the police right away, but then he called the *Moray and Grampian Times* too. He's just a young guy and must have fancied getting his picture in the paper. Anyway, it's all over the local media now and her name's already out there.'

'I guess they'll have taken her to the mortuary at Inverness for the post-mortem and then we'll see what they make of it,' he said, thinking out loud. 'But Steph McNeil questioned her yesterday, didn't she? In fact, my brother Jimmy was acting as Tamara's lawyer. I've not had a chance to catch up with him to see how it went.'

Lexy gave him a puzzled look. 'When you say we'll see what they make of it, are you thinking there might be foul play involved?'

He shrugged. 'Probably not. But she was a murder suspect, so the question has to be asked.'

He was interrupted by the vibration of his phone his pocket. 'Hang on a minute Lexy,' he said, fishing out the device. He glanced at the screen then held it up to his ear.

'Hello Ronnie, how's tricks? Any luck getting a hold of those two so-called suspects that McNeil wanted us to chase up?'

'Not yet guv, but the Gallagher geezer sent me a text after I left him a message, saying he'd get back to me ASAP. But that's not why I'm buzzing you.'

'Okay, tell me more.'

'Well it's about a body found in that river up there. The Spey.'

Frank laughed. 'Talk about coincidences. I hate to disappoint you Frenchie, but you're five minutes too late. The good DC Lexy McDonald got there first.'

'Sorry guv, I don't understand,' French said, sounding puzzled. *'Because I ain't told nobody yet. You were going to be the first.'*

'Now it's me that doesn't understand,' Frank said. 'What's this all about?'

'I was looking at one of them angling websites this morning and I saw a picture of this drowned guy, and I recognised him right away.'

Frank remembered that fishing was one of his DC's enthusiasms, right up there in fact with his great love for West Ham United football club. 'So that's what you do on police time is it? But don't keep me in suspense.'

'A body was found up at the estuary a few days ago and the local police haven't been able to identify him,' French said.

'Aye, I read about that.'

'But they thought he might be an angler, so they stuck his mug-shot out on the internet angling forums and such like to see if anyone knew him. And I recognised him straight away. It's that geeky engineer bloke, you know, from Advance Studios, the one we met. You remember him? Damian Hammond was his name, the fat guy who never looked you in the eye.'

'Bloody hell,' Frank said for the second time in a minute. 'Get onto Inverness nick and let them know that we've got an identification for them. That's good work Frenchie, we'll talk about this again soon. Cheers mate.'

'Sure thing guv, I'll get it done right away,' French answered before ringing off.

'You're looking perplexed sir,' Lexy said after he had slipped his phone back in his pocket.' Something up?'

'You can say that again,' he said, still frowning. 'I learn of two drownings in the space of two minutes, and both connected to our cases. That just can't be a coincidence, can it?'

She shrugged. 'The river's been dangerous in the last few weeks. But no, it is... well, I don't know what it is exactly sir.'

'Not a bloody coincidence, that's for certain,' he said firmly. 'Excuse me Lexy, but I need to track down Jimmy or Maggie to find out what the hell happened yesterday during Tamara's interview. But thanks for letting me know about her. It's a right tragedy, it really is.'

***

He wasn't able to get Jimmy on the phone, that being no surprise given the unreliability of the signal up in the Cairngorm mountains where his brother was based, so he went for Maggie instead.

'Afternoon darling,' he said brightly, when she answered on the first ring. 'And it's *very* lovely to talk to you again.'

'I saw you less than six hours ago, over breakfast,' she said, laughing, *'or have you forgotten already?'*

'Breakfast, what breakfast?' he grinned. 'Listen, this is work. I don't know if you've heard, but Tamara Gray has been found dead this morning.'

'What?' she replied, evidently stunned.

'Aye, that's right. Drowned in the Spey. A fisherman found her body up at the Craigellachie bridge. But she was interviewed under caution yesterday wasn't she? Has Jimmy given you an update as to how it went?'

'Yes, he did. And not very well is the answer. I don't know if you knew Frank, but they've discovered some evidence on a knife they found in a kitchen drawer at that holiday lodge Dougie and Tamara were renting. They're saying it's the one used to tamper with these whisky bottles.'

He shrugged. 'Nah, I haven't heard. But McNeil's not telling me anything so that's no surprise. Anyway, I assume they didn't charge her given they let her go home?'

'They're waiting for the results of the forensics first, but I think they will charge her shortly,' she said. *'Sorry, would have charged her. They let her go, but with conditions of course. Jimmy took her home, and he said she was really upset. Hardly said a word on the journey, and then asked him if he would stay with her because she was really scared.'*

'I hope he didn't,' Frank responded, momentarily concerned.

'No he didn't,' she confirmed. *'But he was affected by it. He was really worried for her, I could hear it in his voice.'* She paused for a moment, evidently thinking about the effect this news would have on her detective partner. *'This is really bad news isn't it? I just don't know how Jimmy's going to take it. But I assume they're thinking suicide? Because if it was, Steph McNeil's going to have some tough questions to answer.'*

'That'll be the working hypothesis,' he said. 'But there'll be a post-mortem of course. Then we might find out for sure. And

I guess they'll be searching the lodge and her social media as well, to see if she left a note or anything,' he added.

'This is just me talking without really thinking,' Maggie said. *'But I can't see why anybody connected with our case would want to murder Tamara.'*

'What about your Cassie?' Frank said. 'She had every reason to hate the woman.'

'I think she hated her husband more than his lover. Besides, Cassie is one person who's actually going to be left in a mess after this.'

'How's that?'

'Because now as it stands, all Dougie's assets are going to go straight to whoever inherits from Tamara. She had indicated she was willing to be more conciliatory over it, but of course we hadn't had time to do anything about it. And it's too late for that now.'

'I thought you said that under Scottish law you can't disinherit your kids? That's still an issue, isn't it?'

'It is,' Maggie conceded, *'but it's all going to be very tangled now. The only people who would benefit if Cassie decides to challenge the will be the lawyers.'*

'But she won't get Inverbeck now,' Frank persisted. 'It'll go to whoever benefits from Tamara's will. That'll be a big blow to Cassie.'

'That's right, and as I said, it's a mess. But I'm not sure that means Tamara's been murdered.'

He thought for a moment before continuing. 'Well I know this is a statement of the bleeding obvious, but I guess this stops your Tamara assignment stone dead, before it even got started.'

He heard her laugh. *'Yes, you could say that. The death of a client often has that effect.'* She paused momentarily. *'But you know what, I can't just leave it here. This whole thing is a crazy tangled web, and I'll go completely mad if I don't find out how the jigsaw fits together, if that's not mixing my metaphors. The Lewis & Clark assignment is paying us well so I can afford to do a bit of pro bono work, for two or three weeks at least. And that's exactly what I'm going to do.'*

After they'd hung up, he reflected that her reaction hadn't surprised him in the least, because he was feeling pretty much the same way himself. This one was developing into one of the thorniest cases he had ever come across, with a historic sexual assault allegation, the murder of a music icon, and now the supposed accidental drowning of two people with unarguable connections to the investigations. The puzzle had really got to him, and like his darling Maggie, he knew he wouldn't be able to leave it alone. The only problem was, unlike his love, he didn't have complete freedom to set his own schedule. But then again, he thought wryly, he had a good idea of how this was going to pan out as far as the murder investigation was concerned. Assuming foul play was ruled out by the post-mortem, Tamara's death by suicide would be taken as an admission of guilt, and DCI Steph

McNeil would high-five her buddy Curran then shut down the file, adding another glittering paragraph to her already impressive CV of collars. Sure, there would be a few journalists speculating that Gray had been driven to take her own life by over-zealous policing, but McNeil and the Police Scotland brass wouldn't give a stuff about that. The result was everything, what was there not to like? That would be their attitude, but this cavalier approach to justice really stuck in Frank's throat.

But then again, what if they were completely wrong, and it was someone else who had killed Dougie McKean? Smiling at his own cleverness, he picked up his phone again and called Jill Smart.

Chapter 23

Anxious to let Jimmy know the news of Tamara Gray's untimely death, Maggie had tried a few times to get hold of him on the phone without success, until she remembered him saying he was mapping a new route up some remote mountain pass that had a Gaelic name he couldn't pronounce and she couldn't remember. So with great reluctance, she'd decided to message him, on the grounds that she'd rather he found out from her than second-hand through the media. That, in retrospect, might have been a mistake, because immediately on receiving her text, he'd broken off his survey and headed back down the glen to his office in Braemar, from where he was now speaking to her.

'I could bloody kick myself,' he was saying, obviously upset. *'She was in a real state when we got back to the lodge, and she asked me to stay with her. I should have done, I really should have.'*

'Don't beat yourself up Jimmy,' Maggie said. 'It's not in the job spec, and I appreciate it could have been, well you know....difficult. Because she was a very attractive woman.' *And you're an amazingly good-looking man,* she thought, *which is why it would have been awkward to say the least.* And besides that, what if he'd stayed the night and then Tamara had thrown herself into the Spey after he'd left in the morning? That would have made the situation a hundred times worse. No, it had been a good thing he had made his excuses and left, despite the tragic outcome.

'But anyway,' she continued, 'I want to carry on with the case, just for two or three weeks, no more. I need to find out who killed Dougie McKean for my own peace of mind. And if it turns out to be Tamara, then so be it. At least we'll know.'

'I got a call from mad Lori yesterday,' he said, evidently keen to change the subject. *'She asked if she could stay in my spare room for a couple of days. What's that all about? And by the way, I told her I don't have a spare room, which I think she knew very well.'*

She laughed. 'Don't you *dare* let Lori hear you calling her that. No, it was just that I was angry with Cassie for not telling me about her affair, and I decided it would be a good idea to put a watch on her house for a few days to see if it *really* was over. And even although everything has changed, it still seems like a good place to start for our new mission. Because our Cassie isn't the woman we thought she was.'

'Sounds like a plan,' he said. *'A lassie called Mhari Brown runs a bed and breakfast in the village, so I'll see if I can get Lori in there. Mhari's one of Stew's friends, in inverted commas, so we should be good for mates' rates.'*

'Stew seems to have a lot of women friends with inverted commas around them,' she said, laughing again. 'And what about a car? Lori will need one so she can park across the road from the gates. I don't suppose she can use yours, because I guess Cassie might recognise it,' she added, thinking out loud.

'I wouldn't let her drive mine anyway,' he said wryly. *'But there's a guy who runs a garage in the village and he's got a*

courtesy car which he'd probably rent out, a battered old Polo or something like it,' he said. *'Mind you, Donnie McQueen's an old chiseller, so it'll cost us.'*

'Not a problem for a couple of days,' Maggie said, 'and the car sounds perfectly nondescript, which is exactly what we want.'

'Alright, I'll get it all sorted then,' he said. He paused for a moment. *'And don't worry about me by the way, I'll be fine. It's just that even after everything I experienced in the army, it's still a shock when somebody you saw very much alive just a day ago turns up dead the next. It always seems a terrible waste. And she was so young.'*

Maggie nodded. 'I know. She was. And that's why we need to find out what really happened up there.'

***

Frank hadn't expected his call to Jill Smart to be easy, and less than one minute into it, it was fully living up to expectations.

'So let me get this straight,' she was saying, just after he had outlined his proposal to her. *'You want me to call the Commissioner to induce him to participate in this... this naked political skulduggery?'*

'That just about sums it up,' he admitted. 'But it's in a very good cause.'

'Which is?'

'Which is to help him go from being just an *acting* Commissioner to being an actual full-fat *proper* Commissioner. I think you'll find our man Trevor will be very sympathetic to *that* cause.'

He heard her sigh. *'Okay, so run it past me again. Slowly.'*

'Right. So, in my opinion, Police Scotland have just made a frightful bodge of that Dougie McKean murder case I've been half-working on. They rustled up a suspect - his lover Tamara Gray -then put her under some pressure to confess. As a result, this poor Gray woman went and drowned herself in the Spey. But the thing was, the evidence against her was thinner than a thin thing, and I think with a bit of proper digging, the whole case will unravel. Which will be very embarrassing for the force up there, and in particular for their hot-shot Chief Constable Ms. Jennifer McCrae.'

'Oh, I get it,' Smart said. *'Your plan is to make Police Scotland and their boss look stupid so that the idea of McCrae replacing Naylor as Met Commissioner is abandoned.'*

'Got it in one,' he grinned. 'It's brilliant, isn't it? And all I'm asking for is official sanction to broaden the scope of our sexual assault investigation just a tiny wee bit, so that we can do some digging into McKean's murder too. Just an extension of an existing case, nothing more. In that way, we can't be accused of running a parallel investigation and tramping all over any other force's turf. And I'm not asking for any extra resources either. Just me, Ronnie French and mad Jessie. Should be enough for what we need to do.'

'DS James is suspended. Or had you forgotten?'

'I was hoping she might be given a temporary reprieve,' Frank said cautiously. 'Just for a couple of weeks.'

'You've worked all this out, haven't you?' Smart said, Frank detecting a softening in her tone.

'Is that a compliment ma'am?'

'I'm not your guv'nor anymore, remember?' she said, laughing. *'And no, it's not a bloody compliment. But just one question Frank. Why are you getting me to do your dirty work for you? Why don't you pick up the phone and call him yourself?'*

He hesitated a moment before answering. 'I spotted him looking at you during that press conference the other day. *Lustfully*,' he added, hastily jabbing the *End Call* button before she could respond.

***

He hadn't expected to get an answer from the acting Commissioner for a day or two, given the guy's reputation for plodding caution in everything he did. Naylor would want to weigh up the pros and cons of the action, judging above all the effect on his reputation, career and pension should his uncharacteristic scheming be uncovered. So acting on the old cliché that it was better to seek forgiveness rather than permission, Frank had decided to push ahead anyway, and there was an obvious place to start. The fact was, it was bizarrely inexplicable that the corpulent body of the studio geek Damian Hammond should be found in the Spey, nearly five hundred miles from his place of employment. Despite the lazy speculation of the local cops, he didn't look anything like an angler, so what the hell had the guy been doing up there? Soon, the results of the post-mortem would be out, and it was odds-on there would be no sign of foul play, meaning that the formal Procurator Fiscal's enquiry would chalk it down to accidental death by drowning. *Aye, sure.* Because if you were planning on murdering someone, what better weapon was there than a powerful river in full spate? A couple of strong assailants could easily overpower a victim, holding his or her head underwater until their last breath was extinguished, letting the river, an accidental but willing accomplice, take care of disposing of the body. Admittedly, there was no evidence that Hammond had been killed, but it certainly made you think.

So he'd set DC Ronnie French and DS Gemma James separate tasks, the former to speak to the victim's distraught parents, the latter to kick off an exploration of his social media activities. Now, a day later, he had scheduled a video call to get their initial reports, a call he was looking forward to very much indeed. Contrary to his expectations, both were already on the line when he joined the call, until he glanced at his watch and realised it was himself that was five minutes late, a consequence of answering an embarrassingly raunchy text from Maggie.

'Sorry folks,' he said, smiling awkwardly. 'Some urgent stuff I had to deal with. So quite a turn up for the books eh, our man Hammond appearing up in the Highlands?'

'And turning up as a stiff too,' French said, deadpan.

'Aye, exactly. So how have you both got on? You first Ronnie. How were the parents?'

'It was bloody awful guv. Their boy Damian was their only child, and they're devastated by his death. I don't think it's sunk in for them yet.'

Frank nodded sympathetically. 'I know, it was a tough mission for you, so thanks for that. But did they have any idea why their son should be up on Speyside?'

French shrugged. *'They had no idea guv. But just talking to them, I got the feeling that he'd been quite a trial for them, their boy. A lot of bullying at school, and bouts of depression and such like. He was still living at home, by the way.'*

'Right, I didn't realise that. What was he, thirty or something like that?'

'Thirty-one,' French confirmed. *'But interestingly, his mum said he'd seemed to be feeling a lot better in the past few months, and that he was quite excited about something. She didn't know what it was, but she said it had come as a great relief to her and his father after all the years of trouble. They wondered in fact if he had found a girlfriend.'*

'But they'd no idea why he'd gone to the Highlands?' Frank repeated.

'No guv. He wasn't an outdoors sort of guy. Always been into music and computer games according to his folks. That was all he did in his spare time apparently.'

'Fair enough Frenchie.' He paused for a moment then asked, 'So what about you Jessie? How have you got on with his social media? Found anything?'

'I found out the guy was a full-on weirdo,' James said unsympathetically. *'One of those incels in fact. He was on some seriously creepy forums, I can tell you.'*

'What's one of those when it's at home?' Frank said, feeling he'd heard the term before, but not being able to recall what it meant.

'It means involuntarily celibates. They're sad losers who can't get a girlfriend, and so they take out their frustration by calling women whores and tramps, and fantasising about rape and worse as a way of getting revenge.'

'Charming. So I'm assuming all of this isn't on Facebook or Instagram or any of the other mainstream services?'

'No way guv. There's a whole bunch of wacky websites that cater for this stuff, where they can peddle their pathetic fantasies.'

'So how come you found it so easily?' he asked, suddenly curious. 'You on some of these sites yourself?'

She scowled at him. *'I found him on Facebook first just by searching for his name. Then I saw he was a member of a Group that I recognised from a rape case I was working on last year. It all looks innocuous, but it's a front, where these saddos meet up online before being directed to the more hardcore stuff. Our perpetrator on my rape case was one of these incels too, and in fact that's how we tracked him down. Our dark web cyber crime team keeps a list of all these dodgy sites, and we found the guy boasting about what he'd done on one of them.'*

'And how did you find Hammond on this saddos' site? Because I presume he was hiding behind a username or handle or whatever you call it, not his actual name?'

She gave a smug smile. *'A bit of lateral thinking guv. I searched for Orla McCarthy.'*

'What?' Frank said, perplexed. 'I don't get it.'

'He was working with her, wasn't he, on that Oran na Mara re-mixing or whatever it was? And for a guy like him, that must have been like all his Christmases coming at once. So I punched her name into the search box, and sure enough, I found a whole thread talking about her. There were a bunch of sick guys fantasising about tying her to her bed and gang-raping her, disgusting stuff like that. But there was one particular guy who was boasting that he had actually met her, and that she was gagging to have sex with him. He was saying she was going to take him out to dinner and he had been promised a blow-job and an all-night shagging session. I mean, that's the sort of delusional bollocks that's all over these sites.'

'But how do you know it was Damian Hammond posting that stuff?' Frank asked.

'His username,' she said. *'SuperDamian. They're all like that. Boastful and arrogant. And seriously thick and deluded at the same time.'*

'Here guv,' French interjected. *'You don't think maybe he was stalking her? That might explain why he was up in Scotland. Because Orla was there too with that reporter mate of yours and his TV film crew, wasn't she? Maybe he was following her all over the country. They do that, them stalkers.'*

Frank nodded. 'That's a very good shout Frenchie. I'll try and give her a ring when we're done and ask her. And good work too Jessie, finding out all that online stuff so quickly.' Given how he felt about the maverick detective, the words stuck in his throat a bit, but you had to give credit where credit was due. 'And whilst you're at it, can you make it a priority to check out his phone records? I guess his actual phone's lying at the bottom of the river now, but his telecoms provider should be able to assist. You can give wee Eleanor Campbell a buzz if you need any help.'

James scowled again, this time at the mention of the forensic officer's name, but said, *'Yeah sure guv, I'll get on it right away, no problem.'*

***

Mention of Eleanor Campbell reminded him of the little jobs she was doing for him, firstly, the verification of the recording of Orla's sexual assault - given heightened significance now that the discoverer of the recording had been found dead - and secondly, the scan of GCHQ's search history database to see who'd been looking up poisons in general and taxine in particular. Anxious though he was for an update from the forensic officer, his immediate priority was now to speak to McCarthy and find out what she knew about Damian Hammond. He picked up his phone and swiped to her number, but after ten or so rings it switched to voicemail. Disappointed, he left a few words asking her to ring him back, augmented by a WhatsApp to the same effect.

He had no similar problem in getting through to Eleanor, she answering on the second ring and her *hello* delivered in an uncharacteristic cheery tone.

'Hello yourself,' he responded. 'You seem full of the joys of the world, if I may say so.'

'No,' she shot back, sounding offended. *'I'm just being like normal.'*

'Good to know. Anyway, just calling for a quick update on all that stuff you're doing for me. Got a minute to spare? Oh and by the way, I'm sorry I didn't do these searches myself. The app just wouldn't accept my password for some reason.'

'So you said,' she said disparagingly, instantly back to what Frank regarded as her real normal. *'Anyway, I did it myself, and there were three incidents of search strings that included the word taxine in the last three months. And...'*

'Bloody hell, that's not many, is it?' he blurted out, surprised.

'Let me finish,' she scolded. *'And I've traced the geolocation of all three.'*

He felt an even stronger *bloody hell* heading towards his lips, just managing to throttle it before it came out. But she had inserted a definite pause in her narrative, so he filled it with a tentative 'Go on.'

'Okay,' she continued. *'So one was from a university chemistry department, and one was from the offices of a pharmaceutical company. The IP addresses are from their internal networks so I think they may be legitimate.'* She paused again, and this time he elected not to fill the gap. *'The other one was from a pub in somewhere called Bath. And this IP was from a personal mobile.'*

He knew he shouldn't laugh but he couldn't help it. 'Nice wee town, near Bristol. They call it Bath because it's got Roman baths, you know, with water in them. They invented them, the Romans did. Before they conquered us nobody here washed themselves. You could smell us in France.' He was unable to tell if the silence at the other end of the line was because Eleanor was annoyed or because she was enjoying the unprompted history lesson. Suspecting the former, he continued. 'Sorry Eleanor, forgive my wee joke. So having this IP thingy, does that mean you can trace the owner? Or was it one of these burner phones?' he added.

'It wasn't a burner, but it went out of service the next day.'

'So what does that mean?'

'The owner reported it missing,' she said. *'So the phone company blocked the SIM.'*

'Ah, I think I get it,' he said, thinking out loud. 'Somebody left their phone lying on a table or something, and our baddie picked it up and used it to do his or her dodgy searching, so that it couldn't be traced back to them.' He paused for a moment. 'But I guess you have the name of the pub? Because they might have CCTV footage we could look at.'

She didn't answer straightaway, he guessing she was searching her notes for a response. Finally she said, *'Yeah it was a place called the Bear and Hound.'*

'So when was this? I mean what day of the week?'

'Friday.'

He sighed. 'So the joint would have been packed out then. Still, not to worry, I'll send Ronnie down there to see if they've still got the footage. Anyway, so you've got all this person's search history then?'

'Like yeah. She started just searching for poisons and then spent a lot of time on taxine. I looked at it myself and it says you get it from yew trees. From the leaves and other parts too. And it says there are thousands of them in church yards around the country.'

'You say *she* Eleanor. What makes you think it's a woman?'

'Because they say poison is the woman's murder weapon of choice,' she responded. *'Everybody knows that.'*

'I didn't,' he said, laughing. 'But I think we'll let the jury remain out on the gender of our poisoner, shall we? But this is great work Eleanor. Thanks.'

'She searched for something else too,' she said, ignoring both his cautionary comment and his compliment. *'Something weird.'*

'Like what?' he asked.

'Like joint enterprise.'

'What?'

'Joint enterprise,' she repeated, adopting her teacher-addressing-five-year-old voice, and leaving a long gap between the two words to make sure he understood. *'Her exact search phrase was, what is the law of joint enterprise?*

'I've heard the term before, but I've no idea what it means,' he said. 'But I'm sure Maggie or Jimmy will know, they trained as lawyers.' He paused again. 'So that was it? Our guy stroke girl nicked someone's phone to make these searches undetectable, then dumped it afterwards presumably?'

'Yeah. The signal went dead about ten o'clock.'

He nodded. 'He or she would have taken out the SIM card and chucked it away. But as I said, this is good work Eleanor.' He was just about to hang up when he remembered the other thing she was doing for him.

'Oh aye, and about that recording. Done your stuff on that yet?'

'My stuff?' she said coldly. *'There's like a ton of complicated tech involved in high-definition audio verification. But yeah,*

I've done it, and yeah, it's definitely Orla's voice on that recording and it's definitely the other guy's too.'

'What other guy? Do you mean Dougie McKean? Because there was a third voice too, the producer. Nicky Nicholson, remember?'

'It's definitely McKean,' she said. *'But I only had one sample of the Nicholson dude to compare with and it wasn't exactly HD quality. But yeah, it's probably him too. The waveforms are close enough.'*

'So that's it then, all nicely put to bed.' It was part-question, part-statement.

'Yeah, defo,' she replied, a little too quickly he thought. Did he imagine it, or was there something in her voice that left room for doubt?

'You absolutely sure?' he asked.

'Yeah, like defo,' she repeated. But somehow, it wasn't one hundred percent convincing. In the course of her update he guessed something had sprung to mind, something that had sown the most infinitesimal seed of doubt. He was probably being needlessly cautious, but he decided it might be best to delay the triumphant press conference for a day or two yet.

Chapter 24

Maggie hadn't exactly been surprised to get a call from Frank, he having developed the lovely habit of calling her at least a couple of times a day, but the subject of this call was unexpected. *What's joint enterprise all about,* he had asked, a question that had her first wracking the deepest recesses of her brain, and then, more productively, reaching for her favourite legal professionals' website. Glancing down at her phone, she re-read what the site had to say about it. *Joint Enterprise is a doctrine enshrined in English common law. It is a law that has been used and evolved over the centuries. It reinforces the notion that if you are seen to be involved in the commission of a crime you could be seen to be equally as guilty as the person who has committed it.* Clear as mud, she thought with some amusement. But scrolling down, another article caught her attention. *One hundred and fifty peers call for joint enterprise law to be scrapped.* Reading on, it seemed that the law was being regularly used in the prosecution of street gang crime, and mainly against urban black youths, leading to hundreds of miscarriages of justice every year, according to the protesting lords.

The article went on to cite some further examples, which did make it a bit clearer - but only a bit, although she assumed that once she had found out exactly why Frank was interested in it, she would probably be able to help him more. But whatever the situation, she was very much looking forward to see him, after hastily arranging a meeting at a location that was convenient for her, but was likely to evoke howls of protest from him. And when he arrived to meet her at the department store cafe, her prognosis proved accurate.

'I always feel a right fish out of water in this place,' he said, smiling fondly at her as he approached her table. 'I'm more of a Primark sort of guy, you know that.'

'No you're not,' she laughed, stretching over to accept his kiss. 'And just so you know, this is where you'll be doing your clothes shopping once we're married.' She nodded towards a huge poster of a rugged and handsome male model that adorned one wall, dressed as if about to go on a shooting or fishing trip. 'You'll look just like him when I'm finished with you.'

'What, am I getting plastic surgery as well?' he laughed, pulling out a chair and sitting down.

'You'll be man at Lewis & Clark's. They'll be using you on these posters instead of that guy.'

He gave a wry smile. 'More of a job for Jimmy I think, in between these expeditions of his. Anyway, I guess you're here because you've sent young Lorilynn up north on that surveillance job?'

She nodded. 'That's right, we've swapped. She's more or less cracked this case. I'm just here to apply the finishing touches.'

'Shoplifting, isn't it?'

'A bit more than that. It's a smooth and sophisticated operation, and it's been costing the store thousands. But I'll tell you all about that later. What I'm interested in is why you need to know about joint enterprise.'

'It's a bit weird, I must admit,' he said. 'We've been looking for folks who were doing searches for taxine, and we found that the person who was doing that was looking at this joint enterprise business too. As I said, weird.'

She smiled. 'Well I know what joint enterprise is, though I had to do a little bit of research to remind myself of the details. As an example, if a crime is committed and a group of people were in on the planning but only one commits the actual crime, everyone associated with it can still be found guilty.'

He looked puzzled, so she tried again. 'Say four people plan and execute a robbery, but in the course of the robbery one of them shoots and kills a security guard. The joint enterprise law means they all could be tried for murder, even although the other three didn't actually do the shooting.'

He nodded. 'Aye, that makes more sense. And now you've told me, I think I kind of knew that already.'

'Yes, cases where it's a factor come up surprisingly often,' she said. 'But the problem with that law is it's wide open to appeal. It can be very hard to get a conviction that'll stick.'

'Because in your example, the other parties can argue that they didn't pull the trigger, so they shouldn't be found guilty?' he asked.

'Exactly,' Maggie said. 'And as a result, it often spirals into a great unholy mess. Great for the lawyers being paid by the hour, but not so great for justice.'

He nodded. 'Well at least I know what it is now, although I'm not sure that helps me right at this minute. But it'll all become clear in time, it always does.'

'I hope so,' she said. 'But isn't it great we're working on the same case again? I think we'll make a great team.' She gave a wicked smile. 'As long as you do what I tell you of course.'

'Always,' he said. 'Anything for a quiet life,' he added, with a mock grimace.

'Cheeky sod. But let me get this straight. You think you can find Dougie McKean's poisoner by just checking the internet for who has searched for taxine?'

'Why not?' he said. 'We've nabbed plenty of would-be terrorists in the past on the basis of them searching for how to make explosives. That's why GCHQ keeps its bloody great database, to keep us all safe. The only thing was, this woman was smart. She went to a crowded pub in Bath of all places and nicked someone's phone to do her searches. And I would bet my pension that she was wearing a hoodie or a balaclava or something, so even in the unlikely event we catch her on CCTV, we won't be able to ID her.'

'So you think it's a woman then?'

He shrugged. 'I don't really know if it's a man or a woman. But Eleanor thinks it's probably a woman on the basis of poisoning being the murder weapon of choice for the so-called fair sex.'

Maggie shook her head. 'That's old-school Agatha Christie thinking. It's just as likely to be a man in my opinion.'

'You're probably right,' he mused. 'Anyway, whether it's a he or she, we need to find out who it is, and sharpish. I'm going to get Ronnie French to go down there and ask a few questions. He likes any assignment that involves pubs, and he likes a train trip too.'

She was thoughtful for a moment. 'Yes, you should do that, certainly. But isn't there another option? It's just came to me, and it might be complete rubbish because I'm not very technical as you know.'

'Better than me though,' he said, laughing. 'So come on, run it past me.'

'Well, obviously our searcher was smart enough to use a stolen phone so they couldn't be traced. But were they smart enough to leave their *own* phone at home? I doubt it very much,' she added, answering her own question. 'Because no-one goes anywhere without their phones these days, do they?'

'True,' he said, intrigued. 'Go on.'

'Phone company databases can pinpoint the location of any phone at any point in time, can't they? I think it's something to do with cell triangulation between three masts or something like that. And they keep that data for a while, don't they?'

'They do,' Frank affirmed. 'It's routine now for us coppers to use it in our investigations. I've used it plenty of times myself as you well know.'

She nodded. 'Exactly. So if our searcher is one of our suspects....'

'And it's a wide field,' he interrupted.

'Yes it is. But if you could compile a list of the mobile phone numbers of everyone who might possibly be a suspect, we could check if they were in that pub on that day and at that time. Or what I mean is, we could get Eleanor to check. On the phone companies' databases.'

'That's brilliant,' he said, beaming a huge smile. 'So we've got Orla McCarthy, we've got Cassie, we've got Tamara, we've got that studio engineer guy whose body we've just found...'

'And there's Orla's boyfriend the record producer, and Clay that American film producer, and the three guys in Dougie's band,' Maggie added.

'And all the band's road-crew too don't forget,' Frank said, suddenly making a face. 'It's a big list.'

'But we've probably got most of the numbers already,' she countered. 'It shouldn't take long to find the others.'

He nodded. 'No, you're absolutely right. I'll make a list of the ones I've got, and then I'll get my mad DS Jessie James to round up the rest of them.'

'I thought you wanted her sacked?' she asked, amused. 'Has the wild-west bandit been granted a royal pardon then?'

'Let's just call it a stay of execution,' he said, pulling a face. 'I've told Jill Smart I don't need any other resources added to the case, so as not to put any unnecessary obstacles in the way of Naylor approving it. So I need to use what I've got.'

'You can use the vast resources of Bainbridge Associates too if you like. Although I'll want paying of course.'

He shot her a cheeky smile. 'Fair enough. I'll buy you an ice-cream, or you can have my body if you like.'

'That's an offer I don't think I can refuse,' she giggled. 'It's a deal. But I want both, just so you know.'

'I'll grab you a cornetto forthwith,' he said, giving a thumbs-up. 'Anyway, tell me all about this big shoplifting conspiracy. I'm a bit short of work at the moment and I could use an easy collar to boost my statistics.'

She raised a quizzical eyebrow. 'I thought you didn't bother about that sort of stuff? That's what you're always telling me at least.'

He laughed. 'I don't really. But they post a wee league table on the notice-board in the canteen, and a man's got his pride. So come on, tell me all about it.'

'Okay,' she said, 'I don't suppose you'll have heard of Fiona Ingleton, but she's a top dress designer. Scottish too. Her designs are in all the fashion magazines at the moment and every woman I know wants to wear them.'

'I bet your pal Asvina's got one then,' he said. 'That's her kind of thing, isn't it?'

Maggie nodded. 'She's got about half-a-dozen I think, and in fact that's how I first got to hear of her. Anyway, they sell them here at Lewis & Clark's. The store is one of Miss Ingleton's biggest agencies in fact.'

'And now they're being pinched.'

'Yes they are. But now we know how it works, mainly thanks to Lori. It's bloody audacious, I can tell you that.'

'How so?'

Maggie smiled. 'So half an hour ago, I went to the dress department and started browsing the Ingleton racks. After a minute or so, the sales assistant who Lori thinks is behind all this came up to me and gave me the usual sales chat, you know, *these dresses are so beautiful and I think they're really your style madam.* Very smooth. Then I said*, yes, it's just a pity they're so frightfully expensive.* She went all coy at that and said, *Actually, I'm not really supposed to be telling you this, but there's a top-secret website where you can get them wholesale, less than half price.* And she slipped me a little business card with a URL on it. *IngletonWholesale.com* it said.' She spun her phone round until it faced him. 'I was looking at it just before you arrived.'

He scrutinised it with furrowed brow. 'Not my area of expertise of course, but it looks very professional.'

She nodded. 'That's because it's been cloned from Fiona Ingleton's official website. The only thing that's different is the prices.'

'So how does this wee scam work?'

'There's two of them in it. The saleswoman's got a pal who poses as a customer. This pal takes a dress to the changing room and then puts it on under her existing clothes and walks straight out of the store, bold as brass. And of course her mate has already snipped off the security dongle. Then they package it up and send it off to the unsuspecting customer, who thinks they're getting an amazing bargain through this super-secret website.'

'They're stealing to order then?'

'Exactly. But it's a dumb crime really, because it didn't take a rocket scientist to work out that it had to be an inside job. Lori had it all figured out in about two days flat.'

'Smart girl,' he said. 'It'll be good to have her on my team.'

'Your team?' she said, grinning.

'Well I need to get *something* in return for my ice cream. They're flippin' expensive now, these cornettos. Nearly two quid each.'

She was just about to retort when her phone rang.

'Speak of the devil,' she whispered to him as she answered the call. 'Hi Lori, how are you? I'll stick you on speakerphone because I've got Frank with me.'

'I just saw a man going into Cassie McKean's house,' her assistant said breathlessly, evidently anxious to get straight to the point.

'Who was it, could you see?'

'Not that well, because he had his back to me most of the time.'

'Sure it wasn't the minister?' Frank asked, laughing. 'They're always sniffing around folks whenever there's a bereavement. Good for recruitment, or so they believe.'

'Not unless they've started snogging their parishioners on the doorstep and putting their hand on their arses,' Lori said.

'Oh, *right*,' Maggie laughed. 'That's pretty conclusive I would say. So what are you planning to do? I don't suppose you can stay outside her house all night.'

'I'll wait a couple of hours to see if the guy comes out again. If not, I'll come back in the morning, nice and early.'

'That's a good plan. This is very interesting, isn't it? In so much that it proves Cassie was lying to us *again* when she said the affair was over.'

'Might not be the same bloke of course,' Frank pointed out.

'True,' Maggie conceded, 'but I would think it's more likely that it is than it isn't. I don't know why I think that, other than woman's intuition.'

'I did get a couple of photographs,' Lori interjected. *'They're not fantastically clear, but I'll send them to you right away. Just a minute....'* There was a moment's silence and then she said, *'Done. You should have them anytime now. There's three of them.'*

***

Lori had been quite right. The photographs weren't that clear, with just the smallest oblique glimpse of the man's features being visible on one of them, recognition not aided by the beanie hat he was wearing despite the balmy early autumn temperatures. But Frank Stewart, lifelong fan and devotee of the Claymore Warriors, had no difficulty in making a positive identification, even from the rear.

'Flippin' heck,' he said. 'That's Jamie Cooper.'

Chapter 25

With the discovery that Cassie McKean had a lover, and that her lover was none other than Jamie Cooper, lead guitarist of the Claymore Warriors, Frank was experiencing that sweet feeling that always arrived at some point in a case, even if you had to wait a bloody long time for it to turn up. It was the feeling that, even if infinitesimally, the tide was starting to turn in their favour. He couldn't say why or even *if* this particular revelation was important to the case. All he knew was that when principal players in the drama were exposed as liars, then there was something serious afoot. Added to this, they had found their poisoner - in *Bath* -even if the identity of that person, be it male or female, was still to be established. Yes, things were starting to move, and if experience had taught him anything, soon the trickle would turn into a torrent. Or at least that was the hope.

Next morning, he was back in what had become his surrogate office, the canteen of New Gorbals police station, awaiting the arrival of his pal DC Lexy McDonald for their regular breakfast catch-up. Earlier that day he had received official sanction from Met Commissioner Trevor Naylor to extend the scope of the Orla McCarthy sexual assault case into looking at the murder of Dougie McKean. Given that good news, he would have dearly loved to have had the excellent Lexy on his team, but that wasn't an option, having promised his boss that the investigation wouldn't need any extra resources. So this meeting was mainly social, although he was hoping their general chat might just pop up the odd fact or two from the official McKean investigation that might be useful to his. Looking up, he saw her approaching his table.

'Well hello DC McDonald,' he said, giving her a puzzled look when he saw she was in uniform. 'Or is it PC McDonald? I hope they've not put you back on the beat for doing something naughty.'

'No sir,' she laughed. 'I'm doing a school liaison visit later today in Paisley. The Super likes us to do these kind of things in uniform. Says it commands authority and respect.'

'In Paisley? I don't think you'll find much of either down there. But does that mean the McKean case is all wrapped up, if you're reduced to performing for school-kids?'

'Yes sir, all wrapped up. They're concluding that Tamara Gray did it to get her hands on Dougie's money, but then killed herself when she thought she was going to get found out. Or out of remorse. They've not quite settled on which yet.'

'Aye, very neat and tidy,' he said, giving a wry smile. 'And is that what you think Lexy? That Tamara killed herself?'

She smiled. 'I'll go and get the coffees then I'll tell you what I think.'

'No cakes?' he said, mildly disappointed, when she returned with just the beverages.

'Think kilt, and how you're going to fit into it,' she said with mock severity.

He shrugged. 'You're right. Anyway, to the McKean murder.'

'Yes sir. So, in a nutshell, I don't buy Tamara's motive.'

'Why so?'

'Well, she wasn't much older than me actually,' Lexy said. 'So I thought, if I was in her shoes, would I marry a guy like Dougie McKean just for his money? And I thought, no I wouldn't. If I was just a gold-digger, I would try and bag someone *way* older than him. Someone who might die of old age pretty soon, not to put too fine a point on it.'

'Makes sense.'

'So then I thought, why *would* I get into a relationship with a guy like him? And the answer's easy. It's the glamour, the parties, the travel, the five-star hotels etc etc etc. All that stuff is very alluring to a certain kind of girl.'

'And of course all of that fancy lifestyle ends if he's dead,' Frank said.

'Exactly. Even if she didn't actually love him, she could have had a bloody good time with him. So to me, she didn't have a credible motive to kill him, despite all the stuff about her getting him to change his will.'

'So who did have a motive?'

Lexy laughed. 'Just about everybody else. Everyone he ever met.' She paused, then laughed again. 'And yes, I know that's not exactly helpful sir. All I can say is that it was quite a *clinical* murder, wasn't it? Which makes me think it wasn't a crime of passion.' She was silent for a moment, evidently thinking about what she had just said, then shrugged. 'I know. Not helpful. But it's the best I can come up with right now.'

He nodded. 'Well I can see your logic Lexy, and I think I might agree with you as to the clinical nature of the crime. I'm only allowed a week or two on the case, so I'll clutch at any straw if it helps me get a result.'

***

His conversation with Lexy had made him resolve to set aside some time to think about motives, but in the meantime, he had some unfinished business to attend to. He had realised earlier that Orla McCarthy still hadn't called him back despite him leaving further voicemail messages, he guessing that with her sexual assault case all but tied up, DCI Frank Stewart of the Metropolitan Police had slipped down the singer's priority list. But this time, she answered within a few rings and began with an apology, citing a mad crazy schedule for not getting back to him sooner.

'That's no problem Orla, I understand,' he said. 'Anyway, this call's on a different matter altogether.'

'Oh is it?' she said, sounding uninterested. *'I just want to thank you first for the way you handled my case. Because I had such a horrible time with the police all those years ago, when I was a teenager, and I thought it would be just the same this time. All you guys would be interested in doing would be covering your arses. But you were different, and I thank you for that.'* She paused for a moment. *'Yash Patel said you were a good cop, but I wasn't sure I believed him at first. But he was right.'*

He smiled. 'Actually, the job of my wee department is to do the exact opposite of covering arses, so you can say you struck lucky getting me. But I guess you can put it all behind you now.'

'Although McKean's dead, I still need everyone to know what he did to me,' she said. *'I want other young women in my position to be inspired to speak out against powerful men, even if they have to wait years to do it. That's why I was so determined to see this through,'* she added.

'Yes, well I'm sure it will inspire them,' he said. 'But if you don't mind, can you spare a few minutes on this other matter?'

'Yeah sure. Go ahead.'

He cleared his throat then said, 'Orla, did you know that Damian Hammond was dead?'

'No,' she shot out. *'God, how?'*

'That's the strange thing. He was found drowned in the Spey just a couple of weeks ago. And nobody's got the faintest idea why he was up there.'

'Good god,' she said. *'What, was it an accident or something?'*

'That's something we have still to establish,' Frank said. 'But the thing is, we wondered if he might have been stalking you, and that was why he was up there at the same time you were.' He paused again for a moment. 'Because we've found certain materials online that suggested he may have had... well let's call it an unhealthy obsession with you.'

'What sort of materials?' she asked sharply.

'I'm afraid they were of a sexual nature,' he said. 'But not hard-core or anything like that. Actually, he was boasting to his mates that you and he were going to be having a cosy dinner date, and that afterwards you would spend the night making passionate love.' It wasn't quite the whole truth, but he didn't think there was anything to be gained by sharing the graphic detail, nor revealing the fact that Damian Hammond's mates were a bunch of these involuntary celibate weirdos.

'That's sick,' she said. *'And I thought he was quite a sweet guy too.'*

'So you're quite sure he wasn't stalking you? And specifically, you're quite certain you didn't notice him at any time when you were up on Speyside?'

'No', she said again. *'Definitely not. I was busy filming my fly-on-the-wall with Yash and Chronicle TV of course, but no, I definitely didn't see Hammond.'*

'And no text messages or emails of that nature?'

'No. I've had them in the past of course, every woman in the public eye gets these pests bothering them from time to time. But not for a couple of years at least, thank God.'

He was just about to ask his next question when he heard music on the line, the unmistakable sound of a live band playing in the background. Despite not being a great fan of Orla's, he had no trouble in recognising the introduction to

Girl in a Taxi, her huge hit of the previous year, which had gained added notoriety by attracting a high-profile law-suit from the makers of an unconnected film of the same title.

'Rehearsing?' he asked. 'Great tune this, by the way,' he added.

'Thanks,' she said. *'Yeah, I'm talking with some folks about a tour. Early days, and we're just having a run through some numbers with my new band to see what it sounds like. My mind hasn't exactly been in a good place lately, but I think I'm ready to get back in the saddle. But we'll see how it goes. Baby steps.'*

'Aye, well fingers crossed,' he said. And then out of the blue, a thought came to him. He hesitated for a moment, then asked, 'Random question Orla, but have you been to Bath lately?'

'Bath?' she answered. *'That's an odd question. But no, I haven't. I'm not sure if I've ever been there in fact.'*

And she was right, it was an odd question. Why then did he think he detected the faintest of pauses before she answered it?

***

From Frank's point of view, nothing much had happened on the case during the preceding couple of days. Ronnie French had been despatched down to Bath to check out the CCTV of the Bear and Hounds pub, where it seemed the search for taxine had been conducted, and DS Jessie James had been given the job of compiling the list of suspects' phone numbers, then working with Eleanor Campbell to see if any of them had been at the pub at the time the searches had been made. He still hadn't a clue as to the significance of the venue, the town of Bath having no obvious connection to any of the suspects nor the victim either, but he was confident the connection would emerge in due course. For Maggie's part, all she could really do was *think*, particularly about the significance of this latest interesting discovery, that of the affair between Cassie McKean and Jamie Cooper, guitarist with the Claymore Warriors. Superficially, it gave both Cassie and Cooper a motive for getting rid of Dougie McKean, but on giving the matter further consideration, Maggie had to concede that it wasn't a very strong one. Plenty of people had affairs, but very few of them felt the need to murder the cuckolded partner in order for it to continue. And the awkward fact was, Jamie Cooper was unarguably one of the biggest losers from McKean's death, the career of the Warriors stopped dead in its tracks with the demise of its charismatic front-man.

But during the period there had been some levity too, with Jimmy making the trip down from Braemar the previous day for the rearranged fitting of their Highland-dress wedding outfits. Frank, as he had dolefully suspected, had added a full inch to his waistline since they'd had the initial rough fitting a couple of months back, a fact that he had been hoping to keep from Maggie, who had been excluded from the event in line with tradition. Not excluded however had been Lori Logan, fresh from her successful surveillance operation, who had insisted on coming along as the bride-to-be's semi-official emissary, and would no doubt report back to her boss in due course. But despite the minor setback, it had been a great afternoon, with his brother in great spirits and keen to remind Frank at every turn what a lucky bastard he was to have bagged a woman like Maggie as his wife. Not that he needed any reminding of *that*. He knew that in meeting Miss Magdalene Bainbridge he'd won the lottery a million times over, and in five or six weeks' time they'd be walking down the aisle of the wee church in Grassington and he would be the happiest man alive.

Now, two days on, it was time for him to get back to work, which meant finding out how DC Ronnie French had fared on his short Wiltshire jaunt, and then to catch up with forensic princess Eleanor Campbell. But just as he was about to select Frenchie's number from his *favourites* list, Eleanor caught up with him instead. And somehow, just by the shrill tone of the ring, he could tell she was going to be angry.

'Well hello there,' he said jauntily. 'What's up?'

'You made me work with that woman,' she said, her voice a couple of semitones higher than normal. *'I hate her.'*

'You're speaking of my DS James, I assume? I tell you Eleanor, she's fine, once you get to know her better,' he said, lying. In fact DS Jessie James was one of these people you liked less and less the more you got to know her, but he wasn't planning on sharing that jaundiced view with his favourite forensic officer. 'Remember that wee team-working course we all went on last year? How embracing different personalities leads to high-functioning teams? Well that's what you have to do with Jessie. Embrace her different personality.'

'I hate her,' Eleanor repeated. *'She treats me like a stupid schoolgirl.'* Takes one to know one he thought, but that was another opinion he had no intention of sharing.

'Ah well, I'm really sorry about that,' he said. 'But I assume you eventually got these phone numbers from her and you were able to do your sweep of the phone databases, or whatever technical magic you were going to do.'

'I had to merge like eighteen different data-sources from twelve different phone companies,' she said. *'And there were over two hundred mobile phones in the pub that night.'*

'Crikey, the place must have been jumping. And I thought Bath was a sleepy wee city.'

She ignored him. *'It was like a mega-complicated bit of coding. I had to borrow a superfast laptop from the labs, and I needed to do regressive cross-curser matching using a sixty-four-bit algorithm.'*

'Good to know,' he said, not quite managing to suppress a laugh. 'And did this display of dazzling coding wizardry produce a result, may I ask?'

'You're taking the mickey out of me aren't you?' she said crossly, evidently detecting his mirth. *'I can always tell when you are.'*

'No no, I'm not, honestly, ' he said, momentarily picturing her sitting at her desk, arms tightly folded and with a face like thunder. 'It's just you make me laugh when you do all that fancy technical talk. It's so earnest, but it's really endearing too.' He paused for a moment, wondering if he should have said that. But the fact was, it was exactly how he felt about her, so why shouldn't he tell her? He said, 'I hope you don't mind me saying it, but you do great work, and I really value it. Even if I do take the mickey a lot. I wouldn't do that if I didn't think we were mates.'

'That's like grossly embarrassing,' she said, but he could tell from her softer tone that she was pleased with the compliment. *'So yeah, I did find a match. But it wasn't easy,'* she added, as he knew she would.

'I didn't for a moment think it would be. But have you got a name for me, or do you have to tear open a golden envelope first? Like in the Oscars?'

'No envelope,' she said, *'but I've got a name. It was Damian Hammond. The recording studio guy. Or at least, his mobile was there. It doesn't mean he was.'*

He drew in a sharp breath. 'Aye, point taken, but bloody hell. So Hammond might be our poisoner eh? I must admit, I didn't see *that* coming, not at all.' He paused for a moment as this new information began to sink in. Certainly, it wasn't a name he'd expected, and he would now have to revise his half-formed ideas of how and why the murder might have been carried out. 'Well thanks a lot Eleanor,' he continued. 'That's bloody good work.'

'There's something else,' she said, and then was silent for a second. Then she said, *'Listen to this.'*

To his utter astonishment, a voice began to narrate a familiar nursery rhyme.

> *Hickory Dickery Dock, the mouse ran up the clock,*
>
> *The clock struck one, the mouse ran down...*

But it wasn't just any old voice doing the narration. *It was himself.*

'Bloody hell,' he blurted out again. 'That's me!'

'It sounds like you. Exactly like you,' she said, evidently amused. *'Except it's obviously not you.'*

'So what the hell is it? he asked, confused.

'Next-generation AI text-to-speech conversion,' she answered. *'I uploaded a recording of your voice into the app and then typed in the rhyme. The technology is like so awesome now, you can't tell the difference with real life. And that's how they did it.'*

'Did what? And who's *they*?' he stammered, still confused.

'I don't know who they are,' she said, *'but that studio recording is a fake. It's AI-generated, defo.'*

'Bloody hell,' he said for the third time, his head now spinning. 'And you're absolutely sure about that? Because I thought you said there was a match?'

'I did. And there was a very good match between the voice samples you got me and the recording,' she said. *'Orla was Orla and McKean was McKean, if you get what I'm saying.'*

'But there was something niggling away at the back of your mind, wasn't there? I got that feeling when we spoke of this before.'

'Like yeah,' she agreed. *'You see, I didn't know how the Fourier voice waveform displayed ageing. I knew it must do it somehow, but I didn't know how.'*

'Sorry, not with you,' he said. 'But that's only to be expected on technical matters. Carry on, please.'

'Your voice changes as you age,' she said. *'It still sounds like you, but it often gets a little bit deeper if you're a woman and often a little higher if you're a man. And that makes the waveform of a recording look a tiny little bit different when you see it on a screen. So I did some research, and I found out what to look for.'*

'So what are you saying Eleanor? he asked, feeling his excitement grow as he anticipated what she might be about to tell him.

'That recording was supposed to have been made eighteen years ago, right?' she said. *'But the voices on it weren't eighteen years old. Like no way. They were from now.'*

And once again he said *bloody hell*, no other response seeming to be adequate.

Chapter 26

There was no doubt about it, Maggie reflected. They had reached the tipping point, that scary but exciting moment in every case where you could almost reach out and touch the solution, where it seemed as if all that was needed was one last push to arrange the disparate pieces of information into a coherent and satisfying whole. It was Frank's recent conversation with Eleanor that had got them to that point she felt, and now it would be the collective application of their little grey cells - with due deference to the famous but fictional H. Poirot - which would get them over the line. Accordingly, they had assembled a crack team at the Bikini Baristas Cafe, and although the investigation of Dougie McKean's murder was now a semi-official Metropolitan Police affair, it amused her that three out of the four individuals occupying a comfortable window table were employees of her own little firm. As they settled into their seats, the cafe's proprietor Stevie glided over, dressed in his usual black T-shirt and pristine white apron, notebook in hand.

'Morning guys, what can I get youse?' he said. 'Is it just coffees, or are you staying for lunch?'

Frank laughed. 'We'll be here all day Stevie. Unless we have a sudden outbreak of inspiration, which is always possible of course, with the big brains round *this* table.'

'Are you including yourself in that?' Jimmy said, grinning. 'Big head, sure. Big brain, I'm not so sure.'

'Leave him alone,' Maggie said in mock indignation. 'He'll be fine after two or three coffees, once the caffeine kicks in.'

'Yup, bring it on,' Frank said. 'And let me just drop a wee message to Ronnie and Eleanor, to make sure they're around if we need to get them on a video call for anything.'

A few minutes later, Stevie returned with their order, which Maggie took as the signal to kick things off.

'So where do we start?' she said, taking a sip of her cappuccino. 'Maybe a quick review of these amazing recent developments, and some thoughts about motive, means and opportunity, the usual stuff?'

'Sounds good,' Lori Logan said. 'And can I add that other thing we've talked about before. I don't know exactly what we call it, but I think of it as previous demonstration of intent, or something like that. You know, somebody shouting *I'm going to beep-beep kill you* or *you're going to beep-beep pay for this*. Things like that.'

'Yes, good point,' Maggie said.

Frank nodded. 'Funnily enough, that reminds me of something DC McDonald said to me the other day. She said this seemed very much like a clinical killing. And I agree. This doesn't feel like a crime of passion, which ties up with Lori's point. Because as far as I'm aware, no-one was going around threatening to kill Dougie McKean.' He took a sip of his drink. 'But I'm getting off the agenda already. Like you say Maggie, let's hear what we make of these recent developments.'

She nodded. 'Pretty sensational ones as well. First of all, Damian Hammond was the poisoner, is that what we think?'

'He was caught doing the research,' Jimmy said. 'That doesn't mean he actually did it.'

'Though he was up in Speyside around the time of the festival,' Lori said. 'So he might have had the opportunity.'

'But why Bath?' Frank said, looking puzzled. 'What's the significance of that?'

'He had a sister there or something?' Jimmy speculated. 'Or one of his weirdo mates lived there maybe?'

Frank shrugged. 'Possibly. But what was his motive to kill Dougie McKean? And why was he searching for stuff about the joint enterprise law at the same time? Any ideas?'

For a moment, there was silence as everyone tried to come up with a plausible explanation for either point, evidently without success.

'Let's just park that for now,' Maggie suggested. 'So, development two, the faking of the sexual assault recording.'

'I've got an explanation for *that*,' Lori said eagerly. 'So this weirdo Hammond is obsessing about shagging Orla McCarthy - I mean, as if *that's* ever going to happen. He knows about the historic assault allegations and thinks, I'll fake this recording to ingratiate myself with her. Because he had the opportunity and the geeky skills to do it, didn't he? Means, motive, opportunity, they're all there, aren't they?'

'And *of course*, that's the motive for him wanting to kill Dougie too isn't it?' Maggie said, nodding. 'To do something really dramatic to prove his love for Orla. It's warped thinking, sure, but I don't know how we missed that. So much for all our big brains.'

'Although isn't it a wee bit of overkill, if you'll pardon the pun?' Jimmy asked. *'If you sleep with me, I'll get Dougie McKean accused of sexual assault and I'll murder him for you too?'*

'Hedging his bets,' Maggie said, then smiled as she recognised the implausibility of that statement. But then again, she knew from experience that some of the most implausible theories had a nasty habit of proving to be true. 'But that doesn't explain why he was found drowned in the Spey,' she added.

Frank frowned. 'Maybe when he told Orla what he had done for her, she laughed in his face. So he went off and killed himself to teach her a lesson.'

Jimmy gave him an uncertain look. 'It is *an* explanation, but not much of one. But I can't think of anything better. Unless it was Orla who pushed him in of course.'

'She said she didn't see him up there,' Frank said. 'And I think I believed her. I'm pretty certain too that he wasn't physically stalking her, or abusing her online either. All his weird obsession was only shared with his other nut-job pals as far as we can tell.'

'So was all of this just in his head?' Lori asked. 'Did he poison McKean then bottle out from telling Orla he'd done it, and that he'd done it for her?'

'Possibly,' Maggie said, unconvinced. 'But let's park this one as well for a minute and move on. So Cassie McKean's affair with Jamie Cooper. Is that important to the case, do we think?'

'She lied to us,' Lori said. 'Once by omission, and once when she said the affair was over. Which makes her an unreliable witness at the very least.'

'She'd put up with Dougie's infidelities for years,' Jimmy mused. 'But now she's found someone herself, and the boot is on the other foot. She can see a perfect new life ahead of her, as long as she gets custody of her kids. With Dougie out of the way, that's no longer an issue.

Frank shrugged. 'Aye, she had a motive all right, but Cooper didn't. With Dougie dead, there's no more Claymore Warriors, is there?'

'That's true,' Jimmy said, looking disappointed.

'But maybe he didn't care about that,' Lori said. 'Maybe he loved her. And the music was rubbish anyway. Anyone would want to escape from *that.*'

'Wash your mouth out,' Frank said, laughing. 'It's a fair point you raise, but as a fan, I can tell you that Jamie Cooper has always been as dedicated to the band as Dougie McKean was. McKean might have been the face of the Warriors, but it was

Jamie's arranging and production skills that shaped their iconic sound, even if he wasn't always given the credit he deserved.'

For the next half-hour, they continued the debate, but without making any significant breakthroughs, Maggie only half-listening as she tested then rejected theory after theory in her head. Until, quite suddenly, the thick fog began to lift. The solution was *there*, almost within reach, if only she could see through the gradually-clearing mist. And at that very second, she knew exactly what she must do.

'Guys...,' she began. But Frank had evidently anticipated the moment, and was ready.

'I know,' he said, laughing. '*I want to be alone.* And sorry for the crap Garbo impression. ' He smiled at the others. 'Come on folks, let's hop round to the Horseshoe and grab ourselves a pint and a pie-and-chips, whilst we leave Miss Einstein here to figure it all out.' He stood up and blew her a kiss. 'And don't forget to send us a wee text when you're done. But no rush, because the beer's great round there. And I hear Jimmy-boy's buying.'

***

Fortified by another coffee and supplemented by a tasty cheese-and-ham croissant, Maggie took out her little notebook and began to scribble, jotting down random facts in a circular pattern which radiated outwards from the centre of the page. It wasn't scientific in any way, but somehow having it laid out in this fashion seemed to help focus her thoughts. Additionally, it helped to highlight all the stuff she *didn't* know. One omission in particular stood out, and to put that right she needed to speak to Eleanor Campbell.

The forensic officer answered with a bright *Hi Maggie*, in sharp contrast to her response should it have been Frank that was calling.

'Hi Eleanor,' Maggie said. 'I won't take up too much of your time, but I wondered if you could help me with something?'

'Like no problem,' she responded. *'Happy to help.'*

'Great. Obviously, it's to do with the McKean murder. So can I ask, did you get a copy of the toxicology report, you know, the one that came out after they analysed the contents of the whisky bottle? I know it would have been a different part of the forensics team that did the work, but I wondered if you got a copy as a matter of courtesy?'

'Yeah, I got it,' Eleanor said. *'Do you want me to send you it? It's quite big.'*

Maggie laughed. 'No no, I doubt I would understand a word anyway. But there's just one question maybe you can help me with. Tell me, did it say anything about the relative proportions of taxine and aspartame that were found in the sample?'

Eleanor hesitated for a moment before answering. *'It would have done I think, but I'm not sure. If you wait for a minute, I can pull it up and have a look.'*

'Great. Take as much time as you need.' There was a delay of several minutes before Eleanor responded, with only the occasional audible burst of keyboard activity to testify the forensic officer was working on it.

'Sorry, it wasn't easy to find,' she said when she returned to the call. *'But I've got it now. Here it is. So there was about a quarter of the whisky left in the bottle, and the analysts assumed that a quarter of the poison solution was left too. Scaling it up, they estimate that there was originally 35 milligrams of taxine administered, the bitter taste disguised by 105 milligrams of powdered aspartame.'*

And as soon as Maggie had done the rudimentary arithmetic, she saw, with a huge sense of elation, that her emerging theory was right. Now, without question, she knew why it was done, and how, and by whom. She knew too why Hammond had travelled to Bath and she knew why he had searched for joint enterprise, and why the studio recording had been faked using clever AI technology. And why, sadly, both Hammond and Tamara Gray had to be murdered.

In short, she knew *everything*. Suppressing a smug smile, she picked up her phone and messaged her lovely fiancé.

No time for that second pint.

Chapter 27

'We're going back to *Speyside*?' Frank said, furrowing his brow. 'There's nothing there now surely? Even the scene-of-crime boys have packed up and gone home from the festival site.'

'Just get your foot down and keep driving,' Jimmy said from the back seat. 'We can do it in two and a bit hours with the wind at our backs. Especially if you make use of those wee blue flashing lights behind the grill.'

'Aye sure, and as long as I don't have to put up with bloody backseat drivers all the way,' Frank replied acerbically.

'Boys boys,' Maggie said, laughing. 'You need to trust me on this,' she added, sounding more assured than she felt inside.

'We always do,' Frank replied, shooting her a fond glance. 'But are you planning to tell us what the hell this is all about?'

'When we get there,' she said enigmatically. 'Because there's every chance I might be terribly wrong. So just sit back and enjoy the beautiful scenery.'

They drove much of the journey in amiable silence, Frank making occasional use of the unmarked car's siren to clear doddling vehicles from their path. From time to time, one or other of the Stewart brothers would try to coax Maggie into revealing the reason for this crazy dash northwards, but to no avail. They tried again whilst making a brief coffee stop on the outskirts of Perth, but all she would say was that there was a high likelihood that Frank would be bringing the

McKean murder investigation to a sensational close by the end of the day.

They reached Grantown-on-Spey just before five o'clock, sailing unobstructed round its bypass, a rush hour being an unknown phenomenon in that remote part of Scotland, before taking the northwards A-road that paralleled the river on its eastern side.

'It was you that put me on to this Frank,' Maggie said suddenly. 'That time you phoned Orla and you heard a band playing in the background. I found that interesting. And something I had been puzzling about suddenly clicked into place.'

'So that's where we're going is it?' he responded. 'To that farm where McKean and the Warriors were rehearsing for their festival show? The one you told me about?'

'That's it. There's a track just off on the left, in about half-a-mile. It leads to the barn and down to the river. Coming up anytime now. Slow down or you'll miss it.'

Quicker than expected they were on it, Frank braking sharply to avoid overshooting the concealed entrance, but the tight turn was negotiated successfully, and soon they were heading gingerly down the heavily-rutted track. A track that was exactly long enough for Maggie to be able to explain everything to Frank and Jimmy.

'Unbelievable,' Frank said, shaking his head. 'But I'm sure glad we radioed ahead to get these uniforms down from Inverness.'

'I don't think there'll be any trouble,' Maggie said. 'But best to be prepared I guess.'

As they swung into the yard, the scene looked much like on her first visit, save for the two marked patrol cars parked alongside a huge *Claymore Warriors on Tour* pantechnicon. Four burly Highland coppers stood around, arms folded, evidently awaiting the arrival of Frank, from whom they were expecting further instructions. He pulled up his car behind theirs and jumped out, brandishing his warrant card.

'DCI Frank Stewart,' he said, smiling. 'Thanks for popping down lads. Good to see you all on this nice September afternoon and I hope you had a nice wee drive.'

'Sergeant Donnie McLean,' one said, returning the smile. 'Is there going to be a rumpus sir?'

'Well, they're called the Warriors, but I don't think there'll be any claymores in evidence. Still, if you're looking for a punch-up, I'll see what I can do for you. But for now, just have your boys hanging about the entrance and looking menacing, in case anyone tries to make a break for it. Because I think they might.'

'Menacing we can do sir,' the sergeant replied, laughing. 'Straight out of the box.'

As Maggie and the Stewart brothers got nearer to the entrance door, from the barn came the unmistakable strains of Oran na Mara, the iconic melody as majestic as ever, driven along by the drums pounding out their irresistible rhythm. But where Dougie McKean's gravelly vocal would normally be, there was something altogether more ethereal, a magical lilt that could only come from the sainted vocal chords of the beautiful Orla McCarthy.

'This is bloody unbelievable,' Frank said, awe-struck. 'I know what we've got to do in a minute, but please, I need to hear this tune right to the end.'

Jimmy nodded. 'We're privileged. Because it's the last time anybody's going to hear this for a while.'

'Maybe ever,' Maggie said. 'Don't forget three people have been murdered. And that's going to attract a whole-life sentence every time, no matter who's in the judge's chair.'

They stood, transfixed, as the epic track wound its way towards its dramatic concluding chords. And then suddenly, there was silence.

'Come on, let's go and do this,' Frank gestured. But as they pushed open the door of the barn, the music started up again. It was *Mountain Dew*, the song Maggie had heard Orla sing with the Warriors the last time she had been here, seemingly impromptu. *Except it hadn't been impromptu, had it?*

'Bloody hell,' Jimmy shouted as he looked around the barn, open-mouthed. 'This is quite a set-up, isn't it? Amazing.'

At the far end of the barn a high stage had been erected, a full-size affair of the type you saw at major arena venues around the world. Dazzling lasers and spotlights illuminated the performers, syncopating in time with the hypnotic beat of the music. Just in front of the stage and to the right, Maggie recognised Yash Patel of the Chronicle and his cameraman Rupert, no doubt here to capture more footage for Orla's burgeoning YouTube channel. Behind the stage stood three huge video screens, the two outer ones showing dramatic shots of what looked like Loch Ness, the footage evidently shot by a drone swooping just a few metres above the water. The centre screen was focussed on Orla McCarthy, belting out the iconic number and looking sensational in knee-length boots and a green velvet mini-dress with a tartan plaid slung over one shoulder. Then one-by-one the camera cut to the other members of the band, the Cooper brothers Jamie and Rab in kilts and cloaks, the drummer Geordie Fisher in shorts and a horned Viking helmet, twirling his sticks showman-like above his head between fills. But suddenly Orla spotted them, instantly raising her hand to bring the music to an abrupt and discordant halt.

'What are you doing here?' she said, speaking into her microphone. 'This is a private rehearsal, didn't you see the sign on the door?' At the same time, she gave Patel a sharp look and shouted, 'Cut the tape Yash. Now.'

'You know why we're here,' Maggie said quietly. 'I'm afraid it's all over Orla. For all of you.'

The singer gave a dismissive laugh. 'I'm sorry, but I haven't the faintest clue what you're talking about. So please could you leave, because we've got work to do.'

'Well maybe this will help to clarify your thoughts as to what we're talking about,' Frank said, stepping forward. 'Orla

McCarthy, James Cooper, Robert Cooper, George Fisher, you are jointly charged with the murder of Douglas McKean and the murder of Tamara Gray and the murder of Damian Hammond. You are not obliged to say anything, but anything you do say....'

'Fuck this,' Geordie Fisher shouted suddenly, throwing his drumsticks the floor and sprinting to the edge of the stage. He jumped to the ground, then started running towards the door. Jimmy made a move to go after him, but Frank held up a restraining hand. 'Let the Inverness boys do their stuff,' he said, smiling. 'They've come all this way after all, and they've been looking forward to it all morning.'

'What's he got to be afraid of Orla?' Maggie asked. 'Are you all hiding some terrible dark secret? Because I'm afraid it's a secret no longer. We know exactly what you did. And why.'

McCarthy sneered. 'You're *totally* deluded, all of you. You can't prove that I murdered anyone. And that goes for all of the guys in the band too.'

Maggie smiled. 'Ah, so you know we're talking about murder, do you? And I suppose you're thinking if they try to use joint enterprise to pin it on all of you, it'll end up in a horrible mess and you might be able to escape justice? Well you might try, but I think it might not be as straightforward as you think.' She paused and smiled again. 'As the old cliché says, see you in court.'

Frank nodded. 'So now it's up to you guys. You can either come quietly, or I'll send in my Inverness boys to grab you. But just so you know, they all got chucked out of last year's

Braemar Highland Games for being too rough. Your choice, but I know which one I'd pick.'

Resigned to their fate, Orla and the Cooper brothers were led, handcuffed, to the waiting police cars, drummer Geordie Fisher already in the back of one of them, awaiting the blue-lit journey back to Inverness. Their task completed, Maggie, Jimmy and Frank slowly wandered out into the yard, then strolled the few yards down to the riverside, enjoying the mighty Spey's roaring grandeur whilst silently reflecting on a job well done. Had they stayed inside, they would have observed the devious smile of Yash Patel, who had captured the sensational arrests on camera.

Chapter 28

Unsurprisingly, things had got pretty awkward afterwards for two of the rising stars of the Police Scotland organisation, which was always going to be the case when it emerged that the woman you had fingered for the murder of a high-profile rock star had herself been murdered, and that the body-count in the case had risen to three, one of them the forced drowning of a sad and lonely studio engineer who hadn't even been on your radar. Regarding DCI Steph McNeil, the general consensus of media and colleagues alike was that she had been seriously over-promoted, a direct but unwelcome consequence of the organisation's diversity-at-all-costs agenda. And far from being talked about as a shoo-in for the post of Commissioner of the Metropolitan Police, people of influence were now asking whether Chief Constable Jennifer McCrae's position was in fact still tenable, given the magnitude of the cock-up she had presided over. Furthermore, Scotland's justice minister, an enemy of McCrae's back to when they had been at school together, had taken no time in exercising little-used executive powers to draft in a Senior Investigating Officer from south of the border to wrap up the case - an act precision-engineered to pile further embarrassment on to the already-beleaguered McCrae and hopefully hasten her resignation.

> Under severe scrutiny too had been Yash Patel of the Chronicle, who struggled to explain how it was he had missed three murders happening right under his nose, during the period when the paper's spin-off TV channel was producing a fly-on-the-wall documentary starring the pop singer Orla McCarthy, now exposed as a callous killer. But

Yash being slippery Yash, the reporter had emerged from the inquests unscathed, and was now salivating over the endless stream of salacious headlines and blockbuster prose that lay ahead of him. *My Time with a Killer - Chronicle Reporter Reveals the Darkest Truths about Orla.* The headlines almost wrote themselves, such was the richness of the material that was available to him, and not for the first time, he imagined himself at a glittering awards ceremony, soaking up the envious applause of his rivals as he stepped up to the platform to accept yet another gong.

Now they were gathered in the New Scotland Yard headquarters of the Metropolitan Police for what had been quaintly labelled a 'drinks reception', a term that somehow reminded Maggie of the old-fashioned cheese-and-wine parties her parents used to host when she was a child back in Yorkshire. Their host was Trevor Naylor - now properly *Commissioner* Trevor Naylor, the *acting* prefix ditched after his appointment had been made permanent following Jennifer McCrae's spectacular fall from grace. Present too were Maggie, Jimmy, Frank and Lori Logan, flown down from Glasgow that morning, and Eleanor Campbell, DCI Jill Smart, DC Ronnie French and DS Gemma James, the latter under strict instructions to go easy on the free booze, but already three glasses of prosecco ahead of the game. A number of representatives of the media had also been invited, although not Patel, who had been purposely excluded by the Commissioner, unimpressed by his connection to Orla McCarthy. Frank and Jimmy had immediately homed in on the impressive buffet, which had included a pile of succulent steak sandwiches, the beef cooked just to the medium side of rare, exactly the way they liked it, served with a biting horseradish sauce and accompanied by a top-of the-range merlot of notable richness. The atmosphere was warm and convivial, Naylor not hiding his gratitude for what Maggie, Frank and the gang had accomplished on his behalf. It had been a clean sweep in his opinion, a historic sexual assault allegation cleared up without a stain on the reputation of the force, and a series of brutal murders smoothly and competently solved by one of his best detectives, working in partnership with a truly excellent private investigations agency. Furthermore, the media had been united in the praise of this new regime at the Met, although Naylor was experienced enough to know that he was still in the honeymoon period of his reign. There was an old adage that all political careers ended in failure, and, he reflected wryly, the same could be said about Commissioners of the Metropolitan Police. Still, he was determined to enjoy it whilst it lasted, and was hoping that his knighthood would come along before it all went sour, as he knew, inevitably, it would.

But now it was time to get on with proceedings. He interrupted the pleasant hubbub of conversation with a clink on his wine glass. 'Good evening all,' Naylor said in his sonorous tones, 'I trust you're all enjoying this little celebration of success, I know I certainly am. How could you not, with these fine supermarket wines being served?' He paused, raising his wine glass and waiting for the obligatory laugh, which arrived on cue. 'And I'm sure, ladies and gentlemen of the media, like me you're all desperate to hear every detail of this most convoluted and complex of cases.'

He paused again, giving a short laugh. 'I of course have had it all explained to me once, which only succeeded in leaving my head spinning. So I'm pretty keen to hear it all over again. Let me therefore without further ado introduce you to Miss Maggie Bainbridge of Bainbridge Associates.' He shot her a warm smile. 'Maggie, if you're ready?'

'Thank you Commissioner,' she said, taking a step into the centre of the room. 'So it's actually quite difficult to know where to start, but I think it's probably best to begin with a profile of the main victim, Dougie McKean, lead singer of the Claymore Warriors.' She paused, taking a sip from her wine glass. 'McKean was a deeply flawed individual,' she began, 'a self-centred and greedy man who had cheated on his wife over many years, and had done everything in his power to grab all the financial benefits arising from the band for himself. As a result, he had made plenty of enemies, so when it emerged that rather than drinking himself to death as was first assumed, he had in fact been murdered, there was of course no shortage of suspects. First on the list was his wife, who had put up with years of abuse in their marriage. There was his new lover Tamara Gray, who had recently become the main beneficiary of his death, persuading him to change his will, such that she stood to inherit a fortune on his death. Then there was the film producer Clay Barrymore, who faced losing millions of dollars as a result of McKean changing his mind about granting him the rights to Oran na Mara in a bid to extort more money out of the film company. And what about his band-mates, who would also benefit from the money and opportunities that would flow from this new and exciting exposure of the iconic album?' She paused for a moment and took a sip of her wine. 'And finally of course there was Orla McCarthy, allegedly the victim of a brutal sexual assault when she was a teenager, and still bitter after all these years because McKean had stolen the Oran na Mara song from her. She had every reason to hate Dougie McKean with a passion. More than most. If she was telling the truth about that earlier assault of course.'

'It was a *massive* list,' Jimmy said. 'I hate to admit it, but I've got some sympathy for DCI McNeil. Her head must have been bursting with all those possibilities.'

'I don't,' Frank said. 'She was so pig-headed and didn't listen to a word I said. She got everything she deserved in my opinion. Traffic duty beckons I'm afraid.'

'Cops don't do traffic duty anymore,' Jimmy said, grinning. 'But I know what you mean. Sorry Maggie, carry on.'

She smiled. 'Yes, there were so many suspects and so many motives. But through all of it, there had been something nagging away in the back of my mind that I just couldn't get straight. Two facts that seemed somehow to undermine Orla's accusation against McKean. The first one was that, apart from that single allegation by her, there had never been a hint or suggestion that Dougie McKean harboured desires for young underage girls. On the contrary, his sexual desires seemed to be stimulated by more mature woman as far as we could tell. And although his present lover Tamara Gray was actually only about thirty, she was very mature in outlook.'

Maggie paused for a moment then continued, 'And the second question I had to ask was, why now? Why did Orla McCarthy leave it until now to resurrect the assault allegations against Dougie McKean? That caused me to look much more carefully at the chronology of the case, and when I did so, a completely different picture emerged.' She smiled. 'I think, ladies and gentlemen, if I walk you through the timing, then it'll all become clear to you too.'

'Go for it Maggie,' Jimmy shouted encouragingly.

'Okay, I will. So let me take you back about nine months or so, when life started to become amazingly exciting for Orla McCarthy. She had won the starring role in a blockbuster Hollywood movie and they were going to re-record Oran na Mara as the title song, with Dougie McKean giving tentative permission for them to use it. All the predictions were that the film was going to be a huge success, and on the back of it, the re-imagined song would become a giant world-wide hit too. Money, fame, artistic recognition, all of it was so close she could almost taste it. In particular, the project was going to open up America for her, where up until then she had achieved only limited success.'

'And then McKean chucked a bloody huge spanner in the works,' Frank said. 'Out of spite, or greed, we're not sure which, he changed his mind about letting them use the song. And since he owned fifty-five percent of the shares in the Warriors' publishing company, there wasn't a damn thing anyone could do about it.'

'That's right,' Maggie agreed. 'Naturally, Orla was devastated, and livid at the same time. So she set out to fix the problem in the most audacious manner.' She hesitated for a moment before continuing. 'Prior to McKean's bombshell change of heart, Orla had been spending some time at Advance Studios, sampling Jamie Cooper's guitar track to use in the new version of the song. And that's when she met Damian Hammond, whom she quickly realised was completely besotted with her, and would do anything to please her.'

'So she came up with a cunning plan,' Lori Logan said.

Maggie nodded. 'Very cunning indeed. Eighteen years earlier, egged on we believe by her father, she had fabricated a sexual assault allegation against McKean, an allegation that was quite properly dismissed by the police at the time on the grounds of lack of evidence. She had done it because she was angry that he had stolen a key part of the song from her, although given what we now know about Orla's track-record as a reliable witness, the truth of that allegation could be questioned too. But now, she saw how that allegation could be resurrected to her advantage. Firstly, she contacts the media and spins the tale of how her mental health is still being challenged by what had happened, and that now, on the twentieth anniversary of the terrible event, it was right that she should finally speak out, so that other young women wouldn't have to go through what she went through.'

Frank laughed. 'Except that it was actually only eighteen years ago. Maths obviously wasn't her strong- point.'

'Just like her truthfulness,' Jimmy added.

Maggie nodded again. 'Exactly. And at the same time, she has induced Damian Hammond to produce and then pretend to discover the fake recording. And on that note, there's something I'd like you to listen to, and with apologies in advance to Commissioner Naylor.' She looked over to where he stood, matching his puzzled look with a seraphic smile. Then she held up her phone so that the speakers faced the audience, and hovered a finger over the screen. 'This is a trick that Eleanor has already played on Frank, but I think you'll all find it both entertaining and illuminating.'

She stabbed the screen, and the plodding but resonant voice of Naylor began to emanate from her phone.

Ladies and gentlemen, it gives me the greatest pleasure this evening to welcome you to historic New Scotland Yard. Although of course, we actually only moved to this new riverside building a few years ago, so it's not really that historic...

'That's me!' he exclaimed, half-frowning, half-smiling. 'Except, it isn't *actually* me, obviously.' Then he laughed. 'Although it's the sort of thing I would say. But do I really sound so *boring*?'

'No, you sound terribly distinguished Commissioner,' Maggie laughed. 'But I used a freely available text-to-speech AI tool to produce your little speech. There's dozens of them available now, and believe me, they're *scarily* realistic. All it needed was a short sample of your voice, and the tool did the rest. Two minutes' work, if that. It was that self-same technology that Hammond used to fabricate the little drama of Orla's alleged sexual assault, seemingly discovered by accident after all those years. He took samples of Orla's voice and of Dougie McKean's, and obviously managed to find some archive recording of Nicky Nicholson, the iconic producer of the album who had recently died.'

'Aye,' Frank nodded, 'and it was that latter fact that made the whole subterfuge possible. Because with Nicholson dead, only McKean could deny its authenticity. And as Mandy Rice-Davies famously remarked, he would say that, wouldn't he?'

'So Orla took her story to the Chronicle,' Maggie continued, 'and to our old friend Yash Patel, who promised to splash it all over one of their Sunday editions. McCarthy's plan was to put unbearable pressure on McKean so that he was persuaded to change his mind about allowing Oran na Mara to be used in the movie. She put it to him that if he was to relent, she wouldn't press charges against him.'

Jimmy smiled. 'But of course, Dougie being the belligerent old sod he was, and being innocent too, let's not forget, told Orla to bugger off.'

Maggie nodded. 'But whilst all of this was happening there had been developments, developments which were set to change the whole course of the affair. Back in London, Orla's manager and boyfriend David Gallagher was slowly beginning to realise what a truly incredible opportunity they were sitting on. His thoughts had turned to a famous British rock band whose career looked to be over when their iconic lead singer had died of Aids, but who had seen an astonishing and lucrative resurgence when they had recruited a new hugely talented and charismatic lead singer. The new singer was a generation younger than the rest of the band, and so had exposed them to a new audience, a younger demographic who became just as devoted to the band as their elders. Gallagher made a few phone calls and confirmed that there would be a huge appetite for a re-imagining of the Claymore Warriors, the majestic songs of the Oran na Mara album being blasted out by the original band, but fronted by the beautiful and captivating Orla McCarthy. The sums involved, he calculated, were stratospheric, he reckoning that a global tour could very easily gross as much as half-a-billion dollars.'

'But we've not charged this Gallagher fellow, have we?' the Commissioner asked, directing a quizzical eyebrow at Frank.

He shook his head. 'No sir, he's totally innocent. He did discuss the opportunity briefly with Orla, but he never ever thought it could actually be pulled off. Because obviously Dougie McKean wasn't going anywhere, so he dismissed the idea. But the thing was, it planted a seed in his girlfriend's head.'

'And that's when things turned darker,' Maggie said, 'because when the Warriors' guitarist Jamie Cooper got to hear of the opportunity, he knew that it was one he had to seize at all costs.' She smiled. 'A few weeks ago, myself, Frank and Lori got together in our favourite Glasgow pub and made a long list of all the possible motives for murder. Not just our murder, but *any* murder,' she added. 'But comprehensive though that list was, we did manage to miss one.'

'Aye, but I thought of it immediately afterwards,' Lori interjected, her eyes shining. 'And I was kicking myself for missing it at the time. I'm not sure what you call it, maybe lust for glory or the need to be famous, something like that? But it can be a powerful motive, definitely.'

'Exactly Lori,' Maggie said. 'The thing was, Jamie Cooper and the rest of the band had always deeply resented the fact that Dougie had continually resisted giving them due credit for their role in creating the Warriors' brilliant music, both artistically but of course financially too. If you asked anyone to name any members of the band, the only name they would come up with was Dougie McKean. And they all hated that.'

'That's when Cooper's thoughts turned to murder,' Jimmy said. 'It all just fitted in so perfectly for him. He was having an affair with Cassie McKean and foresaw a new and wonderful life ahead of himself, with the band resurgent, and him building a great home life with his new love. The only trouble was, Dougie McKean was an obstacle to achieving both of these dreams. With McKean still around, there could be no Warriors Mark Two, nor could Cassie ever be truly happy whilst a battle raged over the custody of her beloved children.'

'That's right,' Maggie said. 'So in Cooper's mind, there was only one solution. Dougie McKean had to die. But he realised that both his band-mates and Orla McCarthy stood to gain just us much as he did from their front-man's death, so he decided to try and recruit them into his dastardly scheme.'

'That must have been quite a conversation,' Frank said, laughing. *'I've just had a wee idea folks. I think we should do away with Dougie. It'll be worth millions to us.'*

'And to his surprise, they were all up for it, ' Maggie said. 'So the question now became how it should be done. You can't exactly google *how to murder someone*, one of them said, *because the spooks are looking out for all that sort of stuff. Not a problem,* Orla said*, I know a poor sap who will do it for us, and it'll never get traced back to us.'*

Jimmy nodded. 'And then I guess someone mentioned the joint enterprise thing, as a sort of insurance policy should it all go pear-shaped and they get caught. So that was added to the things that Damian Hammond was asked to find out. On the promise of a cosy dinner-date with Orla and some wild sex afterwards.'

'That's it,' Maggie agreed. 'But Damian Hammond was very tech-savvy, so was smart enough to know he couldn't do the searches on his own phone or from his work or home computers. His dingy little flat was near Paddington station, so he decided he would just hop on a train and go somewhere he wasn't known, then find a busy pub and steal someone's phone.'

'So Bath was just a random choice?' Naylor asked. 'No more significant than that?'

'That's right. Bath just happens to be on a route out of Paddington,' she said. 'He thought the town would have plenty of busy pubs on a Friday night where he could melt into the background. And so it proved.'

'But he didn't think about switching off his phone so he couldn't be traced,' Frank said. 'Schoolboy error that.'

'And lucky he didn't,' Maggie said. 'Anyway, Orla had told him that they favoured poisoning because McKean's excessive drinking gave an opportunity to disguise the murder as being caused by his over-indulgence. With a bit of research, Hammond decided on taxine. It seemed the poison was relatively easy to extract from the leaves of the yew tree, and quite a small dose would be fatal. And although it had a bitter taste, it could easily be disguised by adding a crushed sweetener like aspartame.'

'There's a yew tree in the yard of that wee church just along from the barn, we found that out afterwards, didn't we?' Jimmy said.

'Yes, and Rob Cooper admitted that's how they got the taxine extract. A pair of rubber gloves, a few leaves and a mortar and pestle to crush them up,' Maggie said. 'It couldn't have been easier.'

'So where did the joint enterprise thing fit in?' Naylor asked. 'Because you found out that Hammond had searched for that too, didn't you?'

She nodded. 'As I said, this was mainly a sort of insurance policy should the murderers get found out, although I think it might also have been to assuage the doubts of Rob Cooper and Geordie Fisher, who were less keen on the scheme than Jamie and Orla. So they came up with the crazy Agatha Christie style twist, wherein each of them would have a syringe to add to the whisky bottles, but three would be a solution of aspartame and only one would be a solution of taxine. The syringes were prepared, then shuffled like playing cards so that nobody knew which one contained the poison.'

'And explain to me again why they did that?' Jill Smart asked. 'I'm not sure that I quite got it first time round.'

Jimmy shrugged. 'I think mainly to salve their consciences, I guess. Because the scheme meant there was a one in four chance that any one of them wasn't technically a murderer.' He paused for a moment, looking uncertain. 'That's if I've got the maths right.'

'I think it was more cynical than that,' Maggie said. 'You see, each one of them will be represented in court by their own barrister, and each one of these barristers will be telling the jury that it is impossible to prove that their particular client committed the murder. I'd be doing the same if I was defending. It's going to be a legal nightmare. They'll all be jailed eventually of course, but I can see there being endless appeals. Great for us lawyers of course, but not for anybody else.'

'Right, thanks,' Jill said. 'I understand now.'

'So to the murder itself,' Maggie said. 'Orla knew that her boyfriend and the American film producer Clay Barrymore had sent cases of Balvenie to McKean in the hope of inducing him to change his mind about allowing Oran na Mara to be used in their movie. And they knew that the cases had been delivered to the lodge that McKean was renting with Tamara Gray. They knew too that if McKean was found to have been murdered, then suspicion would immediately fall on Tamara, who was going to inherit all his wealth and property, having only recently persuaded him to change his will in her favour.'

'And they had already worked out how they could add the poison to Dougie's whisky bottle without it being detected,' Jimmy said. 'Hardly an original idea by the way,' he added. 'The method had been used by the killer in one of these old detective novels from the nineteen-thirties, and Orla had remembered reading it and saw it would still work today.'

Maggie nodded. 'They were super-confident the poisoning would be undetected, but just as a second insurance, they wondered if it might be possible to make the case against Tamara more solid by framing her. As Jamie Cooper told us, he'd been picking up McKean from their rented lodge to make sure he got to rehearsals, and was often kept waiting whilst his singer dragged himself out of bed, giving him plenty of opportunity to plant incriminating evidence at the place. So on one occasion, he took the opportunity to sneak in to the kitchen and take a knife from a drawer, and then he pinched one of the bottles of Balvenie from the box that was lying in a corner. They needed a bottle to practice on, so it killed two birds with one stone. Back at the rehearsal room, the plastic sealing was broken using Tamara's knife, and a small hand-drill was used to bore a hole through the cork. Happy that the method was going to work, they resealed the bottle, and on Cooper's next visit to the lodge he put it back in the box and popped the knife back in the drawer.'

'So now the scene was set,' Jimmy continued. 'On the evening of Dougie McKean's murder, everyone was assembled back-stage. The band were there of course, but

Orla too had muscled her way in uninvited, on the pretext she was filming another episode of her fly-on-the-wall pursuit of McKean, given authenticity of course by the presence of Yash Patel and Rupert the cameraman. And in the usual nervous excitement of the pre-show preparations, no-one noticed Rab Cooper slipping off and drilling a tiny hole in the cork of one of the bottles using a little precision hand-drill. One minute later, the murderers assembled and selected their pre-prepared syringes, not knowing which of them contained the taxine. It was all done in a matter of seconds. The plastic foil seal was glued down, making the tampering undetectable, then Jamie Cooper passed the doctored bottle to the unsuspecting member of the crew who was responsible for keeping Dougie supplied with whisky on-stage.'

'And for two or three days afterwards, they literally thought they had got away with murder,' Maggie said. 'No-one suspected that Dougie had died of anything other than a heart attack caused by his over-indulgence. After all, why should they? He was a notorious drinker and it was a surprise to many folks that it hadn't happened sooner.'

'Until that unfortunate paramedic decided to have a wee dram from the bottle he'd pinched,' Frank said wryly. 'And then suddenly it looked as if it was all going to go tits-up for the killers.'

'Aye, but then DCI McNeil inadvertently rushed to their rescue,' Jimmy said, 'with her sloppy and half-arsed investigation. Once it emerged that Tamara Gray was being cast as the prime suspect, then the killers were handed a second chance to divert suspicion away from themselves.'

'But for that, Tamara Gray had to die,' Maggie said gravely. 'And what better accomplice to murder than the powerful river in full spate? Sad to say, the three members of the band were waiting for her that evening when she returned from questioning at Inverness police station. Once Jimmy had left...' -she turned to her colleague with a forgiving look - '...once Jimmy had left, it took no effort at all to overpower poor Tamara and drag her the few yards to the river, where we assume they held her head under the water until she drowned, and then let the current carry her downstream, where she was found by an angler the next morning. The police bought the line that she had committed suicide, either through remorse or because she knew she was going to be arrested and go to prison for a very long time.'

Frank nodded. 'And it helped that the murderers had been able to perfect their modus operandi when they drowned Damian Hammond just a few days earlier.'

'Yes, that's right,' Maggie agreed. 'Unfortunately for him, Hammond knew too much. He was a loose end that had to be dealt with, so Orla lured him to Speyside for what he believed was going to be the night of his life. She arranged for him to meet her at the barn where the Warriors had been rehearsing.'

'Where as well as his heroine, he found the three members of the band waiting for him,' Jimmy said. 'And that, I'm afraid, was the end of his short and sad life.'

'They must have thought they were in the clear,' Commissioner Naylor said. 'Until you came along Maggie, that was. Tell me, how did you work it all out?'

'It was really just one thing above all that raised my suspicions,' she said. 'It was that day when Lori and I went to the rehearsal barn to meet Dougie McKean, but he wasn't there because he had been drinking. But Orla was there, with Yash Patel from the Chronicle and their camera guy. She was joking about with the band, and then they invited her up to jam with them on one of the songs from the Oran na Mara album.'

'Mountain Dew,' Lori supplied. 'I remember it.'

'Yes, that was it. Orla made this great play about not really knowing the song and not remembering half the words. But then, when they performed it, it was absolutely perfect. No, better than that,' she corrected. 'It was stunning. Completely mesmerising. Off-the-scale in its brilliance. And afterwards, I *knew* it was important, but I couldn't quite put my finger on why.' She paused for a moment. 'That was until all the other stuff about the case began to pop out of the woodwork, and I took the opportunity to sit down and really *think* about everything. That's when I finally realised the significance of that moment in the barn.' She was silent again, then gave a wry smile. 'You see, Orla McCarthy and the Claymore Warriors had been planning for a life without Dougie McKean. In fact, more than that. They had been *rehearsing* for it.'

***

The event had carried on for a good hour after Maggie had finished her explanations, the agreeable atmosphere lubricated by the seemingly unlimited supply of wine that had been provided from the generous entertainment budget of the Metropolitan Police. Scanning the room, she observed Jill Smart hanging on Jimmy's every word, standing closer to him than was generally thought appropriate with work colleagues, and attracting thunderous looks from Lori as a result. Across the room, Eleanor Campbell and DS Jessie James had evidently negotiated a *rapprochement*, as they stood together laughing their heads off at some joke of Ronnie French's. Finally, there was Frank and the Commissioner, also laughing, as her husband-to-be soaked up Trevor Naylor's lavish praise for his work on the investigation. In five minutes' time the Scottish contingent would have to dash back to Heathrow for the late flight to Glasgow, where wonderful Ollie would be fast asleep in bed, assuming their soft babysitter Laura hadn't let him stay up to watch YouTube videos accompanied by his favourite creamy hot chocolate and jam sandwiches. Whatever way you looked at it, it had been a red-letter day, and now they could look forward to a few weeks of relative calm before the red-letter day of all red-letter days.

The day she was to marry her beloved Frank Stewart.

Epilogue

It had of course been the most wonderful of days, Jimmy reflected, as he sat, alone, in the now half-empty village hall, sipping on a malt whisky - Balvenie of course, how could he have chosen any other? His mum and dad and Maggie's parents had gone off to their hotels, the latter in charge of Ollie, and many of the guests were gradually slipping away into the chilly autumn evening, leaving behind just the hard-core revellers, amongst whom could be counted Eleanor Campbell and Lori Logan, who were on the floor laying down some moves to a hypnotic dance beat. The bride and groom had stayed until the band had finished playing, and then they too disappeared off to their nearby hotel. Tomorrow Maggie, Frank and Ollie were flying off to a luxury Mallorca hotel for what would be a memorable start to their official and wonderful life together.

He'd been nervous, naturally, checking in his sporran about a thousand times to make sure he had the rings, and about a hundred times to make sure he had his best man's speech. The loss of the latter wouldn't have been catastrophic - not like the loss of the former - because he could easily have busked something half-amusing, or simply said *my brother's amazing*, which is exactly what he felt about Frank. But he hadn't lost it, and had stumbled through the prepared words with not too much hesitation or repetition, earning some laughs from the guests and a few good-natured looks of disapproval from his brother. Maggie, naturally, had looked amazing, beaming with happiness throughout her wedding vows and barking out *I do* with a gusto that had caused peals of laughter to reverberate around the old church. He had laughed out loud too when Frank had kissed his bride a good half-second before being invited to do so by the vicar, and laughed again when Ollie had stuck his finger down his throat in mock disgust. There had been a *lot* of laughter.

There had been reunions with long-forgotten aunts, uncles and cousins, and pleasant introductions to new folks from the Yorkshire side of the marriage. There were one or two pretty and eligible girls too, as was obligatory at any English country wedding, and one or two who had made their interest in him quite plain to see. Yes, it had been the most wonderful of days, so why was it he had felt an oppressive mist of depression shrouding him throughout? He knew what it was of course, without really having to think about it too hard. It was regret, and no little jealousy too, he reflected, the latter causing pangs of self-reproach. Because had there *ever* been a pair who were so ridiculously well-suited as Maggie Bainbridge and Frank Stewart? You couldn't help but be envious when you saw what they had, a loving and giving relationship that most people would die to have for themselves. And he had had it too, with the beautiful Flora, before he'd screwed it up in a moment of madness. Sure, he'd blamed the war, and Helmand was no picnic, of course it wasn't, but the fact was, he'd had a choice and, fool that he was, he'd made the wrong one. And now it was too late, all too late. *But was it?* Gulping down the rest of his whisky, he took out his phone and swiped to *contacts*, his finger hovering over her number for about the millionth time since they'd separated.

To press or not to press, that was the question.

A note from the author

Dear reader,

I hope you enjoyed reading *Murder on Speyside* as much as I enjoyed writing it. It would be great if you could leave a rating on Amazon, because ratings and reviews are the lifeblood of the independent author. Thank you in anticipation!

Incidentally, some of you may be wondering if I just made up all that AI text-to-speech stuff in the book. Actually, no I haven't! If you google 'AI text-to-speech' you'll come across a bunch of apps that produce spookily-realistic results. Some even let you upload your own voice. Scary!

If you'd like a free Maggie Bainbridge short story for your Kindle or e-reader, go to https:/robwyllie.com/index_fb.php to download 'Murder of the Unknown Woman.' It's just 15,000 words, but it's one of my favourites. I'm sure you'll enjoy it.

Regards

Rob

February 2024

Printed in Great Britain
by Amazon